The Laura Black Scottsdale Mysteries

Books by
B A Trimmer

~~~~

The Laura Black
Scottsdale Mystery Series

Scottsdale Heat

Scottsdale Squeeze

Scottsdale Sizzle

Scottsdale Scorcher

Scottsdale Sting

Scottsdale Shuffle

Scottsdale Shadow

Scottsdale Secret

Scottsdale Silence

Scottsdale Scandal

Scottsdale Sleuth

~~~~

The Aloha Lagoon
Mystery Series

Hula Homicide

Homicide Honeymoon

Scottsdale Sizzle

Scottsdale Sizzle

B A TRIMMER

Editors: 'Andi' Anderson, Linda Annalora, Stacey VandeKoppel, and Kimberly Mathews

Composite cover art and cover design by Janet Holmes using images under license from Shutterstock.com and Depositphotos.com.

ISBN-13: 978-1-951052-04-1
Saguaro Sky Media Co.
070124pb

E-mail the author at LauraBlackScottsdale@gmail.com
Follow at www.facebook.com/ScottsdaleSeries/

*Special thanks to Mike Lee for
his support, encouragement, and advice.*

Scottsdale Sizzle

Introduction

If you've never read a Laura Black Scottsdale mystery, you can start with *Scottsdale Heat*, the first book in the series. If you'd rather start with this book, here are a few of the people you'll need to know:

Laura Black – Laura grew up in Arizona and currently works as an investigator in a Scottsdale law firm. She'd love to make the world a better place and have a full-time boyfriend, but she also has bills to pay.

Jackson Reno – Reno is a detective for the Scottsdale Police Department. He's slowly getting used to the idea of being Laura's boyfriend.

Sophia Rodriguez – Laura's best friend who works in the law office as the receptionist and paralegal. She sometimes helps Laura with her investigations. Sophie's a former California surfer chick and a free spirit who enjoys dating multiple men at the same time.

Gina Rondinelli – Laura's other best friend. She's a former Scottsdale police detective and the law firm's senior investigator. She has a strict moral code and likes playing by the rules.

Leonard Shapiro – Lenny is the head of the law firm. He has little personality and no people skills, but with the help of Laura, Sophie, and Gina, he usually wins his cases.

Anthony "Tough Tony" DiCenzo – Head of the local crime family. Through events over the last few months, he now owes Laura two favors.

Maximilien – The number-two man in the local crime family. He's attracted to Laura and would like to take the relationship further. Laura feels tempted, but she already has Reno as a boyfriend.

Gabriella – A former government operative from somewhere in Eastern Europe. She currently works as a bodyguard for Tough Tony. She takes pleasure in hurting men.

Grandma Peckham – Laura's longtime neighbor who's recently decided it's time to start dating men again.

The Cougars – A group of wealthy, sexy, and fashionable women who like to troll the clubs of Scottsdale looking for athletic younger men for hook-up relationships. Through a series of adventures, Laura, Sophie, and Gina have become unofficial members of their group.

Chapter One

Ask any tourist. Summers in Scottsdale are hot.

Scottsdale is where hot water comes out of both taps. It's where people use oven mitts to open their mailboxes. Summer temperatures have reached as high as a hundred and twenty-two degrees, and that was back before global warming was even a thing.

At the moment, I was trapped in a stuffy closet in George Anson's upstairs master bedroom. I was hot to the point I was about to pass out.

George was a wealthy businessman and a prominent name in central Arizona. He owned seven or eight auto dealerships in Scottsdale and throughout The Valley of the Sun.

I'd seen dozens of his TV commercials over the years. They were usually funny and always ended the same way: he'd look straight into the camera and say, "I'm Honest George Anson, and you can bet my tattoo on it." He'd then turn to show the big tattoo of an anchor on his arm.

I'd been in the process of installing spy cameras in the bedrooms of his north Scottsdale home when he unexpectedly showed up with a woman. I barely had time to hide in the closet before they walked into the bedroom.

George's wife had assured me he would be at his Sun

City dealership for a day-long meeting, but it looked like she'd been misinformed.

George Anson's wife, Debbie, was a client of Lenny Shapiro, my boss. She'd recently hired Lenny to gather evidence that her husband was cheating.

I'd met Debbie at the law office a few days earlier, and she seemed like a nice person. She didn't know who the other woman was, but Debbie suspected the affair had been going on for some time.

She thought they even sometimes cheated in the family home. Although there was no prenup, Lenny was sure that George, being the community big shot he was, would be glad to provide a generous alimony rather than have his sordid affairs become public knowledge.

Using a key provided by Debbie, I'd let myself into the house a little after noon. By twelve-thirty, I'd installed a tiny battery-powered video camera in each of the two guest bedrooms.

I had just walked into the master bedroom when I heard the sound of the front door opening, followed by male and female voices coming up the stairs. I didn't have time to think. I opened the nearest set of folding doors, sprang into the space, and quickly shut the doors.

Based on the dresses and racks of shoes surrounding me, it was clear that I was in Debbie's closet. Unfortunately, the slits in the door were too narrow to be able to see properly into the room. All I could catch were fuzzy shapes and the movement of bodies.

As I heard the clothes come off, I tried to learn what I could about the woman. She had the strong and confident voice of a woman in her late thirties or early forties. From what little I could make out through the door, she appeared to be a brunette with a relatively thin body.

4

I wanted to crack open the door to get a better look at her, but I didn't want to risk being seen. Being discovered could be dangerous, and worse, they'd most likely find a new love nest.

George was a big man, and he wasn't stupid. He'd know why I was there, and I didn't want to get into a fight.

Using my stun gun on him was an option, but that was never a sure bet. If I missed, he'd only get more pissed.

There was also the possibility I would have to explain myself to the police in front of George. I knew from experience things like that tended to mess up an assignment and upset my boss.

George and the woman made it to the bed, and from the noises they made, they were fully enjoying each other's company. After listening to the slurping kissing noises and watching the fuzzy shapes move around using the slit in the door, it became apparent the woman had some pent-up desires she needed to release.

The bed continued to squeak for another few minutes, then the woman suddenly cried out, her voice shaking for fifteen or twenty seconds, her breath coming out in quivering gasps. I was hoping this would be the end of it, but it wasn't long before the entire process started over.

She then repeated it again, and again. She was a passionate love machine, and there didn't seem to be any signs of her slowing down.

Okay, I'll admit, listening to the woman moan for the first half hour did kind of stir me up. My mind kept switching back and forth from my boyfriend, Jackson Reno, an undercover cop for the city of Scottsdale, to Max, a dangerous and exciting man who's second-in-command of the largest crime family in Scottsdale.

I knew from personal experience that Reno could make me moan like the woman on the bed. I wasn't sure if Max would make me moan like that or if my moans with him would be even louder and more frantic.

Honestly, I suspected they would be. Plus, I didn't think Max was the kind of man to lay there and make me do all the work.

Stop thinking about Max! You have a boyfriend.

Unfortunately for me, since no one was supposed to be in the house during the day, the air-conditioning had been programmed to turn itself off during the afternoon heat. This is common in Scottsdale, where summer electricity bills can easily run several hundred dollars a month.

If no one is supposed to be home, the air conditioning will run only enough to keep the plants and animals alive. It must have been ninety degrees in the bedroom, where they at least had a big ceiling fan over the bed. It felt closer to a hundred in the closet.

I stood in the cramped and stuffy closet and listened to them for well over an hour. My eyes stung from the sweat that dripped into them, and my legs started to cramp from trying to stay still.

Hot and tired as I was, I had to hand it to the woman. Her stamina was amazing. I couldn't make out if she had a wedding ring on her finger or not, but I assumed she wasn't getting enough attention at home. A woman like that had some obvious needs.

My legs were starting to give out, so I leaned back against a rack of dresses. I desperately wanted to sit down somewhere out of the heat. My hair was limp, and my T-shirt was clinging to me.

I kept rubbing my eyes to get the sweat out, but that only

seemed to make them sting more. Assignment or not, I wasn't going to last much longer before passing out.

Finally, the woman had worked herself into a state of exhaustion. She fell off George and collapsed next to him on the bed. But instead of getting up right away, they lay on the bed, talking in low voices.

Come on, enough already.

Black spots were dancing in front of my eyes, and I knew it wouldn't be long before I blacked out. I cursed my bad luck that there hadn't been time to install a spy camera in the master bedroom before they'd used it for the afternoon.

If I'd been able to get a video of their tryst, I could have quickly wrapped up the assignment. Instead, I was back at square one.

Almost an hour and a half after they had started, I heard George and the woman get up. They went into the master bathroom, and I heard the shower start.

I eased open the door, and I felt relief immediately as a rush of cool air flooded the closet. I stepped out into the bedroom and stretched the kinks out.

Standing under the spinning blades of the ceiling fan felt wonderful, but listening to them taking a shower made me realize how badly I had to go to the bathroom. Now that my core temperature had started to drop, and the more I thought about it, the worse I had to go. I silently regretted the big Diet Pepsi I had drank right before coming into the house.

I knew I should have snuck out while they were in the shower, but I needed to see if I could get a better look at George Anson's mistress. She was twenty feet from me, and this could possibly be my only chance to discover who she was. I went back into the closet, but this time, I left the door open with the slightest crack.

The woman was only in the bathroom for about five minutes before she came out, got dressed, and began making the bed. With George still in the bathroom and the woman distracted, I took a chance and eased open the closet door, just enough to take a peek.

Now that I had a good chance to look at the woman, I saw she was medium-height with a nice figure. She had great taste in clothes and had spent top dollar on her shoes. When she pulled back her long auburn hair to put it into a ponytail, I noticed a Cindy Crawford beauty mark next to her mouth.

Seeing her face, I thought she looked vaguely familiar. This wasn't unusual for me since I tend to meet a lot of people during the course of my day.

It's rare for me to go into a restaurant or bar in Scottsdale and not recognize *somebody*. Not wanting to press my luck, I carefully closed the closet door and waited for them to leave.

It took another twenty minutes of fixing makeup, pulling on clothes, and cleaning the bedroom, but they eventually left. As soon as I heard the front door close, I bolted from the closet and ran into the bathroom.

Once I finished heeding nature's call, I went down to the kitchen and drank three glasses of disgusting Scottsdale city tap water. But I didn't care about the foul taste. I needed to hydrate.

Sometimes I hate my job.

Since I suspected George and his mistress would continue to use the master bedroom as their main love nest, I went up and installed three of my tiny spy cameras throughout the room.

I hid them well and chose angles that would give the most dramatic effects. I then went back downstairs and took off.

Still feeling dehydrated from standing in the hot closet for over two hours, I stopped by the first convenience store I saw to grab a Diet Pepsi. I'd just made it to the door when two boys in their late teens came walking out.

They stopped, and both looked me up and down. I knew my thin T-shirt was plastered against my body, and I must've looked like someone from a wet T-shirt contest.

"Hey babe, looking good," the older of the two said. His friend stared at my T-shirt and snickered. It was like an old episode of *Beavis and Butthead*.

After all the frustrations of the afternoon, I instantly got pissed. "What are you little twerps looking at? Get the hell away from me before I pound the snot out of both of you."

"Whoa, babe," the older one said. "No need for violence, I was only admiring your awesome boobs."

Sometimes I really hate my job.

My name is Laura Black. I'm an investigator for the Scottsdale law firm of Halftown, Oeding, Shapiro, and Hopkins. Over the years, one of the founding partners of the firm retired to Florida, and two of them died.

The remaining partner, Leonard Shapiro, my boss, has transformed the firm into one of the most successful boutique law offices in Scottsdale. He mainly handles high-profile criminal, civil, and family law cases.

Unlike most lawyers, Lenny loves it when his cases are mentioned in the papers. I've often noticed that whenever one of his cases is featured in the news, Lenny raises his rates another notch.

I keep waiting for him to change the name of the firm, but

I don't think he ever will. Even with all the money he makes, I can't see him spending a dime to change the stationery.

I woke up early the next day and lay in bed while I decided what to do for the morning. I only had one assignment at work, and that now involved nothing more than reviewing the videos from the spy cameras I'd placed in George Anson's house. Since there probably wouldn't be anything to see for a day or two, I knew I was basically going to have the day off.

My bad side reasoned that I could lie in bed all morning and maybe binge-watch a half-dozen episodes of *Say Yes to the Dress*. My good side reminded me there were bills to pay, and I should probably go into the office and see if I could wheedle another assignment out of Lenny.

My good side eventually won out, but that's mostly because my bad side likes to eat, and for that, I need a paycheck. I stumbled into the kitchen, put on a pot of coffee, then made my way into the shower. I wasn't in a rush, so I stood there for almost twenty minutes, letting the hot water pour over me.

After the shower, I went into the kitchen and poured coffee into my *Doctor Who* mug. I was a little surprised that Marlowe, my gray and white tabby, wasn't in the kitchen demanding to be fed.

But since it was after eight o'clock, I knew he was most likely over at Grandma Peckham's, mooching a late breakfast from her.

As I got dressed, a sudden feeling of happiness came over me. It was as if I knew I was going to have a good day. Maybe it was only from the caffeine in the coffee, but I hoped it was a premonition of good things to come.

I locked the apartment, went out to the parking lot, and unlocked my car, a cappuccino-colored Accord. I'd bought it new and successfully paid it off, but it was starting to show its age.

This was mainly due to a few modifications to the body that were not included in the original factory specifications. I sometimes think about getting a new car, something classy, or maybe even a convertible. But it still runs great and who has the money for a new one?

As I drove to the office, I couldn't help but smile. I was still in a great mood, and I started to think it had something to do with the summer heat finally starting to kick in.

Unlike the winter tourists who disappear at the first signs of summer, I actually love the heat. I also love the way Scottsdale empties out when it starts to get hot.

Work had been slow the last several weeks as the city wound down for the summer. As the weather warms up and people leave town, there's also a decline in the number of new clients Lenny takes on. As a result, in the summer, I'm almost always broke.

I drove down the alley behind the law office and pulled into my assigned covered parking space. Covered parking is essential in Scottsdale during the summer months. A car sitting in the full summer sun can easily have an interior temperature over a hundred and forty degrees.

I parked between Lenny's red Porsche 911 and Sophie's yellow Volkswagen Bug convertible. I didn't see the black Range Rover, so I knew Gina hadn't made it in yet. I also knew I wouldn't see Annie's sky-blue Fiesta since she was taking the week off for finals.

Using my key, I entered the office through the heavy security door in the back of the building. I walked past my cubicle in the back offices and up to the front reception area.

Sophia Rodriguez was sitting at her desk looking at pictures of some snowy mountains on her computer. Sophie's the paralegal and the receptionist for the law office. In addition, she's also my best friend.

Sophie grew up in southern California and spent her youth as a wild-and-free surfer chick living in Laguna Beach. For rent money, she'd worked as a catalog model and as a singer in a local punk-rock band.

She got married early and then followed her husband out to Arizona. The husband soon became an ex-husband, but Sophie seemed like a permanent resident.

My best friend is tall and thin, with long black hair going halfway down her back. Her smile dazzles, and whenever we go out, she always seems to attract a crowd of guys.

Where I've come to appreciate the summer heat in Scottsdale, Sophie never has. I don't think she ever will.

She loves Arizona's warm winters, gorgeous springs, and extended falls, but Sophie hates Arizona summers with a deep and sincere passion.

I've noticed that in the summer, she spends a lot of time daydreaming she's somewhere else. Usually somewhere cold.

"Do you know there's a ski area in Colorado called *A-Basin* that's still open?" she asked as I walked over to her desk. "There's one still open in Oregon, too. They have a webcam, and you can see people skiing on the snow on Mount Hood. I wonder what it's like to live somewhere where it snows. I bet people love living where it's icy and cold all the time. I imagine they dance with joy whenever it starts to snow. I know I probably would."

"A lot of them seem to come down here for the winter, so maybe they all don't love it."

"Well, I'd take the snow over living in a furnace."

"But, Sophie," I laughed. "Haven't you heard? It's a dry heat."

Sophie gave me a sour look that made me back up a step.

"If I hear that 'dry-heat' shit one more time," she said. "I swear I'm going to vomit. I don't care how dry it is, when you live inside a big pizza oven, it's fricking hot."

"How'd your date go on Saturday?" I asked. "Weren't you supposed to go out again with Michael?"

Michael was a police officer Sophie had met while helping me with an assignment a couple of months before. Due to some scheduling conflicts, the relationship started out slowly, but now it had started to pick up some momentum.

"Well, I was supposed to have a date," Sophie said, "but the jerk canceled. Something about a change of shift or something. I'm starting to feel your pain with the whole dating-a-cop thing. I ended up going out with the Cougars on Saturday. I would have called you to come along, but I knew you had a date with Reno."

We'd become friends with a group of Scottsdale Cougars a few months before. They were wealthy, middle-aged women who liked to hit the high-end clubs and hook up with guys half their age.

They were a fun group to be with, and Sophie, Gina, and I ended up going out with them two or three times a month. When going out with the girls, we were known as their pumas or "Cougars-in-training."

"How was it?" I asked. "Did you meet anyone?"

"Not really. Don't get me wrong, I love going out with the girls, especially now that Jackie's started to come out again. But I'm starting to think being a puma isn't all it's cracked up to be."

"What's not to like?" I asked. "Between the girls and the guys, you go to the best clubs in Scottsdale, and it doesn't cost you a thing."

"Oh, I love the free drinks and being treated so nicely by the bouncers and everything. The part I'm starting not to like is that I'm only a puma and not a full-fledged Cougar. The guys look at me as more of a consolation prize than anything else. I can see it in their eyes. First, they try with Jackie or Elle. If they strike out there, they take a shot at Shannon, or Sonia, or Pammy, or Cindy. If none of the Cougars are in the mood to flirt with them, they come over to me. I guess I must have a look of hungry desperation that turns a guy on."

"I know Annie never minded being the puma of the group," I said. "But I guess it's not for everyone."

Annie is a college student who works part-time at the law office, filing and doing some administrative work. About six months before, I met her while working on an assignment. She'd been friends with the Cougars even before we got to know her.

"I know," Sophie said. "Going to the clubs is fun and all, but I think I'm starting to lose interest in hooking up with the guys. Meeting a guy and heading over to his place is starting to feel less like fun and more like work. I think I may be looking for an actual boyfriend again. Maybe even a long-term thing."

"Does Michael have any potential? You've been out with him six or seven times now. That's a good sign."

"Well, Michael's nice, and I'm not embarrassed to be seen in public with him, but I'm thinking he's more for hooking-up than boyfriend material. He doesn't really seem interested in anything other than drinks, dinner, and then a hop in the sack. But at least he usually buys dinner."

"Well, what about Milo? You dumped him last month when he wanted to start getting serious. Maybe that's what you're looking for?"

"I don't know. Milo and I get along okay, but somehow, a low-level henchman in the mob doesn't seem like a good move for the long term. Now, if I had a crime lieutenant, like you have with Max, I could be a happy girl. That man's hot. Whatever happened with him? Did you ever see him again after Jackie got kidnapped? That was like two months ago. You got really quiet about giving out the details on him."

"Nope. After we got Jackie back, I only met him one night for drinks. That's been it."

"Well, at least you have Reno. He's a fine-looking man, and you don't need to make up stories when someone asks you what he does for a living."

"Um, well," I said, "about Reno."

"What? What happened to Reno? Is there something you aren't telling me?"

"We sort of had another discussion on Saturday."

"Was it a *little* discussion or a *big* discussion?"

"Sort of a medium discussion."

"Was it about the same thing as always?"

"Yup," I admitted. "He doesn't want a girlfriend he needs to worry about. He says he's constantly waiting for a phone call that I got shot, or stabbed, or kidnapped."

"He forgot blown-up," Sophie said. "You were almost

blown-up that one time, remember?"

"He wants me to go back to being a bartender or something boring like that."

"You'd think he'd understand, being a cop and all."

"That's what I thought, but somehow it only makes it worse. Every time something happens to me, someone in the department rushes to tell him about it, then we have another argument."

"Well, you two always get back together whenever you have a 'discussion.' It'll probably work out. When are you seeing him again?"

"We're supposed to meet tomorrow night for dinner at Frankie Z's," I said. "Hopefully, he'll still want to go. Whenever we have a discussion, he's skittish for a few days."

"Have you decided yet what you're going to wear to Danica's wedding? It's a week from Friday, and I still don't know what I'm going to wear. Gina's not stressed about it, of course. She says she'll root around her closet and come up with a dress. But it's driving me crazy."

"I know what you mean. We got the invitations a month ago, and I still have no idea what to wear. But it'll be great to see Danica and Muffy again."

We'd met Danica and her fiancé Alex during an assignment six months before. There'd been the usual amount of mayhem, but things eventually worked out for the best. We also met Alex's grandmother, a wealthy semi-retired land developer named Margaret "Muffy" Sternwood.

I was a little disappointed I wasn't a closer friend with Danica. She seems like a nice person, and we get along well. Unfortunately, she works nights as an exotic dancer at Jeannie's Cabaret, and our paths almost never cross. I was hoping we could rekindle our friendship at the wedding.

"How's Annie doing?" I asked. "Have you heard from her?"

"Nope," Sophie said. "But since it's finals week, she probably has a lot on her mind. Don't forget she graduates on Saturday, and she expects the three of us to be there."

"It'll be great to see her graduate. I'm also looking forward to the reception at the Saguaro Sky. I've only been there a few times, but it's always gorgeous."

"I wonder if Jackie's had time to do anything new with it yet?" Sophie asked.

Jackie Wade's one of the Cougars we'd recently gotten to know. As a result of an assignment a couple of months ago, we helped her take ownership of the upscale Scottsdale Saguaro Sky Golf Resort. The graduation reception on Saturday was going to be our first time there since Jackie had become the boss.

"I don't suppose any new assignments have come in?" I asked. "I'm beyond broke, and the rent's due soon."

As though he heard me through the closed door, Lenny stepped out of his office. He saw me and smiled, and as always, seeing him smile gave me a creepy feeling.

"Laura, I'm glad you're here. Come on in. I've got something for you."

Lenny disappeared back into his office. Through the open door, I heard the clink of ice cubes falling into a glass. I looked over at Sophie.

"What's up with Lenny?"

"A courier brought over the settlement check from the Bowden versus Martinez case about an hour ago. Lenny's been smiling and in a good mood ever since he got it."

"That lawsuit was settled like nine months ago," I mused.

"We're only getting the check now?"

"The wheels of justice."

I walked into Lenny's office. He was sitting behind his desk with a half-full glass of Jim Beam in one hand and one of his high-dollar Cuban cigars in the other.

He saw me and waved me to one of the two wooden chairs in front of his desk. Leaning back in his chair, he took a long drag on his cigar and blew a huge puff of foul-smelling smoke in the air.

He waved his glass in the direction of the wet bar in the corner of the office, offering me a drink. I shook my head since it was still too early for alcohol.

He shrugged as if to say, *suit yourself.* Setting down his glass, he picked up the check sitting on his desk, gently waving it at me.

"This," he said as he gave a small chuckle. "This makes it all worthwhile."

"The final amount was good?"

"Three-point-seven million dollars."

Damn!

"How much are we going to get out of that?"

He took another puff on his cigar. "Well, you see, that's the beauty of the situation. As of this moment, my fee is whatever I want it to be."

I raised my eyebrows, questioning both his ethics and his sanity.

"But, I thought the fee was agreed to ahead of time," I said.

"Naah, you don't understand. That doesn't matter. The agreement was only meant to ease the client's mind. A beautiful work of fiction. I should know. I wrote it up. This is what matters," he said, again waving the check at me. "For an attorney, this is the magic moment. This is why I worked nights and weekends for almost half a year."

I still didn't get it. Lenny saw my confusion and went on.

"You see," he said, speaking slowly as if he was talking to a child. "The judge ordered the respondent, Bowden, to pay three-point-seven million dollars. Now Bowden has paid it. As far as Bowden is concerned, the case is over, and if he never thinks about it again, he'll be all the happier for it."

"But what about our client?" I asked.

"Our client, Martinez, on the other hand, was never guaranteed to get a dime out of the lawsuit," Lenny said, still with a huge grin. "When I go over tomorrow and hand her a check for over a million dollars, she'll be so floored she isn't going to quibble too much if she gets a million and a half, two million, or three. Whatever she gets, it will be more money than she could have ever imagined getting in her entire life. I can keep whatever I want and call it a fee."

"And no one will complain?"

"Oh, sure, some of her relatives will bitch a little that my fee was outrageous, but the contract she signed states that in case of a dispute over my fee, the entire settlement will be held in escrow until the dispute is resolved."

"In other words," I said, "if she objects, she won't see a dime until it goes through the system, which will take a couple of years."

"Exactly," Lenny said. "Besides, after Martinez starts promising to spread the settlement money around to her family, the 'sue the lawyer' talk will die down. It always does."

Maybe I should go to law school?

"You said you have something for me?" I asked.

"A new client, Lester Murdock, will be in town for a few days. He's cleaning up some issues surrounding an inheritance. It'd be good if he had someone who knows the city to show him around and help him out. I was thinking having you do it would be better than hiring out a driver."

Better? You mean cheaper.

"So, you want me to babysit?" I asked, somewhat skeptically.

"Yeah. But don't think of it as babysitting. Think of it as earning a paycheck. There aren't a lot of cheating spouses needing to be caught at the moment. You have one, Gina's working on two, and that's it. But trust me, with what I'm going to bill this guy, it'll be worth babysitting him for a few days. Besides, you always like doing good deeds and helping to save the world. Maybe helping out this guy will count towards that."

"Somehow, I don't think it will," I said. "Am I only supposed to drive him around?"

"That and help him out. His grandfather died a few weeks ago. They read the will yesterday, and our client apparently inherited some very valuable things. He's in town from Chicago to pick them up. His attorney's an old friend of mine. I got a call this morning to see if I knew someone local to drive him around."

I sighed and registered defeat. "Where's he staying?"

"He's in one of the high-dollar suites at the Tropical Paradise. He got in late last night, but he should be up by now. I'll call him and let him know you're coming." He wrote down the room number and handed it to me.

"It figures," I said with a laugh.

"What? Is there something I should know about the

Tropical Paradise?"

"Nope, it just brings back some memories."

The Scottsdale Tropical Paradise is one of the nicer golf resorts in Arizona. It's owned by a group called Scottsdale Land and Resort Management, Inc., which is run by Anthony "Tough Tony" DiCenzo. In addition to building and running golf resorts, he's also head of the largest crime family in Scottsdale.

Because of certain events that occurred during some of my previous assignments for Lenny, I've gotten to know Tough Tony and some of his associates. This includes his second in command, a gorgeous man named Maximilian.

I've had a few adventures with Max, and I know he's interested in me in a way that goes beyond being strictly professional. Tony has his business offices in the Tropical Paradise, and I've been to meetings with him there more than once. Now, I was headed back to the resort.

Hopefully, I wouldn't run into Tony, or Max.

Chapter Two

I walked out the back door of the office towards my car. As with most mornings in June, the weather in Scottsdale was beautiful.

There wasn't a trace of a breeze, and there wasn't a single cloud in the deep blue sky. The temperature was still climbing, and I knew it was going to be another sizzler.

A perfect day for keeping the tourists away.

I drove up Scottsdale Road and pulled into the main entrance of the Tropical Paradise, where I parked in one of the side lots down the hill from the main reception building. A nearby resort map posted on a sign helped me locate Lester Murdock's room.

Fortunately, it was only about two hundred yards away in a cluster of luxury bungalows. The path to the suite took me past a huge resort pool, the water reflecting the deep blue of the sky.

There were already twenty or thirty tourists sunbathing and splashing in the water. Even though it was still early, the pool bar seemed to be doing a brisk business. The water looked inviting, and I wanted to flip off my shoes and settle down in one of the lounge chairs.

Maybe a piña colada would be a good way to start the day?

Instead of indulging in a cold drink, I continued down the sidewalk between rows of towering date palms. About fifty yards away, a landscaper mowed a patch of Bermuda grass.

I took in a deep breath, both to enjoy the wonderful smell of fresh-cut grass and also to steel myself for the job ahead. A babysitter, I was not.

I climbed the steps to the client's room and knocked on the oversized wooden door. There was a pause of about thirty seconds, during which I could hear movement in the room and someone talking on a phone. The door opened, and there stood Lester Murdock, dressed only in a towel loosely wrapped around his waist.

I immediately noticed that he was gorgeous and had an incredible body. He looked to be somewhere in his late thirties or early forties and was about six feet two inches tall.

His hair was short and dark. A nice tan complemented his deep blue eyes. He was talking on his phone with one hand and holding a cup of coffee in the other.

He waved me in, pointed to a couch, and then to the coffee pot on the table. As he pointed, I noticed his fantastic smile. It lit up his face in a friendly and welcoming way. Turning, he walked into the bedroom, still talking on the phone.

I was grateful the towel had stayed on his waist. I expected it to drop off at any moment, and I didn't want to deal with purposefully seeming not to look, while at the same time maybe sneaking in a little peek.

I can't help it. I like looking at men.

I'd just poured myself a cup of coffee when he walked back into the room. Fortunately, the towel was still in place. He held up his phone and looked at me.

"It's on mute," he said. "Have you ever been to Vail? A

friend of mine's buying a hotel there and wants to know if I want a piece of it. As a businessman, he's solid as a rock, but I don't ski, and I've never been there."

"I spent the night there when I was on vacation in Colorado a few years ago," I said. "It's beautiful. Even though it was summer, I was surprised at how many people were there. We took the gondola to the top of the mountain, and the view was breathtaking."

"Would you buy a hotel there?"

What?

"Um, I guess it would depend on where it was. Vail's a big place. The best hotels seem to be near the ski lifts. The ones further away didn't always look as nice."

He gave me a look that told me he was impressed. Then he hit the button to take the phone off mute.

"Where's it located?" he asked in a serious business voice. "Is it close to the lifts?" He looked over at me and winked.

"About two hundred yards from the gondola?" he repeated, phrasing it as a question as he looked over at me.

I smiled and gave him a thumbs-up.

"Okay," he said into the phone. "I'll take thirty percent. But I'll also need a room at my disposal anytime I give a one-week notice. A nice room. Can you do that? Well, who knows? I might take up skiing. Good, send the paperwork to the office? Okay? Thanks."

He hung up and looked at me.

"Thanks for the tip. Like I said, I don't ski, so I wouldn't have thought of that."

He looked down and realized he was still dressed only in a towel.

"Oh, jeez, sorry. I'm half-naked. I was late getting in last night, and I'm running behind today. Let me get dressed, then we can take off. I don't know what Leonard told you, but I'm on a bit of a treasure hunt this week. Have another coffee, and I'll tell you about it on the way."

Fifteen minutes later, he came out of the bedroom, fully dressed. As he walked closer, I couldn't help but notice his cologne. It was unusual and obviously expensive. Smelling it gave me visions of naked men and lustful feelings. He walked over to me, holding out his hand.

"Les Murdock," he said as we shook. "You must be Laura Black. Thanks for coming out here so quickly. If you're ready, let's go."

He grabbed a folder sitting on an end table, and then we went out the door. I noticed he winced at the thirty-degree temperature increase as we went outside. Personally, I thought stepping out into the warm Scottsdale morning was nice. I'd been getting cold sitting in the air-conditioned room.

In Scottsdale, any building a tourist may enter is air-conditioned down to sixty-eight or seventy degrees. I guess that's the temperature considered comfortable in places like Illinois, New York, or North Dakota.

It's way too cold for me. I keep my apartment at a money-saving and comfortable eighty-two degrees.

Whenever I go to a mall or a movie theater, I always take along a sweater. I've noticed other Scottsdale natives often do the same thing.

We walked through the immaculate resort and made our way down to the parking lot. I hit the remote to unlock the car doors.

As we got closer to my car, Les pulled up short. His gaze took in the crumpled fender, the scraped paint, and the duct-taped mirror.

He took a step closer and looked down at the bullet hole in the driver-side rear fender. Without a word, he went around to the passenger side and was about to open the door when I saw him glance over the gash the hatchet had made in the front fender.

Crap, here it comes.

"Everything, um, okay?" I asked.

"I had an Accord several years ago, back when I was starting out. What a great car. These things are indestructible. It looks like you've had some adventures in this car. I've been known to get into a few adventures myself, and sometimes, I've done more than crumple a fender or two. Is that a bullet hole in the back? Hopefully, we won't run into anything too wild this week."

"Well, you don't know my life, but yes, hopefully nothing too wild. Where're we going?"

"My granddad's house. It's on the side of a mountain."

He gave me the address, and my eyes opened wide.

"Wow, that must be some house," I said as I pulled out of the parking lot. "What exactly did your granddad do?"

"He was an engineer and an inventor. Dad said he was always messing around with stuff. According to family history, he got his first fortune when he patented some advances in air-conditioning systems back in the forties and fifties."

"Your grandfather had some of the original air conditioning patents?" I asked.

"From what Dad said, Granddad's inventions are largely responsible for people being able to live comfortably in places like Scottsdale. Granddad told me that before World

War II, Scottsdale was a small farming community in the desert. The only tourists were tuberculosis patients who came to Arizona for the hot, dry climate. After Granddad's window-mounted air-conditioning systems were introduced in the fifties, people started trickling into the desert. He said the Arizona migration boom really started when his central air-conditioning systems were widely adopted in the sixties."

"He's right about that," I said. "From what I learned as a kid, nobody really lived here at all until about 1950. Then things started going crazy."

"Granddad trained to be a World War II fighter pilot at Falcon Field in Mesa. He came back after the war and lived in Arizona for the rest of his life."

"I've heard that a lot of the flyers from back then ended up here after the war," I said.

"Well, after the money started rolling in from his air-conditioning patents, he went on to make another fortune in real estate. According to Dad, he bought any ranch or tract of land on the outskirts of town that would come up for sale. Granddad thought that when his air conditioners started to become widely used, the city would rapidly expand, and his land would be worth a lot. Since he already had money, he sat on the land as the city grew up around the properties. He sold off most of it about fifteen years ago when land values were so high."

"He must have done well with that," I said.

"More than well, but it partially leads to my current problem. I'll tell you all about it as soon as we get to the house."

We drove west on Camelback, past the Phoenician Resort, then into the high-dollar real estate area south of Camelback Mountain. When we got to Dromedary Road, I turned north and followed the winding road up to a cluster of affluent homes sitting at the foot of the mountain.

When we reached the address Les had given me, I stopped the car and stared. With the possible exception of Muffy Sternwood's, I'd never seen a house so big.

"Are you sure this is the right address?" I asked as I gawked up at the huge house. "It looks more like a castle than a home."

"This is the place. And as big as it looks on the outside, it's even bigger on the inside. There are rooms and hallways going everywhere."

We drove up a long, curved driveway and parked in a front courtyard that could easily hold ten or fifteen cars. The house itself was beautiful.

It was built against the steep side of Camelback Mountain, and I could see that the bedrock of the mountain formed the back wall of the house. There were four floors, each with several archways and balconies.

On the far right side of the house, the third floor had been replaced by a wide, flat terrace protected by a black and gold wrought iron railing. To the left of the house was a tempting tropical oasis with a nice-sized pool and an inviting waterfall. It looked nicer than the pools in some of the hotels in Scottsdale.

Les opened the folder he carried, took out an envelope, and pulled out a key.

As we approached the house, I couldn't help but be impressed. The front entrance consisted of two enormous doors, each almost nine feet tall, flanked by a set of graceful queen palms.

The front surface of each door was covered with a thick copper plate, molded with a scene of a half-dressed Greek goddess being fed grapes by an eager-looking satyr, the little half-man, half-horse of Greek mythology. Maybe it was just me, but the little satyr seemed to be leering at the nearly naked goddess.

Les opened one of the doors and led me into the main entrance hall. The elegant, vaulted ceiling and sparkling chandelier again looked more like something found in a nice hotel than in a house.

"Come on," he said. "If I can remember how to get there, I'll show you my favorite part of the house."

The entry hall had a beautiful curving staircase. We climbed the stairs and then walked down another long hallway, going past six or seven doors, all made of some sort of dark wood.

"Does anyone still live in the house?" I asked as we walked.

"From what the lawyer told me, there's a cleaning staff that comes in twice a week, a pool service, and some landscapers. Other than that, the house is empty."

At the end of the corridor was a set of large double doors. They had a similar Greek Goddess theme as on the front doors. Les swung them open, and we stepped into a beautiful two-story library.

Bookshelves filled with thousands of books extended up almost twelve feet along every wall and reached up to a balcony that curved along the entire back part of the room. There was even a ladder on a rolling track for reaching the books on the upper shelves.

On the left side of the room was a spiral brass staircase

connecting the main floor to the balcony level. The bookshelves along the left wall were interrupted by three recesses on the lower level. Each of these alcoves contained a Greek-looking sculpture.

In the center of the room were several comfortable-looking red leather couches and wingback chairs, just perfect for curling up with a book. The right side mirrored the left but without the sculptures. Three small windows evenly spaced between the stacks of books on the upper balcony provided points of natural light.

Even with all of this, the real statement piece was the floor-to-ceiling window at the end of the room. It must have been fifteen feet high and twenty-five feet wide.

It covered the entire expanse of the wall, revealing a breathtaking view of the city. I could see all the way from downtown Phoenix to South Mountain. I went up to the window and looked out.

"This is stunning," I said.

"Come on," he said. "Let me show you a better view."

"This isn't the best view?" I asked.

"Just wait. You'll see it in a second."

He led me over to a small door in the wall next to the window. We went through the door and found ourselves outside on a wide stone terrace. The same elaborate black and gold iron railing enclosed the front of the terrace, combining architectural beauty with common-sense safety.

Stepping out onto the porch, I felt the heat of the late morning wash over me. I guessed it was now about a hundred or maybe a hundred and five degrees.

The view of the city from the back part of the terrace was the same as from the library. But as we approached the front edge, the view opened up and I could see down the mountain to all the houses below. A faint breeze coming up the side of the mountain cooled the air, just a bit.

Standing at the iron railing, I marveled at the view. Since the air in Arizona is so dry, there's seldom any haze to blur details in the distance.

I had a clear view of the massive skyscrapers of downtown Phoenix, the thousands of individual houses, and the snaking highways full of cars. The city itself seemed to be a living thing stretching across the valley.

I watched as a dozen tiny airplanes took off and landed at Sky Harbor Airport. I felt like a princess standing in her castle, looking down over her beautiful kingdom.

"As a kid," Les said, "I'd come out here with a chair from the library and spend hours reading wonderful books and looking down at the city. I think they got tired of me leaving the good chairs outside because one day when I came out here, there was a kid-size chair and footstool already set up for me. No matter what kind of family squabbles were going on inside, I always looked at this terrace as my own little personal refuge."

"There was a lot of arguing within the family?" I asked, coming out of my princess trance.

"Mostly between my dad and granddad. They fought constantly until right before my father died, about ten years ago. What you need to know about our family dynamics is that my mom died shortly after I was born, so I never really knew her. My sister and I were raised by Dad and a series of nannies. Granddad was a kid during the Great Depression and was part of the World War II generation. But my father was a hippy baby boomer who grew up in the sixties. I've heard he was always somewhat of a socialist, and after Mom died, it only got worse. He kept accusing Granddad of being greedy and hoarding his money from the people. I once heard Dad tell Granddad he should give away his fortune in the name of humanity."

"How'd your granddad react to that?" I asked.

"About like you'd expect," Les said with a laugh. "He'd lecture Dad right back, telling him he was naïve in the ways of the world. Granddad once told my father that when he actually did something with his life, other than bitch about how unfair the world was, they could have a man-to-man discussion. Granddad said until that happened, he'd consider my dad to be a whining child. It was a dispute that went on for years."

"I can't imagine it was easy listening to that."

"Well, I was young and pretty much used to it. What I couldn't figure out was why my father wanted Granddad to give away his house and his money. Even as a kid, I knew Granddad had worked hard to earn it. Giving it away to somebody because they didn't want to work sounded sort of silly."

"How'd you deal with the family tensions?" I asked. "Especially when you were young?"

"Well, as you can see, I had this wonderful refuge. There are thousands of books in the library. My favorites were the international travel books. There must have been a hundred of them, and most were filled with pictures. As a child, I could visit the Taj Mahal in India or the Great Wall in China. Through the books here, I've been to the ancient temple of Angkor Wat in Cambodia and toured the ruins of Machu Picchu in Peru."

"I always loved flipping through the travel books when I was a kid," I reminisced.

"Now that I've been able to make some money of my own, I've been able to visit most of the places I read about here on the terrace as a kid. In some ways, it seemed like I was visiting old friends."

He fell silent, lost in his thoughts. It was obvious that being at the house again was stirring up a lot of old memories.

"Come on," he said. "Let's get back into the air-conditioning, and I'll tell you why we're here."

We walked back into the library. He motioned me to one of the leather couches while he grabbed a nearby chair and moved it closer to the couch. Once we were both comfortably seated, he began to talk.

"Granddad was always one for practical jokes. When the will was read, it seems he wanted to continue his jokes, even in death."

"What did he do?" I asked.

"Some of his wealth was in real estate, mostly this house and a few properties scattered in the cities around Scottsdale. He even owned a bar somewhere up in the mountains. But for the last fifteen years, the bulk of his fortune was in jewelry. It's been both a hobby and a passion. He collected rare and historic pieces of jewelry his entire adult life. He has a necklace documented to be worn by Jane Seymour, Queen of England under Henry the Eighth, and an engagement ring Richard Burton once gave to Elizabeth Taylor."

Damn.

"That sounds like a good hobby to me," I said. "I've always envied people who could afford to do something like that. I can barely afford to collect souvenir T-shirts."

"Granddad always kept the main pieces in a large and ornate wooden box. He called it his jewelry case, but I always thought of it as a treasure chest. He kept the box in the walk-in safe in the master bedroom. I remember when I was a kid, he would take my sister and me into the safe and let us hold some of the pieces. Most of them have full documentation to verify their legitimate sale, authenticity, and history. The lawyer back in Chicago has all the paperwork. That's not the problem."

"So, what's the problem?"

"The problem is, before he died, Granddad hid the chest somewhere."

"Why'd he hide it?" I asked.

"I guess it's just his sense of humor. One last practical joke to play on my sister and me. The will says we'll split the house and the real estate, no matter what. But whoever finds the jewelry first gets to keep it, all of it."

He stopped to look around the library.

"I'll admit," Les said, "it's a nice house. Although I don't know how someone shares a house with his sister, even one this big. But at least that part of the will made sense. Granddad said he put the chest somewhere safe, but in a place we could get to it. He also said we could probably find it on our own, but he left us some clues as to where it was hidden, just in case."

"Okay," I said. "That sounds pretty straightforward. What's the catch?"

"Granddad's will also said that if neither of us could find the jewelry within a year, his lawyer would be instructed to sell it all at auction and donate the money to charity. The bottom line is whoever gets the chest first becomes extremely wealthy."

"Wow," I said. "A treasure hunt to find a chest full of jewelry? It sounds like it's worth millions."

"Tens of millions," Les chuckled. "Twenty, thirty, maybe more. And you're right; we're here like pirates with a treasure map. To be honest, I think Granddad was starting to lose it before the end."

"How'd your sister react to the idea of a treasure hunt? I imagine she's as interested in finding the jewelry as you."

"Yesterday, at the reading, I suggested to the lawyers that neither my sister nor I had time for a treasure hunt. We should just stipulate whoever finds the chest first would agree to split everything. I know we'd both be glad to have the jewelry, but it's not as if we actually need the money."

"I take it your sister didn't agree to split the treasure?"

"Unfortunately, no. We've always been competitive with each other, and this won't be any different. I saw the light in her eyes as they read the will. I'm sure she'll also be in town today to look for the chest. She'll look at this as a way to stick it to me."

"You two don't get along?"

"That's an understatement. I've made a few attempts over the years, but we really haven't spoken since Dad died."

"Okay," I said. "What do we have to go on?"

"Not a lot."

"Well, we have to start somewhere. Did you say there was a safe in your grandfather's bedroom where he usually kept the chest? Maybe we should start there?"

We walked back through the house, down a couple of long hallways, down a wide staircase, down another long hallway, and finally to a wide foyer, stopping at a huge wooden door.

"Your granddad sure did like big doors," I said.

"It was more impressive when I was a kid. I could barely reach the handles, and it always felt like I was opening up part of a wall rather than a door."

Similar to the front doors of the house, this one had an intricate scene of a Greek orgy carved into the gilded wooden paneling. There was the same nude goddess along with the same horny satyrs, but this door also had two half-naked men pawing at the goddess.

The men and satyrs were gazing at the goddess with obvious lust, but it looked to me like she seemed to be rather bored with the orgy. Maybe the goddess was tired of being the center of their lustful attentions, and it didn't really interest her anymore.

My mind drifted to how it would be if I were the goddess and Reno and Max were both pawing at me at the same time. I'd never thought about them both touching me at once. I allowed myself a pleasant few seconds of fantasizing about what would happen next.

Stop that.

"What?" Les asked. "You had the most mischievous smile."

"Oh, just daydreaming."

"I take it you like the carving on the door. As a teenager, I used to pretend I was one of the horny guys who were fondling the woman."

"It's an interesting carving," I said.

We walked into the bedroom, which was instantly illuminated by motion-activated lights. The space was massive, easily thirty by forty feet, with a high domed ceiling. Looking up, I noticed the ceiling was painted to look like a blue sky with fluffy white clouds.

"You like the clouds on the ceiling?" Les asked. "Granddad installed a lighting system years ago. Here, let me show you."

Les walked over to a control panel on the wall and

pressed a button. The main lights slowly dimmed, and hidden lights around the edge of the ceiling caused the clouds over the bed to turn a bright sunshine yellow with a trace of orange.

"This is the sunset program," he said. "It will take about fifteen or twenty minutes for the program to simulate the sun going down. In the meantime, let me show you the vault."

We moved toward a full-length mirror mounted on a wall next to a built-in wooden bookshelf. The mirror was about eight feet high and five feet wide.

Les selected a green book high on the bookshelf and pulled it toward him. There was a slight click, and one side of the mirror popped out an inch. He pulled on the corner, and I watched while it smoothly opened to reveal a small interior room.

This room also had a domed ceiling with a stunning crystal chandelier hanging over our heads. There were two red velvet chairs anchoring the corners of the room with a small white table situated between them. On the table sat a small statue of what looked like a half-clothed Greek goddess.

What is it with Lester's granddad and naked Greek women?

As we walked into the room, I saw the door of a giant safe set in the far wall. It was the same size as the vault at my bank. The door was made of shining stainless steel, probably seven feet high and five feet wide. There was a combination dial and a big handle to turn and open the vault's door.

"Wow," I said. "That's impressive. I've never seen a safe this big in a house. It's bigger than the safes at some of the banks I've been to."

"Granddad said he built the house around the vault. It's a

real Sheffield bank safe. They built it against the mountain. The vault itself goes about thirty feet into the bedrock of Camelback Mountain. He said there's no way someone could simply tunnel into it or come up through the floor."

"Do you think the chest with the jewelry is in the vault?"

"I'm not sure, but I don't think so. The will implied the box was somewhere we could get to, and the vault seems kind of secure. But you're right. Since we don't know where else to look, this seems like the place to start. Who knows, maybe it's been sitting in the vault the entire time, and the will was only another one of Granddad's jokes."

"Okay," I said. "Let's open it up. Do you have the combination?"

"Um, well, that's a problem."

"You don't have the combination? I don't think we'll be able to pick the lock."

"Well, I know it's a three-number combination. I watched Granddad open it up half a dozen times. He once told me the numbers were an important date in his life."

"Okay, what important date? His birthday? The day he joined the Army? Maybe the day he made his first million?"

"I don't know."

I just looked at him. I could see this was going nowhere fast.

"Hey," he said. "Don't give me that look. That's the same look my ex-wife always gave me. I don't know what the date is yet, but I can probably find out."

"Okay," I said. "Let's go back to the bedroom and work this out."

As we walked back into the master bedroom, the sunset program had turned the sky and clouds bright orange. The effect was really beautiful. I could see myself lying in the bed and getting sleepy while the sky slowly changed colors and grew dark.

"Let's think," I said. "We'll need to write down every important date in your granddad's life. There probably aren't more than fifteen or twenty. Then we'll come back here and try them all out. If that doesn't work, I guess we'll hire a safecracker. There must be someone who can open the door to the vault."

"I was thinking the same thing. In fact, I already started a list on the flight out here. I'll need to call the relatives to get the rest of the dates. Hopefully, it won't take too long to get the vault open."

The bedroom sky had gradually started to shift from bright orange to bright red. The red was deepest directly above the bed and still more orange against the side above the door from the hallway.

"That's amazing," I said.

"What comes next is even better. Sit on the bed and look up."

We both went to the bed and sat on the edge. I looked directly overhead at the bright red sky.

Finally, I just leaned back until I was lying back on the bed. Les also leaned back until he lay next to me, looking straight up.

The clouds overhead had started to fade into the darkening sky. As the red dimmed, small stars started to light up. Within a minute, there were hundreds, if not thousands, of stars becoming visible in the sky.

"Amazing, isn't it?" he asked.

"I've never seen anything like it. It's like being in a planetarium."

As I lay next to Les, watching the stars come out, I gradually became aware of the scent of his cologne and that our arms were lightly touching. My brain flashed back to the sight of him in a towel, making my heart kick up a notch.

I began to wonder if he had planned this. How would I feel about it if he did?

Normally, I'd get angry if a guy I didn't know very well tried to seduce me. But in this case, I wasn't upset or even annoyed. Actually, I kind of hoped he would at least try.

Not that it would go anywhere, of course, but it was sort of nice to know a handsome man thought I was still worth the effort. I lightly pressed my arm against his and felt his leg start to rub against mine.

I let it go on for about thirty seconds. Then I opened my mouth to ask him about his intentions.

"What the hell is going on here?"

It was a woman's voice coming from the vicinity of the hallway. She sounded pissed.

As we both quickly sat up, I saw a woman standing in the door to the hall. She looked to be a few years older than Les and was a little taller than I was.

She was thin and had longer blonde hair, parted in the middle. I would have said she was pretty if it wasn't for the fact she was furious. The lights from the sunset program had turned her face a bright red.

"Oh, I should have known," she hissed out. "On Granddad's bed with a woman. That's just great. Don't tell me. You were doing the 'let's watch the sunset' thing? You haven't tried that since you were a teenager. You're pathetic. Do you know that? You really are pathetic."

Les let out a deep sigh.

"Elizabeth," he said, "this is Laura Black. Laura, this is Elizabeth Bright-Murdock, my sister."

I felt my face blushing a deep red, and I was glad the lights of the sunset had helped hide my embarrassment.

"So," Elizabeth said, "I take it after you're through having sex on Granddad's bed, you'll be looking around for the jewelry? I'm assuming it's not in the vault since that seems too obvious. And since I don't see it in here, I'm guessing you don't have it yet."

Elizabeth hit a switch on the control panel, and the bright overhead lights popped back on.

"We haven't been in the vault yet," Les said. "And no, we haven't even started looking around the house."

"What? You needed a quickie first to get motivated to look for the jewelry?"

"It's not like that," Les said. "Laura's from a law office here in Scottsdale, and she's driving me around and helping me look for the jewelry."

"Right," she scoffed. "It's pretty obvious what she's here for. So, why haven't you been in the vault?"

"The door's locked."

"Really? You don't have the combination?"

"No," he said. "Do you?"

There was a pause that seemed a bit too long. "Why would I have the combination? I suppose we're going to need to hire a professional safe-cracker to open the door?"

"Quite possibly."

Elizabeth walked into the room with the vault and, thirty seconds later, came back out.

"You're right. It's locked up tight. Well, while you two

finish up what you were doing, I'm going to poke around the house. Who knows, maybe I'll get lucky too."

"Elizabeth," Les said, "my offer's still good. Why don't we agree that whoever finds the chest first agrees to split the jewelry?"

"Sure, like the way you were going to be helpful when Dad died? When you so kindly offered to handle the settling of his estate so we'd both get an equal share? How'd that work out for me?"

"You know that wasn't my fault."

"Right. Well, you look for the jewelry your way and I'll look for it mine. We'll see who finds it first."

She turned and stalked out of the room, only pausing to hit the light switch to start the sunset program again.

"I'm sorry about that," Les said, his face again lit with the yellow-orange glow of the sunset.

"Is she always that angry?"

"Well, as you heard, we haven't always gotten along. I don't think this is going to be any different. Okay, how do we start?"

"I agree with your sister," I said. "Let's walk through the house. We'll feel pretty foolish if the jewelry's sitting in a bedroom down the hall, and your sister goes in with a pillowcase and picks it all up."

Chapter Three

We spent the next three hours going from room to room throughout the mansion. We looked in a dozen bedrooms and in at least twenty closets and wardrobes.

We looked in the kitchen, the pantries, the parlors, the formal dining hall, the breakfast nook, the game room, the offices, and the library. We went outside and searched the garages, the pool, and the gardener's shack.

We then searched hallways, stairs, an elevator, and even the attic. We went down to the basement, where there was a huge wine cellar and a laundry room, and we even started poking through a stack of old boxes we found.

Finally, we had to admit neither the chest nor the jewelry were anywhere obvious. We passed Elizabeth several times as we searched, but she apparently wasn't having any better luck than we were.

Eventually, we ended up back in the library. Feelings of annoyance and frustration were washing over me.

"It's pretty obvious the jewelry isn't anywhere in the open," I said. "Since it's hidden, we'll need to sit and think logically about where it could be."

"That seems reasonable. How do you want to go about it?"

I looked at my watch. "It's already after three. Are you

hungry?"

"I was thinking the same thing," he said. "Is there anywhere nearby?"

"I know the perfect place. We're about ten minutes from The Oasis at the Phoenician. It's gorgeous, and I know you'll love it. It's also a good place to talk and think."

We made our way through the house and out to the courtyard. A red Chevrolet was parked next to my Accord, and I assumed it was Elizabeth's rental. As we stepped out into the sunlight, I felt the desert heat wrap around my body like an old friend.

We drove back down the winding mountain road and turned east on Camelback. After a mile, we came to the beautiful tropical display marking the entrance to the Phoenician Resort.

We pulled into the resort and drove to the guard shack. The guard spent a few seconds eyeing my beat-up car. I felt a little annoyed when his eyes lingered on the bullet hole in the side of my trunk.

Haven't you ever seen a bullet hole before?

The guard directed us to park in the visitor's garage. We took our time as we walked past the fountains and through the lush grounds to the main pool complex.

Even though it was now over a hundred and ten degrees in the shade, there were at least fifty women and half as many men laying out and getting some sun. I saw that not all of them had used enough sunblock, and several of the tourists were turning red. Dozens of cabanas surrounded the pool, most of which were being used by people who didn't want the full effects of the sun.

We wound our way past the sunbathers and through the pools to The Oasis, a bar and grille set in the middle of the three levels of the resort's pools. I couldn't think of a more lovely and relaxing spot.

I'd been here several times before, most recently with Reno. It made me smile to think of being here with him.

We were seated at a table near a splashing waterfall. I ordered a Diet Pepsi and a black Angus burger. Les had a beer and the blackened mahi-mahi. The waitress brought our drinks, and we had a chance to talk while we waited for the food.

"We're focusing on the vault," I said. "Do you know anywhere else your granddad could have hidden the jewelry or where he might have left a clue about where to find the chest?"

"It's been a few years since I've been in the house. I think it's been the same with Elizabeth. But as we went through the house today, we looked everywhere I could think to look."

"The room with the vault can only be accessed if you know to pull the green book on the bookshelf," I said. "Do you think there are any other hidden rooms? Maybe your granddad thought you knew about one of those, and he put the jewelry there?"

"It's possible. Granddad always loved things like that. Having another secret room somewhere wouldn't surprise me."

"What about the other properties he owned? We're concentrating on the house because it seems the most obvious. But maybe he moved the jewelry chest to one of those?"

"From what the lawyer said, there're five other properties. Four of them are undeveloped land somewhere in the desert near places called Carefree, Pinnacle Peak, and Queen Creek. The other's a bar. I remember Granddad once said he owned a saloon in a place called Whiskey Row, wherever that is."

"Whiskey Row's up in Prescott," I said. "That's a town up in the mountains about an hour and a half from here. It's nice."

"Maybe we should go up there and look around."

"Maybe, but let's first get into the vault. You said the combination is an important date in your granddad's life. You've started a list of those dates. If you think you could call other family members to get the rest of them, I can drop you off at your hotel, and you can get that done. When you're ready, we'll go back over to the house and try them out. I imagine your sister will be doing the same thing. Are you sure we can't work with her?"

"You saw how she was, and this was one of her better days. I don't think we can expect any cooperation from Elizabeth."

After our lunch, we spent a few minutes walking around the resort, mainly looking at the tropical plants, the fountains, and the pools. As always, being surrounded by the beautiful scenery lifted my spirits and gave me the motivation to press on.

We eventually reached my car and left the resort to go back to the Tropical Paradise. As we turned north on Scottsdale Road, I noticed there was a dark blue rental sedan behind us with two big guys in it.

I normally wouldn't have given it a second thought, but they appeared to be the same two guys in the same dark blue car that had followed us down Camelback Road as we drove to the Phoenician.

"I don't suppose there's a reason why anyone would want to follow you?" I asked.

He turned and looked back at the car, now about fifty yards behind us.

"None at all. Are you sure they're following us?"

"No, but they look familiar. Maybe I'm being paranoid."

I dropped Les off near his room at the Tropical Paradise. The two guys in the blue rental sedan had followed us up Scottsdale Road until we got to the resort, but they didn't follow us in.

Les and I agreed that he'd make calls to his relatives and get as many of the important dates in his granddad's life as possible. I told him I'd pick him up again at eight o'clock to head back to the house.

We'd then try as many of the combinations as possible. With any luck, we could wrap this whole thing up in one day.

I drove back to my apartment, found a parking space near the back entrance, and went in. My apartment building started out as a hotel back in the seventies.

It was then converted into condominiums in the nineties. It was later switched over to apartments at about the same time people were getting worked up about the latest stock market crash.

After converting the building to apartments, the maintenance budget took a dip, and now the place could really use a facelift. But it's close to where I work, and the rent is reasonable. Well, it's reasonable for Scottsdale, anyway.

I was sitting at my kitchen table, sorting bills, and feeling vaguely depressed about my finances when someone knocked on my door. I tensed briefly, then realized it was the gentle knocking of Grandma Peckham, my next-door neighbor.

I'd met Grandma the day I moved into the apartment a little over three years ago, and I'd liked her from the start. I'd heard the same soft knocking at my door and had opened it to find a small, thin woman with curly purple hair, a big smile, and mischievous blue eyes. Grandma handed me a Diet Pepsi as a housewarming present, and we've been friends ever since.

Today, I opened my door to find Grandma Peckham holding my cat, Marlowe, who was asleep and limp in her arms. She walked in and placed him on my couch. Marlowe didn't wake up, but he did a long stretch, then rolled over and curled into a ball.

"I'm going to be out for the rest of the day," Grandma said, "so I thought I'd bring Marlowe over. I wouldn't want him to singe his little paws on the balcony."

Grandma and I share a common wall between our bedrooms, and we have doors leading out to a shared balcony. We've both installed cat doors so Marlowe can come and go as he pleases.

We leave the cat doors open year-round, but Marlowe won't go outside in the summer heat. He hates the temperatures in the summer as much as Sophie.

I can't say I blame him. When the outside air temperature goes over a hundred and ten, I can only imagine how hot the concrete of the balcony gets.

"Are you doing anything fun tonight?" I asked.

"I'm having a gentleman caller take me out to the movies. We're going to see a new Tom Cruise film."

"Is this a new guy or somebody you've seen before?"

"Well, I know we've been out before. But honestly, I really don't remember a lot about him. There've been so many men lately that they're all starting to blur together."

"Any of them stand out so far?" I asked.

"Well, I did go out with this one eager beaver about two weeks ago. Land sakes alive, that soldier was ready for active duty. But I'm not just looking for that anymore. I'm also looking for someone who respects me as a person. I've even started thinking about traveling again. It might be nice if I had someone to do that with."

A couple of months before, Grandma had decided the best way for her to get some action in the bedroom was to put an ad on the internet. She'd picked out a website called *Naughty-MatureBabes.com*, where the personal ads were full of pictures of naked seniors.

Grandma took several naked selfies and posted her ad. As a result, she's had a steady stream of horny older guys who were also looking for some intimate companionship or at least a steady booty call.

"Is there anything you do remember about him?" I asked.

"Well, he used to be a dentist from Cleveland. He has some family out here, and he moved to Scottsdale after he retired."

"Do you remember what he looks like? Tall, short, thin, fat?"

"I think he took me out to dinner last time. But I can't remember anything else about him. I guess I'll have to let you know."

I made myself a tuna fish sandwich on twelve-grain bread for dinner. As I was mixing the ingredients, Marlowe loudly reminded me how much he also liked tuna. I plopped a spoonful into his bowl, and we both had a nice snack.

I looked at the clock and saw I wouldn't need to leave for an hour, so I took the opportunity to call Reno. We'd had what I called a "discussion" on Saturday night about my job and how it was too dangerous.

Before the discussion, we'd made plans to meet again Wednesday night at Frankie Z's, our favorite restaurant. About halfway through the discussion, I'd gotten angry and left in a huff. Since it was currently Tuesday, I thought I should call Reno and make sure the date for tomorrow night was still on.

I sat on my couch and hit the speed dial for Reno. He answered on the third ring, and I could tell he was in his car.

"Hey," I said. "Is this a bad time?"

"No, I'm heading over to headquarters on Indian School. We're having a citywide meeting on some of the Mexican drug gangs that are popping up in The Valley. Now that we're losing control of the southern border, some of the gangs in northern Mexico have picked up their operations entirely and relocated to Arizona. I'm one of the detectives assigned to advise a task force that's exploring ways to deal with it."

I shuddered when I thought of my recent close encounter with a Mexican drug syndicate called the *Muerte Negra*, or in English, the Black Death. The leader in Arizona was a vicious man named Carlos "The Butcher" Valentino.

I wasn't sure how much Carlos knew about my involvement in helping to bring down a rather large shipment of drugs the gang had brought into the country. I sometimes wake up in a cold sweat, fearing he'll piece together the information and decide to come after me personally.

"Hey, Laura, did I lose you?"

"No, sorry. Thinking about an assignment. Are we still on for tomorrow night? Frankie Z's at seven-thirty?"

"Well, yes, if you're sure you still want to. I wasn't certain after the way you left on Saturday."

"I know. I was angry. But you implied my job wasn't important."

"I'm sorry, that wasn't my intent. I only worry something will happen to you. You sometimes meet up with some rough people in these assignments you do for Lenny."

"You want a girlfriend who's boring? And besides, don't you deal with the same things? Like every day?"

"I have a gun and a badge. Not to mention the backing of the entire Scottsdale Police Department. You only have Sophie."

"I have a gun, remember? You got me the Baby Glock for Christmas a year and a half ago. Besides, I also have Gina. So, in a way, I also have the backing of the Scottsdale Police Department."

"Well, I can't argue about Gina. It was a loss to the department when Lenny lured her away by offering to double her paycheck. She's one of the best detectives I've ever worked with. I'm glad she's there to help watch over you."

"So, are we good?" I asked.

"Yes, we're good. And you're right. I couldn't handle a boring girlfriend. Frankie's at seven-thirty?"

"Perfect. I can't wait."

I hung up the phone and sat on the couch for a few minutes, petting my purring cat. Having a nice conversation with Reno put me back in a good mood.

I hadn't meant to throw in the part about him not wanting a boring girlfriend, but now that I'd said it aloud, I began to realize it was true. I think deep down Reno liked having a girlfriend who could handle herself.

I think the only thing bothering him was the thought that someday I might get myself into more trouble than I could handle. Then I'd end up getting hurt, or worse.

I guess that's a reasonable attitude for my boyfriend to have about me.

Playing treasure hunt in the big house all day had made me feel a little grimy. Since I still had about forty-five minutes before I had to leave, I decided to take a quick shower, blow dry my hair, and fix my makeup. I then said goodbye to Marlowe and was out the door.

As I walked down the hallway toward the stairs, I saw an older man, wearing a dark grey suit, white shirt, and a black tie. The suit was about two sizes too big for the man's thin body. He had on a pair of thick black-framed glasses, and he was lifting them to squint at the numbers on the apartment doors.

"Are you looking for Mary Peckham?" I asked. "I'm Laura Black. Grandma Peckham's my next-door neighbor."

"Why yes, I am," he said in a bright, cheerful voice. He held out his hand in greeting. "I'm Robert Henderson the third, but you can call me Grandpa Bob."

We shook hands, and I led him back down the hallway to Grandma's door.

"I heard you're going to a Tom Cruise movie tonight."

"I think so," he said. "But if she doesn't want to go to that one, she also talked about liking vampire movies, so maybe we'll go to one of those."

"Grandma said you two met on the website. How's your experience been with that?"

"It hasn't been half bad," he said. "I've been able to meet some Cracker Jack women. It was my daughter who suggested it. She knows I've been lonely lately. Besides, the family thinks it'll be safer this way."

"Safer?" I asked.

"Well, you see, after my wife passed, the kids have been worried I'll marry some Clyde-hopping-Jezebel, and they'll be out an inheritance. I can't say I blame them. I've still got a few good years left in me. It might be worth an inheritance to be treated like a king by some good-looking younger gal who doesn't mind spending time with an old geezer like me. They think if I just date around and don't get serious with anyone, they'll still get the money after I'm gone."

I walked the man down to Grandma's door, told him to have fun, and then walked down to my car. The sun had just set, and the horizon was on fire with oranges and reds. It reminded me of the bedroom at the house on Camelback Mountain.

The drive back up to the Tropical Paradise was uneventful. If someone was following me, I couldn't make them out.

I again parked by Les Murdock's bungalow. I didn't want to park too close to the main building where Tony DiCenzo had his business offices.

It wasn't that I was avoiding him, exactly. It's more like talking to Tough Tony isn't something anyone should do unless there's an actual need. Too many things could go wrong.

As I got out of the car, I heard the sound of a Caribbean band with a steel drum coming from the direction of the big resort pool. As I walked closer to the bungalow, I saw the band playing on a small stage near the pool bar.

Now that the sun had gone down and the temperature was barely over a hundred, people had come out to enjoy the evening. I'm not sure how many pools the Tropical Paradise has, but the one next to Les Murdock's room seemed to be the main one for the resort. There were the happy sounds of splashing, talking, and laughter.

I stopped in front of the gate that led down to the pool. Looking over the scene, for some reason, the ongoing party made me a little sad.

Listening to the band, the people, and the splashing waterfalls, I was again tempted to grab a drink and lay on one of the lounge chairs next to the pool. Then, I would simply forget about life for a few hours.

Instead, I had work to do.

I knocked on Les Murdock's door. He answered, and this time, he was fully dressed. Somehow, that vaguely disappointed me. His hair was wet, and I assumed he'd just gotten out of the pool or maybe the shower.

I've noticed tourists take a lot of showers. There's something about walking around all day in the dry desert heat that makes them feel grimy.

"How'd the search go?" I asked. "Were you able to come up with the dates?"

"Um, yeah," he said. "I called several relatives and came up with a pretty good list. I circled the three I think are most likely."

Something about his voice seemed a bit odd. Like maybe he was stressed or nervous. Perhaps it was only the anxiety of the whole treasure hunt thing, but it sent up tiny red flags in my head.

He went to the table and handed me a notepad with a list of maybe twenty dates and notations on it. Some of the dates were underlined, one had stars next to it, and three of the dates were circled.

There were also a couple of small doodles of dogs in the margins. Les stood next to me and pointed at the first date he'd circled.

"This one, December 20, 1923, was the day he was born. It seems kind of obvious, but you never know." His finger slid down to the next circled date. "He was married on June 19, 1948. It seems reasonable he'd regard his anniversary as important, especially after my grandmother died. And this one, March 21, 1949. It's the day Dad was born. I know Dad and Granddad never got along, but maybe Granddad regarded the date as important anyway."

"Those seem reasonable," I said. "Okay, let's head over to the house and try 'em out. If none of the three works, we can go through the entire list, one by one."

We left the bungalow and walked down the path to my car. The pool party was still going full force. If anything, it looked like more resort guests had joined in.

I saw there was a new group of at least a dozen women who were all dressed in identical pink shirts. They looked like part of a bachelorette party.

They stood in a circle, laughing and tossing back shots. As we passed by the gate, Les stopped for several seconds and looked in, just as I had.

"That looks like a nice way to spend the evening," he said. "From what I can tell, they have a party here every night. Honestly, it's been a while since I've done anything just for fun. Let's go open the vault. Maybe we can get the jewelry and be back before the party's over."

We drove down Scottsdale Road, and traffic was light. As we passed Lincoln, I saw the same dark blue rental car again following us at a distance. When we turned west onto Camelback, the blue sedan turned with us, now about three cars behind.

"Your friends are back," I said.

"What friends?" he asked. He then seemed to catch on, and he turned around to look.

"They're a few cars back, but they've been with us for at least four or five miles. Are you sure you don't know who they are?"

"No idea. Are you sure they're following me and not you? I do a lot of business deals, and I'm always pissing off someone, but I don't think I've pissed off anyone enough to have them follow me around in Arizona."

"You came into town to look for several million dollars worth of jewelry. Who else knew you'd be here and knows what you're looking for?"

"Um, only the lawyers and Elizabeth."

Again, I picked up something in his voice. Maybe the guys in the car were making him nervous, or maybe it was something else.

I hate it when a client hides something. It makes my job harder. I hoped whatever he was hiding wouldn't get me into too much trouble.

But it usually does.

As we pulled into the empty courtyard of the house, I watched as the two guys in the car pulled off the road. Apparently, they already knew where we were going, and they didn't want to confront us directly. I hope it stayed that way.

We entered the house and made our way back to the master bedroom. Les hit the light switch, and the large room was once again brightly lit. I was surprised when I felt a brief pang of regret when Les didn't hit the button for the sunset program.

I really need to spend more time with Reno.

We walked to the bookshelf next to the big mirror, and Les pulled on the green book, releasing the door to the vault room. I heard the faint click, and the door swung silently open.

As we walked in, I noticed one of the two chairs had been overturned, which seemed odd. As far as I knew, Elizabeth was the only other person to go into the room after we'd left it earlier.

Les set the list down on the table. I noticed the small Greek statue that had been on the table was now gone.

"There was a figurine on the table, and now it's gone," I said.

"What'd it look like?"

"It was about a foot tall and made of white ivory or plastic. It was sitting on a small granite base. It looked like a Greek goddess of some type. Like the one on the bedroom door."

We both started to think the same thing at the same time.

Damn.

"I hope this doesn't mean Elizabeth's already been here," Les said.

"Well, there's one way to find out. Let's open the door."

Les walked to the vault and tried the handle. It was still locked.

"Tell me," I said. "If the chest with all the jewelry was in the safe and Elizabeth did get it out, would she tell you she had it, or would she just take off?"

"Oh, I'm sure she'd call me," Les said. "She couldn't help but gloat. She'd want to rub my face in it."

"Oh, *would* I?"

We both turned and saw Elizabeth standing in the doorway leading back to the bedroom.

"Hello, Elizabeth," Les said. "Did you come back to say you have the jewelry?"

"If I had the jewelry, why would I be here? I'd have everything locked up tight, and I'd be calling Christie's auction house to have them start the sale."

"Have you been here since we left this afternoon?" I asked.

"I took off right after you did and only got back a few minutes ago. I saw your car in the courtyard and came straight to the bedroom. Is that important?"

"Well, if you haven't been here since this afternoon, how

did the chair get knocked over, and where did the statue go?" I asked.

Elizabeth took a few seconds to look around. "Well, it wasn't me. Have you opened the vault yet?"

"We're about to," Les said. "The combination's an important date in Granddad's life. I made a list of several possibilities and narrowed it down to the most likely three. Since you're here, you might as well help us."

Les glanced at the list, set it down on a nearby table, then went over to the vault. He started turning the dial to the combination. Elizabeth picked up the list and read through it.

After Les entered the date of his granddad's birthday, he tried the lever to open the door. He yanked on it a couple of times, but it was still locked tight. He released a small sniff of frustration before turning back toward Elizabeth, who was still holding his list.

"It's this one," she said, pointing to a date near the bottom of the list. "It's the one you put stars next to. May 15, 1955, that's the day his patent lawsuit was settled. It was in his favor, and it meant he was entitled to the millions of dollars that had been sitting in escrow for years."

"How do you know that's the right date?" I asked her.

"One day, back when I was eight or ten, I was with Granddad while he was opening the vault. As he was dialing the combination, he told me the day he won his lawsuit was the day that changed his life. I've always assumed that date was the combination to the vault."

"So, if you knew, why didn't you open it sooner?" Les asked.

"Well, I would've opened it as soon as you left this afternoon, but I didn't know the exact date. I had to call around to the relatives, the same as you did. I was hoping to get back here and open the vault before you two showed up again. But since the date's already on your list, I imagine you're going to try them all anyway. Who knows? Maybe we'll end up splitting the jewelry after all."

"I told you at the lawyer's office that's what I wanted," Les said. "Let's hope it's in here."

Les went back over to the vault door, and we called out the numbers five, fifteen, and fifty-five as he spun them on the dial.

As he finished entering the combination and was about to pull the lever to unlock the vault, he instead turned toward Elizabeth, swept out his hand, and bent at the waist in a grand bow.

"Would you like to have the honors?" he asked his sister.

"Cross your fingers," she said.

She pulled down on the lever, and it smoothly rotated without a sound.

"Okay," Les said. "Let's take a look."

He pulled on the handle, and the massive door swung open. The accompanying creaking and popping noises indicated just how heavy the door was.

We saw that the door to the vault opened onto a short and narrow hallway, maybe twenty feet long. Beyond loomed a large dark room. Next to the door was a light switch. Les flipped it, and the hallway and vault became so bright that it made me squint.

Again, Les offered to let his sister go in first. She took a deep breath and entered the vault with Les close behind. Elizabeth walked down the hallway and had taken two steps into the vault room when I saw her body go rigid.

"Oh my god!" she squeaked. Unfortunately, she didn't

sound excited. It was more like she was startled or frightened.

Les and I hurried in behind her. The vault was bigger than I expected, probably twelve by fifteen feet. It was ringed with wooden drawers and shelves covered in red velvet.

The first thing I noticed was that there was no chest full of jewelry. The second thing I noticed was a man lying face down and motionless in a pool of blood on the floor.

Shit.

Chapter Four

Elizabeth was still staring down at the body, the shock causing her to shake uncontrollably. Les walked over to the man on the floor and bent down.

He grabbed him by the shoulder and rolled him over. As he did, we could see that the top of the man's forehead had a massive and bloody wound.

The man was in his mid-forties and big. Even without the blunt force trauma, no one but his mother would have ever accused him of being handsome.

The blood on his face was still partially wet, and it looked like he hadn't been dead for very long – a couple of hours at the most. He was lying on top of the missing statue from the outer room.

Les walked around the body and moved the statue to one side so he could bend down and listen for a heartbeat. I knew there wouldn't be one, but watching him go through the motions seemed like the right thing to do.

Les pressed his head against the man's chest for several seconds, followed by pressing his fingers against the man's neck. He looked up at us and shook his head.

Why is it always me? Why can't somebody else find the dead body?

"What do we do now?" Les asked.

I sighed deeply, hoping to convey to everyone I wasn't happy about finding another dead body.

"We need to call the police," I said. "Don't touch anything else."

Les stood up and started to walk out. I looked over at Elizabeth. She was still rigid and shaking. Her eyes hadn't left the body since she'd entered the vault.

"Go on out," I said to Les. "We'll be out in a second."

He didn't waste any time arguing. He almost ran out of the vault. I was glad he left. Elizabeth was letting all her emotions come to the surface.

Les was seemingly trying to remain above the whole thing, but I could see there was deep fear and maybe even some panic in his eyes. I didn't want them both to lose it at once.

"Hey," I said as I walked over to her. "Are you going to be okay?"

She looked up at me, her eyes were red, and two tears slid down her face. She reached out her arms to me, like a toddler.

I instinctively held out my arms and hugged her. She held me in a tight grip for almost a minute while her body shook.

Finally, she started to calm down. Her breathing was still fast, but she was no longer quite so terrified. She let go and took a step back.

"I'm sorry," she said, shaking her head and sniffing back the tears. "I've never seen a dead person before. Well, not one like this."

"I understand," I said. "It's not an easy thing to see. Are you ready to go into the other room? It'll help not being next to him."

"Yeah, okay. But give me a second. My whole body's

numb. If I try to walk now, I'll probably fall over."

Elizabeth had turned her face away from the body and was taking slow, deep breaths. I took the opportunity to look around the vault.

Lining the walls were several rows of wooden drawers, their faces exposing only glimpses of their contents. Not wanting to leave any fingerprints, I used a pen from my purse to pull open a few of them.

Unfortunately, they were all empty. The red-velvet-lined shelves also didn't have a lot on them.

There were two small Greek statues and three vases. There were also several unadorned mannequin busts, like those used in high-end jewelry stores to sell their expensive necklaces. It felt a little creepy with all those blank faces looking down at the body.

Suddenly, I spotted a card propped up on a small stand, centered on one of the shelves. I walked over to take a look at it. It was elaborately inscribed with small, neat cursive writing:

Congratulations on making it into the vault!

Okay, that's weird.

I didn't take the time to read the rest of the card. Instead, I pulled my phone out of the back pocket of my shorts and quickly snapped four or five pictures of the vault.

I then made sure to take two good pictures of the card with the writing on it before helping Elizabeth back to the bedroom. Les was sitting on the bed, the same bed where we'd been watching the sunset just a few hours before.

"Let's go out to the front courtyard," I said. "The police will appreciate it if we don't touch anything else. And there's the real possibility that whoever killed the guy is still somewhere in the house."

At that thought, Elizabeth's eyes opened wide with fresh terror, and she hurried out the door. Les and I followed close behind. We quickly walked through the house and made it to the courtyard without incident.

An ornate wooden bench sat next to the front doors under a vine-covered ramada. Elizabeth sat on the bench while Les stood next to her. I pulled out my cell phone and called in the murder.

"The police will be here in a few minutes," I said, starting a speech I'd made so many times that I knew it by heart.

"I know we just found a murder victim, and that's terrible enough. But now we'll need to go through the formal police process, and that's almost as bad. Realize from the start that this will take most of the night."

"Do you really think we'll be here that long?" Elizabeth asked in a quiet voice.

"The police don't arrive all at once," I said. "Different people will come and go throughout the night. Whenever a new detective or technician shows up, they'll want to ask us the same questions all over again. Try not to get angry or defensive with them."

"What if they lean on us to confess to something?" Les asked.

"If they ask you something you don't want to answer, tell them you'd like to discuss your answer with counsel first. Then we'll call in Lenny."

"Leonard handles criminal matters?" Les asked.

"Yes," I said, "but remember, innocent people typically don't have anything to hide. Get everything out right away. The will, the jewelry, the treasure hunt, plus any personal issues or history between you two. Everything."

As I spoke, Elizabeth was nodding with understanding.

She'd stopped crying and seemed to find her equilibrium. Les was staring into the courtyard as if in deep thought.

Within three minutes, the first patrol car pulled into the courtyard.

I halfway expected my friend Chugger McIntyre to step out of the car, but since we were over the city line and into Phoenix, it was an officer I didn't know. He introduced himself as Officer Ramsey.

I told him there was a body in the upstairs vault. He collected IDs from each of us and told us to wait where we were.

A second patrol car arrived while he was talking to us. Again, I didn't know the officer, but she said she'd watch over Les and Elizabeth while I showed Officer Ramsey the location of the victim.

I led Ramsey into the house and up to the bedroom. As we moved through the hallways and up the stairs, both of us kept a sharp eye out. He was likely looking for signs that the murderer was still on the premises. I was looking for any sign of a chest full of treasure.

We passed through the master bedroom to the room with the vault. I stood outside the vault while Officer Ramsey went in and surveyed the condition of the room. Why the chair had been knocked over was still a mystery, but the statue could now be accounted for. I didn't see anything else amiss.

After Officer Ramsey verified that the dead guy really was dead, he led the way back down to the courtyard. Leaving me with the others, he turned around and went back into the house, presumably to search for additional victims and to begin the process of securing the scene.

The officer in the courtyard started the formal process by giving each of us a clipboard with several standard forms on it. I sat next to Elizabeth on the bench, and we started writing.

After filling out the first form, I glanced over at Elizabeth. She seemed okay for the moment, but I could still hear her breathing very fast. Her hands shook as she wrote.

It made me think back to the first dead body I'd found. That was almost three years ago. I was with Gina, working on one of my first cheating spouse assignments.

Unfortunately, during that assignment, the husband ultimately decided that killing his wife would be quicker than a divorce. After Gina called in the murder, she sat me down and gave me the talk about what to do when the police showed up for a murder investigation.

Since Gina had spent several years as a detective in the Scottsdale police department, she knew the drill. I've used the same speech for others several times since then, including tonight with Elizabeth and Les.

"Hey, I'll be here the whole time," I said to Elizabeth. "If it ever starts to overwhelm you, let me know, and I'll talk to them. This is routine to them, and sometimes they don't see what it's doing to the witnesses."

Elizabeth nodded her head, and we continued filling out our forms.

Over the next five hours, there was a steady stream of patrol cars, unmarked detective's cars, supervisor's cars, and a forensics van. The Maricopa County Coroner showed up at about midnight but had to wait another hour before forensics released the body.

Since the house was so big, the detectives called in for more help to go over the property. It looked like they were going to be at it for some time.

The detectives were efficient, but they didn't let us go until almost two thirty in the morning. They asked us to keep them apprised of our movements in case they had additional questions.

So far, they didn't seem to look at us as anything but the unfortunate witnesses who'd found the body. I took that as a good sign.

Elizabeth took off in her rental car. The police then called a cab to take Les back to his hotel. I was grateful for that.

I started home and called Lenny. Being woken up put him in a bad mood, but he perked up when I told him I'd discovered a body. His mood turned sour again when I informed him the police hadn't arrested Les, and it didn't look like he was involved.

As I pulled into my parking lot, I had to shake my head to clear it. I was mentally drained. Between the late night and being grilled by Lenny, I was more than ready to call it a night.

Walking into my bedroom, I noticed Marlowe wasn't lying on the bed. He must've been spending the night at Grandma Peckham's.

I didn't waste too much time or energy thinking about it. Instead, I tossed my clothes into the laundry basket, pulled on an oversized ASU Sun Devil's T-shirt, and crawled into bed. I was asleep as soon as my head hit the pillow.

I'd finally made it to Hawaii and was sitting on Waikiki Beach. Diamond Head was to my left, and a row of beach hotels was stretched out to my right.

The air was warm, humid, and smelled like tropical flowers. The ocean was a deep blue, and the waves gently pounding on the beach were soothing and relaxing. My plan was to sit on the beach for the rest of the afternoon, watching the sunset and then finding an amazing place for a big seafood dinner.

This is just about perfect.

I sat on my lounge chair, taking in the people and the scenery. I hadn't been this relaxed in months, and I felt great.

Over the sound of the ocean, I started to hear faint music. It was a light and catchy tune, but for some reason, it made me a little sad. As it went on, I realized it was a song called "*S & M*" by the singer Rihanna.

For some reason, knowing the significance of the song made me even sadder. I became so sad that the beach started to fade and swirl around me. The sky above the ocean dissolved and gradually became the ceiling of my bedroom.

No, no, no. I love the beach!

Unfortunately, the beach was gone, and now all I heard was Sophie's ringtone. I rolled over and picked up the phone from my nightstand. I had to look at the screen twice to push the right button.

"Sophie, why are you calling me?" I mumbled. "I'm dreaming about Hawaii. What time is it?"

"It's almost eight thirty," she said in her always happy voice. "You need a big clock in your bedroom, so you don't have to ask me what time it is whenever I wake you up. By the way, you sound terrible. You should try to sound a little more cheery when you wake up. I read on Yahoo that how you wake up sets your mood for the entire day."

"I'm sorry," I said, still in a grumpy mood. "But so far today, I'm not feeling very cheery. Why are you calling me?"

"Why can't you ever leave the office without finding a dead body? Do you know how much paperwork I need to do whenever you find a dead body? I've been doing paperwork all morning, and I'll probably be doing paperwork all afternoon."

"Hey, it's not like I went looking for another dead guy," I said. "We just stumbled across this one. And you think you have problems? Reno's going to shit kittens when he finds out about this. The murder was across city lines, so it may take a day or two, but you know he'll eventually find out. I don't think he's over being upset about the last one I found."

"Lenny's real disappointed that Lester Murdock wasn't arrested. You know how much he likes having a rich client charged with murder."

"I know," I said. "He was cranky last night when I told him Les didn't seem to be involved."

"Ever since he got in this morning, Lenny's been making calls to his police contacts to see if they're looking at anyone in particular. He said he wants you to come in as soon as you can. He's starting to catch the scent of a big fee out there, and he doesn't want it to slip away."

"Well, I won't be able to help him a lot with this one," I said. "The dead guy was locked inside a vault that no one had the combination to."

"So, what are you saying? Was he transported *Star Trek*-style into the vault? That would cause a stir. Or maybe you're thinking there's some sort of space alien involvement? You know, I once saw a movie about a bunch of twenty-somethings who could walk through walls. Maybe you're thinking something like that happened?"

"No, but I don't have a clue who did it."

"Too bad, we've never had an assignment involving

space aliens. That would've made my day a lot more exciting. The only aliens we deal with around here speak Spanish. I'll tell Lenny you'll be in as soon as you can. I'll be pretty vague, so you can take your time."

"Thanks," I said. "Let me make a pot of coffee, and I'll be in as soon as I can."

"But for real," she said. "Next time, don't call him at two thirty in the morning talking about a rich client and a murder. Lenny said he's been awake since you called. I think he got all excited thinking about collecting another big fee. By about three this afternoon, he's going to get tired and cranky. Do you know who he'll take it out on? Me, that's who."

"Now that there's a dead body," I said, "I don't know where it'll lead. We might need to start checking into both Lester and his sister, Elizabeth. Would you have any time to start a file on them?"

"I'm way ahead of you. That's the first thing Lenny wanted me to do when he came in today. Like I said, nothing but paperwork today. But I should have some information when you get in."

"Thanks, you're the best."

"I know. But don't leave me alone with Lenny for too long today. You know how he gets when he's waiting for something to happen. He'll get that pulsing vein-thing going in his forehead. You know how gross that is. I also don't want to see him pacing in front of my desk all morning."

I switched off the phone and stretched until I started to wake up. Marlowe sauntered into the bedroom, jumped on the bed, and settled on my chest. He was purring, demanding to be petted.

I got up and put on a pot of coffee. Marlowe followed me into the kitchen and reminded me that he was nearly dead from starvation.

I ignored his food demands. I was still a little queasy, and I didn't want to deal with listening to him throw up his breakfast.

After a long, hot shower, I looked at myself in the mirror. I was a little shocked at how bad I looked.

The worst things about getting up early after a late night were the bags under my eyes. It took me almost twenty-five minutes, but between the blow dryer and my makeup drawer, I started feeling better about myself.

I went into the kitchen and poured the pot of coffee into *The Big Pig*, my oversized travel mug. I plopped a spoonful of Turkey Deluxe dinner into Marlowe's bowl.

As always, he attacked the food as if he hadn't been fed for several days. I grabbed a couple of chocolate chip granola bars for breakfast and headed out the door.

In the Sonoran Desert surrounding the city, the flowers and hurried growth that had appeared after the brief winter rains were now long gone. It hadn't rained for several months, and the few rivers snaking through the city had become bone-dry ditches.

In the mountains north of the city, the tinder-dry forests had been shut down since mid-May to any activities other than day hiking. Even at that, several forest fires were already blazing away, and more were sure to start at the slightest provocation.

From Scottsdale, you could see the distant towers of smoke reaching up into the sky along the northern horizon. But having lived here all my life, I knew this was as it should be.

May and June were the months when the forests burned. It happened every year like clockwork.

Instead of calling it late spring, it should be called fire season. I knew by the end of June, rain clouds would start to appear over the northern mountains in the late afternoon.

By the middle of July, the clouds would make their way down into Scottsdale, and the annual summer monsoon thunderstorms would begin. With the rain, the fires in the mountains would all go out, and the forests would gradually open back up.

It's like "The Circle of Life."

I always looked forward to the afternoon rains of the summer monsoon season. It wasn't so much for the rain, which the deserts always need, but more for the change in the daily routine of heat, blue skies, and sunshine. Besides, being from Scottsdale, I'm always a little fascinated to see water just falling from the sky.

The drive to the office was uneventful. I turned into the alley behind the office and parked in my space.

In addition to the red Porsche, the black Range Rover, and the lemon-yellow Volkswagen, there was also Annie's sky-blue Ford. Like my Accord, Annie's Fiesta had been around for a while and had a few creases and dents on the body. Although, I've seen her drive, and I'm pretty sure she didn't get her dents the same way I did.

I went in through the rear security door. The back offices were quiet, so I made my way up to the front reception area.

Sophie sat at her desk, typing out a report. Gina was talking to Annie next to the main conference room. Lenny had his door closed, which could mean either he was on the phone, or he needed some naptime.

"Hey, girl," Sophie said as I walked up to her desk. "I'm glad you made it in. Lenny's already starting to get cranky. From now on, you should always try to find your dead bodies in the daytime. It'll make things in the office go a lot smoother for me. It's creepy how he was in the vault. I mean, what if you hadn't been able to find a way in? He could have been there for years."

"It was the last thing I expected to see," I admitted. "We were hoping for a treasure chest full of jewelry, and instead, we found a dead body. Has there been any word on an ID for the corpse? With Les and Elizabeth standing there, I didn't think I should go through his wallet."

"Not yet, but I'll give you a call when we find out. Speaking of a treasure chest, what are they going to do with all of that jewelry when they find it?"

"I imagine they're going to put it up for auction, well, most of the pieces, anyway. Apparently, it's worth twenty or thirty million altogether. Are you getting visions of needing some new jewelry?"

"Well, you'd think a small finder's fee would be in order," she laughed. "You know, maybe a couple of necklaces or some earrings. Even a gold brooch with a few accent diamonds would be good with me."

"Jewelry?" Annie said as she and Gina walked over to Sophie's desk. "I heard about the treasure chest and what was in it. It's a shame you didn't find it yet."

"What are you doing here?" I asked. "Aren't you supposed to be studying for finals? How many more do you have?"

"I needed a break, so I came in to catch up on the filing." As usual, Annie was full of smiles and good cheer. "I'm down to my last final. It's on Thursday. With any luck, I'll graduate on Saturday. I hope everyone can still make it." She then looked expectantly at the three of us.

"We wouldn't miss it," Gina said.

"Are you kidding?" Sophie said. "I already bought new shoes for it. Of course, after I got the shoes, I realized I didn't have a bag to go with them. So, I got a new bag, too."

Annie looked at me. "Well?" she asked.

"Of course, I'll be there," I said, mentally crossing my fingers and hoping nothing would come up to prevent me from going. I've been known to miss out on things like weddings, birthday parties, and funerals. It's a part of the job I really don't like.

"Are the girls all still coming?" Sophie asked.

"I only got a tentative yes from Shannon and Sonia's in Europe for the summer. But everyone else should be there."

"How are the plans for the reception going?" Gina asked.

"Still no problems," Annie said. "The graduation ceremony will be over at about three, and we'll meet on the Hohokam Terrace at the Saguaro Sky at about four. The reception is from four to six thirty. The girls wanted to have a band, but since there won't be more than about fifty or sixty of us, I thought a DJ would probably be better. We aren't having a formal dinner, but there shouldn't be a lack of food. Make sure to come hungry."

"That won't be an issue," Sophie laughed.

"I'd better go back and get to studying," Annie said. "Accounting has never been my strongest subject, and the final will be a bitch."

"Good luck," Gina said.

"Yeah," Sophie said. "The next time we talk, you'll have a new degree."

"Thanks. Cross your fingers for me," Annie said as she headed to the back offices.

"You know," Sophie said after Annie had left, "I might need to buy a new skirt too."

Gina looked over at her with a look of motherly concern.

"It's not my fault," Sophie said, a little exasperated. "I never know what to wear around the Cougars. I know they're our friends and all, but I always feel underdressed whenever I'm around them."

"I don't think it's only the clothes," I said. "For me, it's the perfume. I haven't even asked the girls what they wear since I'm sure I'd never be able to afford any of those perfumes."

"I know what you mean," Sophie said. "Being around them is sort of like being in the perfume section of a duty-free shop. Also, they always have on at least a hundred thousand dollars' worth of jewelry. It's hard to compete with that, no matter how nicely you dress."

"Jealous?" Gina asked us both.

"Of course," I said.

"Absolutely," Sophie said with a laugh.

Lenny's door was still closed. Gina went into the back offices to work on a report while I stayed up front with Sophie.

"How'd your date with Michael go last night?" I asked.

"Him? I'm going to drop that loser. I told you the past couple of dates have only been dinner, then a hop in the sack.

Well, last night, he picked me up at my place and didn't even want to take me to dinner first. I think I've only become a booty call for him."

"I'm sorry to hear that. Are you still feeling those long-term relationship urges?"

"Yes, and they're getting stronger. Going to Danica's wedding isn't going to help. It's a week and a half away, and I'm already starting to get excited about it. Speaking about long-term urges, how are things with you and Reno?"

"We talked last night, and things are good. Of course, that was before I found the dead guy. I don't know how I'm going to tell Reno about this one. For some reason, whenever I find another dead body, I get a lecture."

"I still think he should be a little more understanding. In his line of work, he finds dead bodies all the time."

"That's what I think too, but he still doesn't see it that way. What have you found out so far on Lester and Elizabeth Murdock?"

"Well, Elizabeth's the easy one. Elizabeth Murdock seems to have a normal life that includes growing up in Chicago, Ivy League education, getting married, and then getting divorced. She works in advertising at a big Chicago firm. No kids, her credit's clean, and she's never been in any legal trouble. It looks like she split a sizeable inheritance with her brother when their father died. That was about fifteen years ago."

"What about Les?" I asked.

"Lester Murdock's more of a problem. He also grew up in Chicago, also has an Ivy League education, was married, divorced, but his current situation is murkier."

"He seems to be doing well," I said. "When I was with him yesterday, he bought part of a hotel in Vail."

"Well, yes and no. Yes, he seems to be well-off, and no, he doesn't seem to actually own anything."

"You're confusing me."

"Yes, he lives in a big house and drives a nice car. But the title to both the house and the car seem to be held in some sort of trust. He has several hundred thousand dollars in available credit, but he doesn't show an income. I don't know what to make of it."

"You know what I'm thinking?" I asked.

"I know. Use the secret software."

The previous year, Lenny helped the Drug Enforcement Agency with an investigation that had apparently gone well for the Feds. I'm not sure what Lenny's fee was, but soon afterward, a nondescript man came into the office and installed a program onto Sophie's computer.

He gave her a security key fob along with two separate passwords to access a secret database. We never could figure out exactly what the database was called or where it came from. All we know is that you can get amazing amounts of information on almost anyone by simply typing in a name.

"I hate using the secret software," Sophie said. "I know someday I'll punch in the wrong name, and we'll get a visit from the Men in Black. No matter what Lenny did for the Feds, eventually they'll realize we shouldn't have it."

"But until then," I said.

"I know, use what we've got. I'll do a deep dive and let you know what I find out."

Lenny's door opened, and he stuck his head out.

"Laura," he said, sarcasm heavy in his voice. "I'm so glad you could make it in. If you aren't too busy, let's talk about the mess from last night." He then disappeared back into his office.

"I can see how this is going to go," I said.

"Have fun," Sophie said.

When I walked into Lenny's office, I spotted half a dozen cigarette butts in the ashtray on the corner of his desk. Whenever he's nervous or stressed, Lenny tends to chain smoke. He's also been known to take a glass or two of Jim Beam.

I sat in one of the two wooden chairs in front of his massive desk and waited for him to start.

"What have you been able to find out since you called me last night?" he asked.

"Nothing new. I still need to talk this out with Gina. I'm meeting Les at noon to go over where we stand."

"Do you think either our client or his sister had anything to do with the murder?"

"I don't think so. The body was in a locked vault, and neither one had the combination."

"What? I thought you said they both had the combination to the vault. Lester had it written on a notepad, and Elizabeth confirmed the combination before he used it to open the vault."

It's so fricking annoying that Lenny remembers everything I tell him.

"Yes, but until they opened the vault, neither of them knew it would actually work."

"What about the jewelry? Are you any closer to finding

that?"

"The vault was only the first obvious place to look. We'd already been through the house but didn't see any signs of it there."

"Alright, the results from the crime scene haven't started to come in yet. You said everyone had their fingerprints and DNA taken at the scene last night, so that should speed the process along. We should know in a day or two who else was recently in the vault. We should also know the ID of the dead guy later today or tomorrow. They're currently notifying next of kin."

Lenny then leaned forward and started speaking slowly. This always annoyed me, but there didn't seem to be anything I could do about it. "Next time, it would be helpful if you could pull an ID before you call the cops. It would make things go a lot smoother here."

"Won't the police get upset if I touch the body?"

"People touch the body all the time; look at what Lester did. He all but gave the guy a full body massage, and nobody's said boo about it. If you could sneak a peek at the ID next time, it'd give us a leg up. I'm sure the cops would get over it."

I nodded, and that seemed to be good enough for Lenny.

"Go find out what you can," he said. "If Lester Murdock's involved, I want to know about it sooner rather than later."

I left Lenny's office and went over to Sophie. When she looked up at me, I could see she was concerned.

"How're you doing?" she asked. "From what I caught, Lenny's mood hasn't improved a lot."

"I hate talking to Lenny when he's like this," I said. "It puts me in a bad mood for hours."

"Try not to let it bother you. Think about finding a treasure chest. That should put a smile on your face. If nothing else, think about going to the Saguaro Sky on Saturday and stuffing yourself on Jackie's hors d'oeuvres and champagne."

Chapter Five

I left Sophie as she was starting the log-in process to get into the secret database. I then went into the back offices and found Gina in her cubicle, typing out a report on her laptop.

"Hey, would you have a minute to talk about this one?" I asked.

"Sure," she said. "I figured you'd stop by."

"There's something creepy about finding a dead guy in a vault that's supposedly been locked for weeks, if not months."

"I know what you've already told Sophie," Gina said. "But tell me more about the victim. Could you tell how long he'd been dead?"

"It didn't seem like he'd been there for very long. The blood on his wound was still sort of wet when Les rolled him over."

"Did it look like rigor mortis had started to set in?"

"I don't think so. He seemed pretty limp."

"So, we're only talking about a few hours. That would put the time of the murder sometime after about three yesterday afternoon."

"That's after everyone had left. But I don't see where the dead guy fits in with any of this."

"As I see it," Gina said, "the motive for the murder is most likely the millions of dollars in jewelry. People have committed murder for far less. What about opportunity? Did either Les or Elizabeth have time to go back to the house, open the safe, and kill the guy?"

"Well, both of them had the time," I said. "I can't account for Elizabeth from roughly three until we saw her at about nine. She told the police she went back to her hotel and only went out for dinner before coming back to the house. I dropped Les off at about five o'clock and picked him up at eight."

"Three hours is more than enough time. You said that Les is staying at the Tropical Paradise. That's one of Tony DiCenzo's hotels. They'll most likely have security cameras all through the parking lots. If you asked, I imagine they'd be able to tell you if Les left his room last night before you picked him up."

"Yes, but I'd rather not ask. The further I keep from Tony DiCenzo, the better off I'll be."

"Okay, you're probably right, but let's still keep it as an option. What about Elizabeth? Do you know where she's been staying?"

"She's at the Hyatt Regency Scottsdale at Gainey Ranch. She has a rental, so she probably wouldn't have taken a cab. For Les, I thought I'd start with the cab companies and work backward. See if they made any drop-offs at the house and then see where the cab came from."

"Okay, that's a plan. It sounds like either one had an opportunity. What are your feelings about Les and Elizabeth? Do you think they're involved with the murder?"

"Elizabeth and her brother don't get along. At first, I thought she was being unfair to him, but now I'm not so sure. As I've gotten to know her, she seems alright."

"What about Les?"

"That's a harder call. He seems okay, but I keep getting an undercurrent that something's off. He's not sharing all he knows. I'm not sure what to make of everything yet. I understand Les and Elizabeth have been arguing with each other for years. Apparently, they're both well off, and neither of them actually needs the jewelry. It's more like this treasure hunt is only the latest thing for them to fight about."

"After you confirm the movements for the two of them, your best bet will be to find out who else knew about the will and the jewelry. If neither Lester nor Elizabeth is involved with the murder, it'll mean there's at least one other person or group involved. What about the two guys you said have been following you? Any idea how they're involved?"

"Not yet, but they seem to know more about what's going on than I do."

"They're driving a dark blue rental?" Gina asked.

"Well, it looks like a rental. There are half a dozen stickers on the driver's side of the windshield."

"This should be simple. When you pick Lester up today, I'll follow behind and get the license plate. If the same two guys are still following you, we should be able to track them down from the rental agreement. If we can't get the IDs directly from the rental agency, we'll hand the information over to the police and have them do it. It'll slow down the process, but we'll eventually get an answer."

"That will help," I said. "One other thing. We're assuming the treasure chest is still somewhere in the house. If the police seal off the entire residence, it will make it harder to look for the jewelry."

"I'll talk to Lenny about that. Since we're representing one of the two people inheriting the house, perhaps we can persuade the police to only seal the master bedroom and the vault. That'll keep the rest of the house open for exploration."

"Perfect," I said with a sigh. "Now I just need to find the jewelry and avoid the murderer."

"Well, when you first started working here, you said you wanted something more exciting than being a bartender at Greasewood Flat. You can't say this is boring."

"Yes, but is it bad to want exciting without a murderer skulking around?"

"What else do you have to go on for this treasure hunt?"

"I knew they wouldn't let us back in the vault for a week or two, so I took some pictures. I would've loved to have gone through all the drawers, but I'll see what the pictures show."

"When are you picking up Les?"

"I told him noon. I figured he'd be up and ready for lunch by then."

"Alright," she said. "Let me know when you take off."

I plopped down on my chair and downloaded the pictures from my phone to my desktop computer. The pictures from the vault didn't show a lot more detail than I'd seen the night before. The mostly empty shelves contained nothing more than two Greek-looking statues and three vases.

Next, I looked at the pictures I'd taken of the card that'd been propped up on the shelf. I was glad I'd taken two pictures from different viewpoints since the light from my flash had masked some of the words.

By comparing both pictures, I could make out the entire message.

Congratulations on making it into the vault. As you can see, the jewelry isn't here. I've hidden it somewhere in the house, but not anywhere out in the open. If you need another clue, look below the coffin rock as seen from Dobbins Lookout.

Dobbins Lookout? I thought to myself. What could be up there? It's only a place on the top of South Mountain where the tourists go.

I'd been there several times over the years, mostly when someone came into Scottsdale for the first time, and I wanted to give them a great view of the entire city. I couldn't imagine what could be there that hadn't already been picked over by the hundreds of tourists who went there every day.

"Hey, Gina," I said. "I'm ready if you are."

"Did you find anything in your pictures?"

"Sort of, but I'm not sure what to make of it yet. The card in the vault said a clue to finding the treasure is below the coffin rock as seen from Dobbins Lookout."

"Do you have any idea what that means?" Gina asked.

"None at all, but I guess we'll find out soon. Follow me up to the Tropical Paradise and I'll get Les. With any luck, you can find out who my tail is. Maybe we can start to get some answers on this."

The drive up Scottsdale Road to the resort was uneventful. I saw Gina had positioned her black Range Rover about a hundred yards behind me, but I didn't see that anyone was following me. It seemed more reasonable that they had an eye on Les at his hotel and would wait until he left to make their move.

Les met me at the door to his room. I could tell he hadn't gotten a lot of sleep the night before.

He had dark circles under his eyes and an overall disorganized look. There was a pot of coffee on the table, and he absent-mindedly offered me a cup.

I didn't want to make Gina wait too long, but I also wanted to make sure Les was up to going out again. I poured myself a coffee and took a chair at the table.

Les poured one for himself, then leaned against the counter. It seemed to steady him.

"How're you doing today?" I asked. "It's never easy to find a dead body. Going through the police procedure is even worse, especially when it lasts until two in the morning. You did really well for your first time."

"Thanks," he said with a small snort of disgust. He held up his coffee mug in a toast. "Here's to hoping there won't be a second time."

"I'll drink to that," I said as I took a sip.

"Where do we go from here?" he asked. "The jewelry wasn't anywhere I could see in the vault. Plus, I don't think the police are going to let us back in to look around."

"We're working on having the rest of the house, outside of the master bedroom, to be released so we can explore the rest of the rooms. We'll find out later today or tomorrow. I didn't get a chance to look through more than a couple of the drawers, but I don't think the jewelry's in the vault. There was a card on one of the shelves. I took pictures of it last night and looked at them this morning. The card says the next clue to finding the treasure is below the coffin rock, as seen from Dobbins Lookout. I thought we'd go up there and look around."

"Why couldn't Granddad have made this more straightforward?" Les asked, a little annoyed. "All of this running around seems rather pointless."

"It probably made him happy to think that you and Elizabeth would be hunting down his treasure together after he was dead. Maybe he thought it would make the two of you closer. Who knows?"

"Maybe you're right. I assume Elizabeth doesn't know about the coffin rock or Dobbins Lookout?"

"As far as I know, it will only be you and me up there, along with a couple of dozen tourists."

"Where is Dobbins Lookout?" he asked.

"It's at the top of South Mountain. You have a great view of it from your terrace outside the library at your granddad's house."

"Okay," he said. "Let's go up and take a look."

As always, Les winced when he stepped out of his room. The temperature was again over a hundred degrees and still rising.

We climbed into my car and took off down Scottsdale Road. I had a cooler full of water bottles in the back seat, and before we left, I handed him one.

"We'll be walking around in the heat," I said. "Stay hydrated, and you'll be okay. If you start to feel dizzy or if you notice you've stopped sweating, drink some water."

Traffic was heavy for the middle of the day, and I couldn't see the tail. We made it almost down to the turnoff for the Loop-202 freeway when I got a call from Gina.

"You said two big guys in a dark blue rental sedan?"

"Yes," I said, "but I haven't seen them."

"They're about four cars behind you. You should be able to see them now, behind the white pickup truck."

I glanced up into the rearview mirror, and there they were. "Looks like the same guys and the same car," I said. "Did you get the plate?"

"Yes, and I'll head back to the office and have Sophie run it. It doesn't look like they want to get too close to our client today, so you should be okay. But keep your eyes open anyway."

"Let me know when you get something?"

"I'll call you first thing."

"Gina will let us know when she finds out who's been following us. Are you hungry?"

"Actually, I'm starving. I've been thinking about the man we found last night, and I haven't had anything at all today."

"What are you up for? Want to stick with something bland?"

"Actually, I was hoping to try something local. Are there any restaurants around here I couldn't find in Chicago?"

"Sure," I said. "We'll be driving right past a place called Los Dos Molinos. It's some of the best New Mexican food you can get in the city. Although I should warn you, they don't do mild sauce. It can get kinda spicy."

"Not a problem," Les said. "I go to Mexican places all the time in Chicago. I'm always dumping hot sauce on everything."

I pulled into the lot of Los Dos Molinos, and we went in. The waitress directed us to a booth in the corner and handed each of us a menu. Les seemed to enjoy the music and the colorful decorations covering the walls and ceiling.

"This is what a Mexican place should look like," he said. "What's good here?"

"Everything. I'm doing a *machaca* burro, enchilada style. That's where they put Hatch green chili sauce on top."

"What's *machaca,* and what's Hatch green chili?"

"*Machaca* is a type of marinated shredded beef; it's good. The chilies come from the Hatch Valley in New Mexico. If you like spicy, you'll love the sauce they make from them."

Les thought it sounded good, and we both ordered a machaca burro with green chili sauce. We munched on chips and salsa until the food came out.

When the waitress sat the plate in front of me, I didn't wait. I took a big bite and was rewarded with the throat-tightening tingle from the Hatch chilies.

I was about to shovel in another bite when I heard Les coughing. I looked up and saw his face had turned red.

He put his fork down, coughed again, and downed about half his glass of water. I noticed beads of sweat had broken out on his forehead.

Tourists, won't they ever learn?

"Too spicy?" I asked.

"Not at all," he wheezed out as his color gradually returned to normal. "But, you're right. This isn't like the stuff they have in Chicago."

He took another bite and again winced from the heat. But I also noticed he was starting to appreciate how good the flavors were. By the time he was halfway through his burro, he was wolfing it down as fast as I was.

It looks like I've ruined another tourist for real Southwestern food. The stuff he gets back in Chicago will never taste the same again.

After lunch, we drove the rest of the way south on Central Avenue until it wound its way into South Mountain Park. The two men in the blue car followed us through the entrance, then pulled into a side lot off the main road.

South Mountain Park is the largest city park in the United States, covering some 16,000 acres of mountains and desert landscapes. There are a dozen hiking trails, and they're all popular with the locals.

At the base of the mountain, you can rent a horse and meander along miles of winding trails. It's a great place to come if you want to experience the real Sonoran Desert without traveling too far from the city.

Except for some TV towers, the highest point you can drive in the park is Dobbins Lookout. There, you'll find a big parking lot with several women sitting on blankets selling Native American jewelry to the tourists. The lookout also houses an observation area and a stone ramada large enough to fit twenty or thirty people.

I parked my car, and we spent a couple of minutes putting on sunscreen. I pulled out a sun hat and asked Les if he wanted a hat from the assortment in my trunk. He picked one with a wide brim and settled it on his head as we walked down to the stone ramada.

As with the view from Les' granddad's house, it felt like

you could see every detail of every building. The view was completely clear, and the city itself seemed to be alive.

Like most people, Les was fascinated with the mountaintop view of The Valley. I showed him where his granddad's house was on the south side of Camelback Mountain, then pointed out downtown Scottsdale, Chase Field, Sky Harbor Airport, the University of Phoenix Stadium, and the campus of ASU.

"The view from up here is similar to the view from the terrace at Granddad's house," he said. "But we seem to be higher up, and you can see a lot farther. It's amazing to be able to take in a city this big in one glance."

"The note in the vault said the next clue is under the coffin rock," I reminded him. "I suggest we look around for anything that looks like a coffin."

We spent about twenty minutes walking together, looking for anything that could be the right rock. Eventually, we separated, and each of us followed whatever seemed promising. I saw a lot of stones, but nothing that looked like a coffin.

I went back to the parking lot to get a broader view of the lookout. I was thinking maybe the buildings or the footpaths would form a casket shape, but I didn't see anything looking even vaguely like a coffin.

After about an hour, I met up with Les, who was back at the ramada. His face was flushed and I could see the heat was getting to him.

"Any luck?" I asked.

"No, not a thing. Since this mountain is nothing but thousands of rocks, with a cactus between each one, you'd think somewhere out here was one shaped like a coffin, a casket, or even a sarcophagus. For the last half an hour, I've been loosening my standards on what that would look like, but it's still nothing doing."

"I haven't seen anything either. You'd think coffin-shaped rocks would be pretty common, but I guess not."

"Well, what's next?" he asked.

"Well, we know the treasure chest is somewhere in the house. Let's find out when the police will release the crime scene and then go back and look for it."

We walked back to my car and opened the doors to let it air out. Opening a door in a car that's been sitting in the Arizona summer sun is roughly the same sensation you get when you open the door to a hot oven. There's a big *whoosh* of heat, followed by several seconds of hot air escaping outside.

Once the car was aired out sufficiently, we climbed in. I cranked the AC to high and got a fresh bottle of water for each of us. We sat there for several minutes, letting the cold air wash over us.

I'd just put the car in gear to back out of the parking space when the theme to the old TV show *Wonder Woman* started blaring out from my cell phone.

"It's Gina," I said, "hold on."

I put the car in park, slid the button, and held the phone to my ear.

"Those two guys who're following you," Gina said, "I think they're Feds. The license plate shows the car's part of a motor pool of private vehicles confiscated by the government. They're about to be put up for auction."

"Any idea which part of the government they're from?"

"Not yet. The car was transferred to the general accounting office about three months ago. Any Fed could use it. Sophie's doing a deeper search on the license plate, but so far, that's what I know."

"I'll ask Les about it, but it doesn't make a lot of sense."

"I agree, but remember, the Fed's aren't the bad guys. Maybe you could meet up with them and let them know that you know who they are. You could even offer to help with whatever it is they're doing."

"Yeah, maybe," I said, not quite convinced.

"By the way, Lenny talked to the detective in charge of the murder, and they've agreed that only the bedroom and vault will remain secured as a crime scene. You'll be allowed in the rest of the house without restrictions sometime tomorrow morning."

"Thanks," I said. "I'll let you know what I find out."

I disconnected and looked over at Les. "We need to talk. Why would the Feds be following you?"

He looked at me with a strange look on his face.

"Feds? Is that who's following us? I have no idea why they'd want to follow me. I haven't done anything worthy of the attention of the government."

Again, maybe it was only my suspicious nature, but the way he said it rang alarm bells in my head. I could tell this assignment was going to be long and difficult.

When we first entered the park, I noticed the Feds had turned into a parking lot near the entrance. They must have looked at their maps and seen there was only one way in and one way out of the park. But if Les was acting squirrely about whatever he'd been hiding from me, I decided we should ditch the Feds, at least for the afternoon.

I pulled out of the parking lot at the Dobbins Lookout and took the turnoff to San Juan Road. On a map, the road dead-ends at a small scenic lookout, but right before the overlook, there's a dirt side road that wasn't going to be on anyone's map.

I took the dirt road as it snaked and bounced its way down the hill, through an arroyo, until we were dumped into the bedroom community of Laveen. From there, we made our way over to Scottsdale and Lester's hotel.

The Feds were nowhere to be seen. For some reason, that fact made me happy. I then dropped Les off in the parking lot next to his room.

"Relax this afternoon and tonight," I said. "Have a big dinner or maybe go for a swim. If they're having another party by the pool tonight, you should go and have a nice time. You've been through a lot the last few days. The house should be released by tomorrow morning. I'll be over about ten o'clock. We can go over and look around again."

I drove back to the office feeling a little guilty. I knew I shouldn't have ditched the Feds, but somehow, I couldn't help myself.

As Gina had reminded me, I knew they weren't the bad guys. I just don't like having anyone following me, Feds or not.

I parked in my spot and went in through the rear door. The back offices were quiet, so I walked up to reception.

Gina had pulled a chair up next to Sophie's desk, and it looked like they were working on one of Gina's reports. I was going to ask Sophie how she was coming on my report, but I didn't want to disturb her while she worked with Gina.

I was about to go back to my cubicle when my phone

started ringing. I looked down in surprise when I heard the theme from *The Love Boat*, the old TV show from the eighties.

Two months before, Sophie had set Max's ringtone to the theme from the show. It was her idea of a joke.

My heart skipped a beat. Then I started to panic.

I wanted to answer it, but not in front of Sophie and Gina. I looked over at them. The panic must have shown in my eyes because Sophie started laughing and clapping her hands.

Gina grabbed a pen from the desk to use as a microphone, stood up, and started singing the theme to *The Love Boat* along with the ringtone.

"Shut up," I said. I could feel my face growing hot. Sophie started singing with Gina, grabbing her water bottle to use as a microphone. They were dancing, singing, and laughing as I got more annoyed.

As the song finished, they were both singing into their microphones, their arms stretched wide. Sophie and Gina then had a fit of the giggles as they both collapsed into their chairs.

"You both think you're funny?" I asked. My face still felt hot, and I knew it was bright red.

"Why didn't you answer it?" Sophie asked, still laughing and wiping tears from her eyes. "We wanted to hear you talk to Max."

"I panicked," I said. "It's been two months since I've talked to him. I wouldn't know what to say. I don't even know if talking to him is a good idea or not."

"It sounds like you still have feelings for him," Gina said.

"It's complicated," I said.

"You mean it's complicated because you're with Reno, but you also sort of want to be with Max?" Sophie asked. "Complicated because you know Reno's the safe choice, but Max's a dangerous bad boy with a hot body? Complicated because you feel like you're settling with Reno when Max could be perfect for you? Or maybe it's complicated because you could have a real future with Reno, complete with kids, and all you'd get with Max is visiting hours at the state prison in Florence?"

Gina looked over at Sophie and raised her eyebrows.

"Yup," I admitted. "That about covers it. Reno and I have a good thing going, and I won't do anything to mess that up. I know Max isn't a good choice for a boyfriend, well, until I get around him. Then I want him to rip my clothes off."

"I know you're attracted to him," Gina said. "But it's never a good idea to get romantically involved with a criminal. I've seen it too many times. It's easy to get pulled into their world of crime, and that never ends well."

You don't know the half of it.

"I hear what you're saying," I said. "I'll be careful around Max."

My phone made the trumpet-fanfare sound, indicating Max had left a voicemail.

"Well, good luck with that," Sophie said. "We've seen you with him, remember? The first time you two kissed, you about had multiple orgasms."

"I can control my reactions to him," I said. "Well, mostly."

"Maybe you can control yourself," Gina said. "But I'd still play it safe. If you see him again, only meet in a public location, preferably in the daytime."

"Yes, Mother," I said.

I went to my cubicle in the back offices and listened to the voicemail. Hearing Max's voice after all this time still made my heart pound. As I listened, I started to tingle and grow warm all over.

"Laura," said Max's deep and powerful voice. "Forgive me if I've disturbed you. This is Maximilian. I'd like to meet with you if you have some free time in the next few days. It concerns business. Well, it *mostly* concerns business. Please give me a call when you have a moment."

I am so going to regret this.

With my heart pounding, I punched the button for Max's cell phone. After two rings, he answered.

"Laura, thank you for returning my call. Hopefully, I didn't catch you in the middle of anything."

"No, I was with Sophie and Gina. But I really didn't want them to hear every word of our conversation. You already provide them with too much to gossip about."

"Oh really?" he asked with a laugh. "You'll have to tell me sometime what they talk about. But as to why I called, I'd like to meet with you sometime in the next few days, if you have some free time. I have some questions about the people you met with about two months ago."

A hard knot suddenly formed in my stomach. Two months before, I'd come face-to-face with Carlos Valentino, also known as Carlos the Butcher.

He's the local leader of a violent drug cartel from Mexico called the *Black Death* and definitely not a nice man. At the time, it looked like Tough Tony and Carlos the Butcher were going to be in a war with each other for control of the drug trade in Arizona.

This was something I wanted no part of, and I was actively avoiding any involvement. I was lucky to have escaped from Carlos the first time. I had no desire to see the man again. Ever.

"Laura?" Max asked. "Did I lose you?"

"Sorry, I sort of got lost in my thoughts for a minute. Actually, I'm probably free tonight. Where should we meet?"

Like maybe your place?

"I've been trying to get you to a Different Pointe of View for months."

"That's in one of the Hilton resorts. Are you checking out the competition?"

"Not at all. I like the view of the city. Dinner?"

"Um, maybe not dinner," I said, remembering Gina's advice. "Why don't we meet up there for drinks out on the patio at the Terrace Room? It has the same great view, and we can talk without anyone listening."

"Perfect. Would eight o'clock work for you?"

Again, I started to panic. What time was it now? I looked at the clock on my desk and saw that it was already after five.

That would give me less than three hours to go home, get cleaned up, get dressed, and then drive up to the resort. If I hurried, I could just do it.

"Alright," I said, in a voice I hoped sounded both sexy and confident. "I'll see you at eight."

I walked back to the front offices. Sophie and Gina both stopped talking when they saw me.

"Well?" Sophie asked.

"Well, what?" I asked innocently.

"Don't keep us waiting," Gina said. "What'd Max

want?"

"Um, we're meeting for drinks tonight at the Terrace Room at the Pointe Hilton Tapatio Cliffs Resort."

Sophie started giggling, and Gina shook her head with concern.

"What?" I asked. "It's only for drinks, and it's in public. He wants to ask me about what happened two months ago. They apparently still have some questions about it."

"Just be careful," Gina said.

"Just use birth control," Sophie laughed.

I sighed with exasperation. "I don't know why I tell you two anything."

I drove home, took a shower, blew my hair dry, and then spent almost half an hour trying to figure out what to wear. Part of me kept saying it really wasn't a date and Max only wanted to talk.

If that was the case, I could wear some capris and an oversized T-shirt. The other half said yes, it was a date, and I'd better look the part. At last, the date side of me won out, and I went to my closet.

I pulled out my little black dress. Black typically isn't the color for summer in Scottsdale, but I usually look good in it.

Unfortunately, when I looked at myself in the mirror, I could see a roll of back-fat showing above my waist. I was slightly grossed out about how bad I looked, so I took off the dress and tossed it on the bed.

Time to go back on the diet.

Out of desperation, I pulled out my short black skirt that hung slightly above my knees. It's my favorite evening skirt, and I save it for special nights on the town. It's made of a silky miracle fabric that never wrinkles or keeps a stain, plus it has little silver rainbow sparkles that flash as I move.

Saying goodbye to Marlowe, I ran out the door.

Chapter Six

Both the Terrace Room Lounge and the Different Pointe of View restaurant are located on top of a hill overlooking a long canyon at the Tapatio Cliffs Resort in north Phoenix. The views from both the restaurant and the lounge are spectacular.

My favorite view was from the outdoor patio at the lounge. Here, you sit at the top of a steep overlook and look down the canyon to the sparkling lights of downtown Phoenix and beyond to South Mountain.

Once inside the resort grounds, I wound my way up to the restaurant at the top of the hill. The parking lot was almost full, and I had to park near the back.

The temperature was down to about a hundred and five and was slowly falling. There was even a lovely light breeze blowing around the hot air. The sun was about to set, and the western sky was already starting to change colors.

As I walked closer to the restaurant, some of the dormant feelings I've had for Max started to awaken. Over the past two months, I'd learned to keep thoughts of him in a place I reserve for things like red Ferraris, beach houses in Maui, and winning the Powerball.

I wondered why Max had asked to see me. Was this really about the horrible events of two months ago, or was it only a ruse to get together with me?

I guess we'll find out.

Walking into the lounge, I saw it was relatively crowded for a Thursday night. I worked my way through the tables and walked out onto the patio.

Although there were several groups of people on the terrace, it wasn't quite as busy as the air-conditioned inside. Most of the people on the patio probably lived in Arizona since they seemed to be unconcerned about the temperature.

It didn't take me long to spot Max. He'd already gotten us a table near the edge of the overlook.

When he saw me walking toward him, he stood and held his arms out to me. I did my best to stay calm and not run to him. This was even though I had an overwhelming desire to jump into his arms, wrap my legs around his waist, and then spend about twenty minutes kissing his handsome, upturned face.

Stop that! You already have a boyfriend.

When I finally got to him, he wrapped his muscular arms around me, and I couldn't help but hug him back. I seemed to drift into a dream world.

I was enveloped in sensations of desire, happiness, and of feeling safe. I wanted to bury my face in Max's chest and not let go.

I realized my feelings were deeper than how good his arms felt or how great he smelled. I wanted to wake up with him, cook his breakfast, and do his laundry. I even wanted to…

"Laura?" Max asked, "Are you alright?"

Crap.

"Oh, um, sorry," I managed to say as I took a step back.

"I was sort of spacing out for a second."

"Well, it's good to see you too." He gave me a small half-smile and quietly laughed as if he'd been reading my thoughts.

We both sat down, and a waitress came to take our drink orders. I requested a scotch with one ice cube, and Max did the same. We both sat in silence, enjoying the view.

The sun had dipped below the mountains to the west, and the sky was on fire with iridescent yellows, oranges, and reds. I briefly thought about laying on the bed with Les at his granddad's house as we watched the ceiling turn bright with the colors of the sunset. That seemed like a long time ago, even though it had only been on Tuesday, just two days ago.

"Thanks for coming out to meet with me," Max said at last. "I know it's been a couple of months since we've talked. I can understand if you'd like to put the business with Carlos and the drug cartel out of your mind."

"I wish I could forget about it," I said. "I still have nightmares about that day. I'm thankful we were able to get Jackie out of there in one piece. It could have easily gone the other way. I know I've already thanked you for rescuing us, but it goes deeper than a thank you. You literally saved our lives."

"Don't worry about it. I was glad we could get you out. You did well that day. People who can remain calm and keep their wits in a stressful situation are rare."

The waitress brought our drinks, and we again sat in the quiet of each other's company while we watched the western sky fade to a brick red. Overhead, the stars were beginning to come out. In the distant valley, the lights of the city were starting to come on.

For the first time in days, I felt wonderful. Part of it was the beauty of watching a sunset on the patio at the lounge, but I knew it was mainly because of Max.

It felt good being next to him. I wanted to start chatting about his life and ask him what he'd been up to the past couple of months.

I wanted to ask if he was lonely or if he'd found a girlfriend. I wanted to learn about his family and what his secret desires were.

But deep down, I knew Gina was right. Getting too personal with Max was probably a bad idea.

"Well," I said. "You wanted to talk about Carlos and his men?"

Max looked at me for a second. It reminded me of the cop-look Reno would give me. The one where I knew he could read my mind. The look on his face quickly faded to mild disappointment.

"Um, sure," he said. "Well, we have indications Carlos will be making a major move against us soon. Tony wants to act before things get out of hand. Unfortunately, we have only limited information about who Carlos has working for him, which makes it harder to set up our defenses. All we have are vague descriptions of men that could be almost anyone."

"I'll help if I can. But there was nothing special about any of them. They were all men in their twenties or thirties. Most of them had short dark hair and brown eyes, and most of them had a mustache. But I know that describes about half the men in Scottsdale. If you had some pictures, maybe I could point them out."

"Do you have any names? Even first names would be helpful."

"Other than Carlos, I didn't hear anyone's name."

"Is there anything remarkable about any of them? A scar

or unusual tattoo?"

"The little guy who threw the hatchet at me got a face full of wasp spray. It made his right eye bloodshot and gave him a dark red rash on the right side of his face. But that was two months ago, and he's probably healed up by now."

"Thanks. I didn't think you'd be able to add a lot, but I needed to ask."

"There's something I've been worrying about," I said. "Do you think Carlos will be able to piece together that I was sort of responsible for getting his shipment of heroin confiscated and all those men arrested? Not to mention getting his car blown up. Whenever I hear a noise in the middle of the night, I can't help but think they're coming for me."

"Well, technically, his Ferrari didn't blow up. We set it on fire, and it burnt to the ground. Besides, it was Gabriella who thought that one up." He sat back and chuckled at the memory.

"Jerk, you know what I mean."

"To answer your question, no, we haven't heard of anything like that. A lot of things went wrong for Carlos that day, and you seemed like a minor player. As far as he knows, it was either Tony or the police who were the cause of the drug seizure and the arrest of his men. There isn't anything to connect you other than you were there."

"I guess that makes sense," I said.

"But so you know, I'm keeping an ear open for any talk on the street about you. I'll let you know first thing if I hear anything. If something comes up, we can put you in a safe house until any nastiness blows over."

"You're watching over me?"

"Of course. Um, well, we owe you and wouldn't want to

see anything happen to you."

"That's it?"

"Well, *I* wouldn't want to see anything happen to you either. I've grown rather fond of you over the last six months."

My heart did a flip-flop, and I started to tingle all over.

All right, keep calm. You knew this was going to happen.

"You're sweet," I stammered out. "I'm glad you're out there watching over me."

I could see this wasn't the answer he was looking for. He looked at me for a few seconds, again seeming to read my mind.

The waitress stopped by the table and dropped off two more drinks. I hadn't ordered another one, but I was glad to have it. I sipped on the fresh scotch, and it seemed to help.

We both spent a few minutes watching the lights of the city. As always, it seemed like you could almost reach out and touch them.

"Okay, what else do you want to know?" Max asked.

"Well, there is one other thing that's been bugging me. Tony says he owes me two favors. I appreciate it and all, but I'd rather he didn't owe me anything. I keep wanting to give Tony back his favors, but he's not very receptive. What's going on with that? I don't want to upset him."

With the change of subject, Max relaxed. He was now back on familiar territory.

"There's one thing you have to understand about all men in powerful positions," Max said, "not just Tony. They make deals all the time, and yet nothing is written in the form of a contract."

"What do you mean?" I asked. "How can anyone do business like that?"

"I've often seen Tony make a deal to spend millions of dollars based only on a handshake. When you do business like that, your word and your reputation are what you live on. To Tony, giving you his word was the same as having a twenty-page contract signed, witnessed, and notarized."

"I guess I never thought of it that way," I said.

"When he told you he owed you two favors, it was binding to him. It's a debt he owes you. He'd never think of reneging on the obligation. To be honest, it'll also never enter his mind that you don't want him to owe you. If you told him that directly, it would probably hurt his feelings. That usually isn't a good thing to do."

Yikes!

"So, what do I do?"

"Just go with it and never use the favors. Besides, I know the business you're in and the risks you take. A favor from Tony might be useful someday."

"That's what I'm worried about, that I'll need to use them someday. I don't think I ever want to become that deeply involved."

Max barked out a short laugh. "I hate to tell you, but you already seem to be at least sort of involved. Between diamonds and drug smugglers, you always seem to be in the middle of everything we do."

"Please don't take this personally, but I really hope I'm never involved with you, well, in a business sense, ever again."

Max caught my qualifier and perked up. He held up his glass.

"To never being involved, in a business sense, ever again."

I held up my glass and clinked it against his.

After a few more minutes, we had run out of business things to talk about. I could see Max wanted to get more personal with me but was doing his best to be a gentleman about it. At last, the waitress brought the check, and Max tossed down some bills.

"Can I walk you out to your car?" he asked.

You can take me to a hotel.

"Thank you," I said. "But that's probably not a good idea. Every time we walk together, I end up kissing you."

"Is that such a bad thing?"

"Well…"

"Still having a hard time sorting out your feelings toward me?"

No, that's the problem. I know exactly what I want to do with you.

"Yes, sort of."

"Alright, we've had this discussion before. I think you know how I feel about you. Are you going to Alex and Danica's wedding next Friday?"

Again, the tingles flooded all over my body.

"Of course, I wouldn't miss it. All three of us will be there."

"Good," he said. "I'll be there as well. You don't need to have clear feelings to dance with me. I'll look forward to that."

Great, one more thing to stress about.

I woke up a little after eight the next morning. I lay in bed and stretched until I was mostly awake.

I was feeling better than I had in days, and I knew a lot of it had to do with my date with Max the night before. Thinking about how good he smelled and how great it was to be in his arms started to get me going.

Reluctantly, I stumbled into the shower. I stood with my head completely submerged in the flow, allowing the warm water to cleanse my mind.

After the shower, I blew my hair dry, put on a pot of coffee, and started thinking about Reno.

Thinking of him evoked a different set of reactions: thoughts of protection, being cared for, and long-term stability. Stability has been a rare commodity in my life, and it's something I crave.

I knew I could be happy with him, and he seemed to be happy with me. I'm pretty sure we both love each other, although neither of us spends a lot of time vocalizing how we feel.

He does amazing things for me, and I know I should be happy. I don't even think of being with other men. So why do I keep thinking about Max?

How did life get so complicated?

I went into the kitchen and poured myself a coffee. Marlowe loudly squeaked to remind me this trip to the kitchen had better be all about the cat.

I plopped a spoonful of Seafood Deluxe dinner in his bowl, and he scarfed it up in less than a minute. I didn't want to listen to him throw it up, so I went back to the bedroom.

I glanced at the clock and saw it was already after nine. I knew I needed to leave soon to get up to the Tropical Paradise by ten.

The thought of having the Feds following us around all day was still giving me the willies, but as Gina had said, they weren't the bad guys. I knew she was right, but I also didn't want federal law enforcement watching my every move. I had an idea and called Les on his cell phone.

"How are you doing today?" I asked.

"Actually, I'm feeling great. I slept in until eight. You were right about needing some time to recharge. I spent most of the night at the party down at the pool. It was nice. They had a new band, and this one mostly played reggae. I was half tempted to give you a call and see if you wanted to come down so you could enjoy yourself as well."

"It sounds like it was fun," I said. "Maybe next time. The Feds are probably parked outside of the resort entrance, waiting for you to leave. Having them following us around is a variable I'd rather not deal with today. There's a big maintenance building for the golf course less than a mile away from your room. I'll pick you up there. We'll then leave the resort on a road they'll never think to watch."

I explained where the building was, and Les punched the destination into the navigator on his phone.

"My phone says I can walk there in seventeen minutes."

"Alright, see you at ten."

The drive up to the hotel was uneventful, but I was also

starting to get some mixed emotions about my destination. When I'd picked out the building where I was going to meet Les, I chose a place I knew would be away from the prying eyes of the Feds. I didn't realize how I would feel about going back there until now.

Well, it's too late to change it now.

The meeting place was a big steel building used to repair the maintenance equipment of the golf courses in the area. I'd only been there once before, about six months earlier.

At the time, it was the location of an exchange of diamonds between members of the Russian mafia and two brothers from a group called the Consortium. Tony DiCenzo had agreed to provide both the building and the security for the exchange.

Unfortunately, the deal had gone badly. As a result, some people were killed, and the building had blown up. Fortunately, the Consortium had offered to pay for a new building, at least partially in an effort to gloss over the questionable details of the accident.

With the help of the navigator on my phone, I drove up Scottsdale Road but turned off just past the resorts. I drove down a couple of side roads, the last half-mile being a narrow maintenance road.

It ended in a dirt parking lot in front of a large red metal building. I seemed to remember the old building had been blue. The red was an improvement.

I parked and got out of my car. It was already a hundred and five degrees and promised to be another scorcher. Les was walking down a footpath from the direction of the resort. He came around the building and got into my car.

"I'm glad you're here," he said. "I wasn't sure I was on the right path, and this is the middle of nowhere. How'd you know about this place?"

"Well, you know me. I get around."

The drive to the house on Camelback Mountain was uneventful and thankfully free of any sort of tail. As we pulled into the courtyard, I saw the crime scene tape had been removed from the front door.

From what Gina had said, I knew the master bedroom would still be sealed, but the rest of the house would be open. Les pulled out his key and unlocked the deadbolt on the front door.

"Where should we start?" he asked.

"Well, from the note, we know the jewelry's somewhere in the house."

"We've already looked everywhere. Plus, I'm sure the police have been over everything as well."

"That's true," I said. "But when we looked the last time, we were in a hurry trying to beat your sister at finding the chest. I've been thinking about it. Since your granddad put the vault in a hidden room, perhaps he has another one somewhere else."

"How do you want to do it?" he asked.

"Let's start in the basement and go room to room to see if we can find it. Maybe we'll get lucky."

We first spent an hour and a half in the basement. There

were fifteen or twenty old boxes and crates lying in two large piles.

From our previous search of the basement on Tuesday, I didn't think any of them had been handled in several years. But realistically, the chest could have been in any of them.

Going through the boxes was dirty and dusty work, but at last, we finished. Unfortunately, there was no treasure.

We then went outside and looked around the pool. The date palms and queen palms provided plenty of shade, and the waterfall made a relaxing sound.

Although lovely, there wasn't anything of note at the pool other than a wet bar, some comfortable lounge chairs, and a small metal bust of Lester's grandfather sitting on a marble pedestal by the back wall. The bust, although noteworthy, was much too small to contain the jewelry, even if someone had carved out the middle.

We looked in the bar refrigerator, and it was fully stocked with a nice selection of German beers. I made a mental note to come back and lay in a lounge chair sometime soon, preferably with one of the cold beers.

We spent the next two hours examining every room in the house. We lifted carpets and looked behind paintings. We pulled on books and tapped on walls. We even banged on pipes and pushed on the backs of closets.

Frustrated by our lack of progress, we both seemed to agree we were getting nowhere. Since we were near the library, we decided to go in there. Les headed straight for the door leading out to the terrace.

We stepped outside and were welcomed with a fresh blast of heat. Les flinched, but I could tell his mind was elsewhere. We both walked to the edge of the terrace and looked down at the city.

"I don't remember it being this hot when I came here as a kid," he said. "We didn't always come in the summer, but even when we did, it didn't seem this brutal."

"Summers in Arizona are special," I said. "It's already over a hundred and ten, maybe even one fifteen. It's a day that's going to sizzle like bacon in a frying pan."

"Do you ever get used to it?"

"Well, sort of. I don't even notice anything under one ten. When it feels hot, I mean really hot, like now, I know it's closer to one twelve or maybe one fifteen. But temperatures this hot only last a couple of months. For the rest of the year, we live in a paradise, and the rest of the country pays top dollar to visit. It always seems like a small price to pay."

"I'm not sure I could live here. I'm a Chicago guy. When this is over, I'll probably give the house to Elizabeth and see if she'll give me the land. I could probably sell those properties faster than the house anyway."

As he was talking, I could feel the assignment slipping away. We weren't any closer to finding the jewelry, and I could tell Les had pretty much given up on it. I knew his sister Elizabeth had no idea where to look. I also knew I couldn't hide from the Feds much longer. When they caught up with us, they'd stick to us like Velcro.

It was the same with the police. They were going to want to interview him again in a day or two. If they arrested Les for murder, there was no way he could remain involved in hunting down the jewelry.

It annoyed me that Les had information that might help, and he was keeping quiet. The more I thought about it, the angrier I became.

Les was still gazing out over the city, and his thoughts seemed to be drifting. I reached up and grabbed Les by his big shoulders, turning him to face me like he was a two-year-old who wasn't paying attention.

"Look," I said, "I know you're holding things back from me. If you truly want to find this treasure, I need you to tell me what's going on. I'm not a cop, I'm not your wife, and I'm not a priest. I'm the person who's trying to help you. You've got to tell me what you know, or else we'll never get anywhere."

He stood in silence for almost a minute, turning away to look back out at the city as he considered my words. I could tell he was thinking about what to say. He seemed to come to a decision, then turned and looked at me.

"Okay, you're right. I guess I should be straight with you. If we're going to do this, there are some things you should probably know about me. Let's go sit where we can talk."

By mutual agreement, we made our way back into the library. I knew Les felt safe there, and it seemed like the right place to begin our conversation.

As we entered the massive room, the air-conditioning hit us like an icy blast. Les walked to one of the red leather wing chairs and sat down. I pulled another one close to it. He composed himself before he started to talk.

"You should know I've been deeply involved with some pretty bad guys over the last few years. At first, it was exciting, and I made a lot of money. But, as I grew older, I'd come to realize it was something I didn't want to spend the rest of my life doing. I'd had enough of that life and told them I wanted out."

"What happened? Were they upset?"

"No, not upset. But they told me I was obligated to stay. If I wanted out, I'd need to buy out my contract. Since I knew too much about the organization, I'd either need to pay them off and never say a word to anyone, or I'd need to disappear, as in permanently disappear. Unless I wanted a bullet to the back of the head, I owed them money. A lot of money."

"How much?"

"Three million dollars."

"Wow. Okay. I understand that part. But that doesn't explain the Feds."

"The government wants me to testify against my associates. They've been following me for weeks, supposedly to keep an eye on me and keep me out of trouble. They've promised me immunity and a witness relocation. But, unless I pay off the money first, there'll be a contract out on me for the rest of my life."

"But if the government changes your identity and moves you somewhere that's secret, how could they get to you?"

"That's true, and it might work out okay. But this is still the government we're talking about. They seem to mess up everything they touch. I'm not sure I'm willing to bet my life that they'll get it right this time."

"But even if you pay off what you owe, won't they still be upset if you testify against them? That sounds even worse than being in debt."

"Well, if I can pay them off with this jewelry money, I should be okay. From what I understand, in addition to me, the FBI is also pressuring five of my former associates to testify. If one of them turns first, there won't be any further demands on me. That's what I'm hoping for."

"I assume the government has some sort of leverage over you to testify?"

"The Feds are threatening to charge me with various crimes unless I cooperate. The only things they can prove are relatively minor. I won't get anything more than a light sentence, probably two or three years. After that, the slate will be clean with both the government and my former associates. I can get on with my life. Plus, if we do find the jewelry, I should have enough left over for a nice nest egg. It will go a long way towards starting my life over after I get out of prison."

"Now I'm confused," I said. "You already have money. When we first met on Tuesday, you bought part of a hotel in Vail. Can't you sell some of that stuff and use the money for the guys in Chicago?"

"I'm sorry to say the hotel story you heard was a sham. I knew you'd be coming to the room, so I made up that thing about the hotel. It was a spur-of-the-moment decision. I was on the phone talking to an old friend in Chicago when I saw you walking up the stairs. I told him I was trying to impress a woman and asked him to roll with it."

"So why the deception?"

"I wanted you to think I still had a lot of money, so you'd help me. There's no way I can pay the legal fees I'm piling up with both the lawyer in Chicago and with Leonard over this inheritance thing. But I knew I was going to need somebody local to help me out, or else I wouldn't have a chance against my sister."

"So, you just need the jewelry."

"That's right. With the money I'll get by selling Granddad's trinkets, I can buy my way out of a lot of trouble."

"But we need to find the jewelry first."

"Yes, that will be a helpful first step. And, as long as you want to know my secrets, I should probably mention one other thing. It's about Tuesday night…"

"Lester," said a high-pitched man's voice coming from

behind us, "I think you've said enough."

We both turned in the direction of the voice. It belonged to a skinny guy dressed all in black, like a military commando. He wore black boots, black cargo pants, and a tight black T-shirt.

The man had a shrunken face, dark eyes, and long black hair pulled into a ponytail. He looked to be somewhere in his mid-twenties and had the malnourished body of someone who'd taken a lot of drugs.

He was standing just inside the door leading out to the hallway, holding a pistol, pointing it directly at Les. From the size of the hole in the barrel, it must have been a 10mm or maybe a .45 caliber. Either way, it wasn't good news.

How long had he been listening? Did he hear that Les might testify for the Feds?

"Morningstar's getting annoyed with you," the man said, and he laughed a thin, high-pitched giggle. There was no humor in the creepy little laugh. "You and I need to go for a ride. We need to talk about your future in light of recent events." Again, he let out a creepy giggle.

"Come on, Magic," Les said. "You don't need the gun. You already know I'm working to find the jewelry so I can pay everyone off. It's somewhere here in the house. I think it would be more constructive to find the jewelry first. Then we can all get together. If I'm off having a meeting with Morningstar, the jewelry could be recovered by someone else. Then we're both screwed."

"Unfortunately," Magic said, "after what you did to Frankie the other night, I think it's gone beyond a simple payment to set things straight. You're a hard man to find, but Morningstar sent me to fetch you. I think he's tired of waiting and wants to personally explain how things stand for you now."

"Hey, I didn't do anything to Frankie."

"Well, that's not how I hear it. Come on, you have a date with Morningstar. You can tell him all about it."

He waved the gun as our invitation to get up. He made me go first and had Les walk three steps in front of him. Since I was in the lead, I wondered what the odds would be of getting shot if I tried to make a run for it.

I also thought about the bulletproof vest Max wore the last time he was shot. It had probably saved his life. Maybe a bulletproof vest would be a good accessory at times like this.

Okay, I guess Reno has a point about my job being somewhat dangerous.

We walked through the house and out to the courtyard. There was a nondescript white rental sedan parked next to my car.

Magic used his gun to wave us to my Honda and told Les to get in the front driver's side. After Les was seated, the guy looked at me. I could tell he was deciding what to do about the woman who had no business in his affairs.

"Give me the keys and then get in the back," he quietly said.

I dug through my purse and handed him the keys. I was briefly tempted to pull out my Baby Glock, but with his gun already trained on me, it wouldn't be a fair contest. Besides, if he wanted me in the backseat, I could play it cool, take my time, and perhaps get the drop on him.

I walked to the back of my car with the man right behind me. I reached out to open the door when a sudden bolt of pain struck the back of my head.

Bright lights and black dots danced in front of my eyes. I felt myself falling. Then I knew no more.

Chapter Seven

I slowly came swimming back to consciousness, gradually becoming aware I was somewhere dark and cramped. The air was hot to the point that I was having a hard time breathing. I couldn't tell how long I'd been out, but it seemed like it'd been quite a while.

I was curled up in a fetal position and couldn't seem to move. My eyes burned and stung from the sweat running into them. The back of my head hurt like hell, and I had a bitch-kitty of a headache, pounding to the rhythm of my heart.

As I felt around, I suddenly knew I'd been placed in a coffin. At this thought, I started to panic.

I'm normally not bothered by closed spaces, like an airplane or an elevator, but being trapped in a coffin was way beyond my comfort level. I remembered a scene in the movie *Kill Bill* where Uma Thurman had been placed in a coffin and then buried alive. That vision suddenly became all too real for me.

I tried to yell for help, but what came out instead was a long, frightened scream. I spent almost a minute in stark terror as I imagined my slow and painful death, trapped below the earth, unable to move and slowly suffocating.

I kicked out with my legs and attempted to move my arms, but they were tightly pinned behind my back.

Gradually, my panic subsided to below the surface, and I became determined to find out where I was and how I was going to get myself out of this cell.

The first thing I noticed was it was not completely dark. There was a faint light coming from the side of my tiny prison, somewhere above my head.

From what I could tell, I was in some sort of box or container, and it seemed to be made of metal and plastic. I could also tell the walls were not lined with satin.

At this, I realized I wasn't in a coffin. That helped reduce my panic down to a manageable level. I next tried to free my hands, but by feeling around with my fingers, I could tell I had on a set of handcuffs. These were likely the ones I kept in my purse.

Great. I hate it when this happens.

My heart rate started to slow as the terror receded. Unfortunately, the air was still hot, and it hurt to take in a breath.

The last time I'd felt heat like this was when I'd gotten dumped in the middle of the desert on a hot July afternoon and had to walk almost ten miles to a truck stop on the outskirts of Gila Bend. I almost hadn't made it then, and I was getting the same dizzy feeling from breathing in the heat.

The next thing I noticed was the faint smell of oil and gasoline. I also began to hear the sounds of traffic. They'd probably been there all along, but in my fright, I hadn't registered them.

My eyes were becoming adjusted to the dim light, and as I looked around my prison box, I saw some faint shapes that were starting to make sense. There was a piece of plastic on the side of my box that had a bundle of wires going into it.

I also saw I was lying on what looked like one of my old

blankets. It had colorful cartoon characters on it from when I was a kid. It was one I always kept in my trunk for emergencies.

Am I locked in my own trunk?

The only thing that didn't make sense was the light coming from above my head. Then I realized if this were my car, there would be a bullet hole right about where the light was coming from.

I'll have to thank Max someday for shooting up my car.

Knowing I was locked in my trunk helped narrow down my options, but it still didn't get me any closer to getting out. I knew there was an emergency trunk release that would open the lid, and then I could crawl out.

Unfortunately, in my cramped fetal position, there was no way I could roll over to pull the release. I tried to bend down so I could pull on it with my teeth, but I couldn't move my head more than a few inches in any direction.

I silently regretted all the stuff I'd crammed into my trunk over the years. If it hadn't been for that, I could've probably twisted around enough to free myself.

If my bag was somewhere in the trunk, perhaps I could dig out my handcuff key. Maybe I could even use my Baby Glock to shoot open the trunk, assuming it was still in my purse.

I looked around in front of me and felt around behind me for my bag. But I quickly concluded that even if it was in the trunk, I couldn't reach it.

Realizing I was out of options, a wave of sadness and desperation washed over me. I was locked in my trunk, slowly baking in the heat, and I began to think I might die.

Maybe Reno had been right, and maybe I should've gone back to being a bartender. Nobody ever tosses their bartender in the trunk of a car and then leaves her to die if their drink isn't made right.

Desperate to get out, I began blindly searching around with my fingers, looking for anything I could use to pull the release or even pry open the trunk. As I was feeling around behind my back, my hand brushed against the back of my capris.

As it did, I felt something hard. It took a second to register – my phone was still in my back pocket.

My phone? Okay. Interesting.

I maneuvered my hands around and tried to pull the phone out, but with my legs curled up, it was tightly wedged into the pocket. I then reached down with the tips of my fingers and pushed up on the phone from the outside of the pocket. It still didn't budge.

In desperation, I grabbed the top of the pocket and pulled as hard as I could. There was a ripping sound, and I felt the top of the pocket loosen.

Okay, that's a start.

After another few minutes of ripping my pants to make the hole bigger, I pushed up on the phone from the outside of the pocket. My fingers began to ache, but the phone finally started to slide out of the top.

Slowly, I began to work the phone out. My cuffed hands were slippery with sweat, and it took several attempts to get a grip on it, but I gradually eased it out of my pocket.

I was panting from the effort of pulling the phone out and was getting seriously lightheaded from the heat. Knowing if I passed out, I probably wouldn't wake up again, I cradled the phone in my hands.

Okay, now what?

Since the phone was behind my back, I couldn't see what I was dialing. Even worse, my phone had a smooth glass face. There was no way I could feel around to push nine-one-one.

Well, it's a smartphone. Maybe I can talk to it?

I pushed the one button I could find, and the phone beeped to let me know it was waiting for a voice command.

"Call nine-one-one," I burbled out.

"I'm sorry," the phone said. *"I don't understand what you mean."*

All right, I told myself, calm down and speak slowly and clearly.

"Call nine-one-one."

"Okay, call nine-one-one. Are you having an emergency?"

"Yes!"

"Thanks. Do you need the fire department, the police department, an ambulance, or the border patrol?"

Border patrol?

"Police," I shouted to the phone.

"Okay, police. Is there an intruder in your home?"

"No."

"Thanks. Have you been robbed?"

"No."

"Okay. Are you reporting an illegal alien?"

"No."

"Thanks. Have you been kidnapped?"

"Yes!"

"Okay, you've been kidnapped. I'll call the police."

"Thank you!"

"I'm sorry you've been kidnapped. Would you like to listen to some soothing music while I call the police? Bruno Mars has a new album out, and I can download it to your phone for only $8.99."

"Just call the fricking police!"

I finally got through to the police and told them what happened. They said they'd send help right away. From the GPS in the phone, they said I was parked on Pima Road, just north of Indian School.

The next ten minutes were some of the longest in my life. My legs and arms were cramped from being pinned in the same position for so long.

The hot air burned my lungs with each breath. My eyes had stopped stinging, but that was only because I'd become so dehydrated that I'd stopped sweating.

My core temperature was rapidly rising. Within a few minutes, I knew I'd pass out again, this time with heatstroke.

As I waited for rescue, I thought about Reno and how he'd scold me about this. Even after everything that had happened to me in the last two hours, the thought of that made me smile.

The minutes went on, and I fought to stay awake. But it was a battle I was slowly losing.

I started thinking about lying in a cool swimming pool. The pain was gone, and I was floating.

It was a wonderful and peaceful feeling. I decided floating was nice. I told myself I'd float for a while, and then everything would be okay.

I was startled awake by the loud banging sound of something hard hitting the top of my car. Trapped in the trunk, it sounded like fireworks were going off next to my head.

"Hey, Laura, are you locked in your trunk?"

The voice sounded familiar, but it took me a few seconds to put the voice with a name.

"Chugger? Is that you?" I noticed my words were coming out weakly with a touch of panic. "Yeah, I'm stuck in here. Get me out. Hit the trunk release on the dash."

"Your car's locked. I'd need to break a window. Isn't there something in there you can pull to open the trunk?"

"I can't get to it." I noticed the panic sound in my voice had risen a notch. "My hands are cuffed behind my back. It's hot, and I can't breathe. The bullet hole isn't letting in a lot of air."

"Okay, hold on," I heard him say.

Less than a minute later, I heard the sound of metal on metal, and I felt my car rock. With a loud metallic popping noise, my trunk lid opened.

I felt the rush of cool air, and my eyes felt the sting of the bright sunshine. Gradually, as I got used to the brightness, I saw Chugger standing there with a crowbar in his hands.

"Sorry about your trunk," he said as he pulled me out. "You'll probably need to replace the latch. I've got an old bungee cord in the cruiser you can have. It'll work to keep your trunk lid shut until you get it fixed."

Great. One more thing wrong with my car.

I leaned against the side of my rear fender on wobbly legs. I looked back into my tiny prison and saw my purse had indeed been thrown in the trunk with me.

"The keys to the handcuffs are in my purse."

Chugger reached in, pulled my bag out, and then used the key to unlock the cuffs.

I noticed Chugger's partner, Arny Montoya, was also standing next to my car. He was using his walkie-talkie to call into the station. I heard him say they'd freed me from the trunk, and I appeared not to need EMS.

Chugger then helped me into the backseat of his patrol car. Arny handed me a fresh bottle of water, which I downed in several large gulps.

After about five minutes of sitting in the back of the air-conditioned patrol car and sipping on another bottle of water, I was again able to think clearly, and my voice started to come back. Unfortunately, the headache was still there, and a large bump had formed where the guy had hit me with his pistol.

"Thanks for getting me out of there," I croaked. "I think I had passed out again."

"I'm glad you were able to call us," Chugger said. "Who did this to you? In my mind, putting someone in a trunk on a hot day like this is attempted homicide."

"I'm not sure. I've never met him before. But it somehow ties in with an assignment I'm working on."

"Arny found your keys. Somebody tossed them in the ditch next to your car. I'd suggest pressing charges this time. Give the okay, and I'll call it in."

"No. I'm out of the trunk, and I'm alright. I don't want

this to become official. As a favor to me, please don't report it as an attempted homicide. It'll mess up any chance I have with Reno. He's been touchy about my job lately, and hearing about this would probably finish it."

"Hey, I've known you since the first grade at Navajo Elementary. I'd hate to see anyone get a second chance at killing you. I know how you feel about pressing charges, but I worry that someday your luck will run out. But sure, if it's important, we can leave that part out of the report."

"Thanks, Chugger. Is there a way not to mention my name in the report? Finding out I was locked in my trunk will still be enough for Reno to give me another lecture."

"Sorry, you already called nine-one-one, plus we called the license plate in first thing. You're a public record. Not much we can do about that now."

Great.

Chugger and Arny took off. I sat in my car for a few minutes and waited for the world to stop spinning.

I found the bottle of Advils I kept in the car and downed four of them, along with another bottle of water. After about fifteen minutes, I felt somewhat better, so I drove over to the office.

The bungee cord Chugger had given me worked to keep the trunk closed. Unfortunately, every time I hit a bump, I heard a loud thump as the lid bounced up and down. Each time it thumped, I felt a fresh bolt of pain in my head.

I parked behind the office and saw the only car there was Sophie's yellow Volkswagen. I went in through the back door and walked up to the front offices.

Sophie was working away at her computer and didn't see me until I was almost on top of her. She then looked up with a start.

"Jeez, I thought you were Lenny. Don't sneak up on me like that." She then looked closer at me. "Damn, you look terrible."

"I'm having another shitty day," I admitted.

Sophie looked me over from top to bottom.

"Well, no knife wounds. No gunshot wounds, either. But your hair's a little funky, and your clothes are a mess. Is that dirt, or grease all over your top? Either way, it's probably ruined. You don't smell bad this time, so you didn't get peed on by a dog again. You stunk really bad the last time that happened."

"Hey, that was two years ago. How long are you going to remind me about that?"

"Like, forever. It was hilarious. Let's see, your makeup's gone, and you have some fresh handcuff scrapes. I'm thinking kidnapped."

"They took Les, and I got tossed in the trunk of my car."

"I hate to tell you," Sophie said, "but whenever you take on someone as a client, they tend to get kidnapped. Remember Alex? Oh, there was Jackie, too. Maybe you're bad luck or something?"

"It's not funny. A guy pistol-whipped me, and my head's killing me. Would you look and see how bad it is?"

I turned so Sophie could examine the lump. She stood and felt around on my head where the pistol had struck me. I winced every time she touched the bump.

"Well?" I asked.

"Well, I always took you for the kind of person who

matched their panties and their shirt. But your shirt is yellow, and your panties are blue."

"Why are you looking at my panties?"

"It's not like I'm trying to look. But you have a hole the size of a paperback book in the back of your pants. Half your ass is hanging out."

"What about my head?"

"Well, the good news is they didn't break the skin this time. No blood anywhere. The bad news is you have a lump the size of a walnut. Maybe this time you should have it looked at, by a real doctor."

"No, it's okay. It'll go down in a day or two."

"Seriously?" she asked.

"If I go to the hospital, they'll just poke at it, take an x-ray, and tell me I need an MRI. After all of that, they'll tell me the lump will go down in a day or two and then send me a bill for fourteen hundred dollars. Besides, that would take all night, and I'm supposed to go out with Reno in a couple of hours."

"What about the guy that did this to you? Are the police getting involved, or did you forget to press charges again?"

"You know that having the police snoop around will only drive everyone underground. The guy wasn't after me personally. He had no clue who I was. I was only someone who was in his way. Besides, Reno would flip if he found out what happened."

"You know, it's a good thing you always pass out at the slightest tap to your skull. Otherwise, the guy would have needed to beat you senseless, and you'd be a mess. Although I've been thinking, we should probably start a concussion protocol on you whenever you take another blow to your head, like they do in the NFL."

"Shut up," I grumbled. "Where's Lenny? I need to tell him about this."

"He's down at the Phoenix district station sniffing around to see what he can find out about the murder. He should be back soon."

"When's Gina coming back? I could use her advice."

"She's up in Sedona chasing down a lead in one of her cheating spouse cases. There was a fresh credit card hit from a hotel up there."

"It figures. This assignment is really getting weird. What have you found out about Lester and Elizabeth?"

"Nothing on Elizabeth. She seems to be just as she appears. She has a job at a respectable Chicago marketing firm. She has a nice car and a nice house. Both are paid for. One unusual thing is that she has three brokerage accounts with about a hundred thousand in each. She opened these up not too long after her dad died, about fifteen years ago. The brokerage accounts each started out at about a million dollars, but they all fell rapidly to where they are now."

"Les and Elizabeth talked a little bit about their dad's inheritance. Apparently, Les did something peculiar with that, and it pissed off Elizabeth. Do you know why they lost so much?"

"Not yet. I'm still looking."

"What about Les?"

"Les opened up three brokerage accounts at the same time as his sister. His also started out at a million dollars per account, but they all gradually went down and have been zeroed out for several years."

"As if he slowly pissed it all away?"

"Looks like it."

"What else did you find out about him?"

"His apartment and car are leased by a financial group out of Chicago. The secret software says the group is a front for an organized crime outfit based in south Chicago. Not nice people."

"Okay, that explains some things," I said.

"You're thinking the Chicago gangsters are down here? So, why exactly are Chicago gangsters in Arizona? That might piss off Tough Tony."

"Les owes them money, plus they know about the jewelry. I'm assuming the jerk who shoved me in my trunk was one of these Chicago guys. What did you find out about Les last night? Was there a cab from the Tropical Paradise to his grandfather's house?"

"I've been making some calls. Not only did Les take a cab from the Tropical Paradise to the house on Camelback at about six-thirty, he had the cabbie sit there and wait for over half an hour. He then took the same cab back to the hotel at about seven-thirty."

"Okay, so Les was at the house and had just gotten back to the hotel. He would barely have had time to take a quick shower before I showed up."

I got the sinking feeling in the pit of my stomach that happens whenever a client of ours is found to be caught up in a serious crime.

"Damn," I said. "So, it's possible Les was involved with the murder."

"Well, that'll make Lenny happy. You know how much he loves rich clients who kill someone."

"Unfortunately, I also found out that Les is flat broke. Worse, he owes a lot of money to the gangsters."

"But what about buying a hotel in Vail?" Sophie asked.

"He made that up. He didn't want us to know how badly he needed the money."

"You know, that's going to piss Lenny off something fierce. Poor clients can't pay their fees. No fees means no Lenny, and that means no us."

"I know. But there's still twenty or thirty million dollars in jewelry floating around somewhere. Maybe we can keep Lenny focused on that."

I needed to tell Lenny what was going on, but I couldn't until he came back. I've learned when he's outside the office, he doesn't like to talk on his cell phone unless it's something important. Telling Lenny the new client couldn't pay his fee didn't strike me as something I wanted to tell him over the phone.

I went back to my cubicle and turned on my computer. Since I had some free time, I decided to go through the surveillance tapes from George Anson's house.

I'd hid the cameras on Monday, so they'd been transmitting pictures for almost three full days. The office computers now had a file downloaded from each of the five video cameras placed in the various bedrooms.

I began to go through the videos, starting with the two guest bedrooms. I knew these would be the easiest since George and his mistress seemed to prefer the master bedroom. By hitting the fast-forward button, I was quickly able to scan the events from the last seventy-two hours.

In less than fifteen minutes, I'd determined that neither of the videos from the guest bedrooms showed any activity during the previous three days. I erased the videos and made a notation of the time and date when I erased each one.

This was per the terms of the contract the client had

signed. It wasn't in anyone's interest to have unrelated sex tapes of the client in our possession.

I then went to the files with the videos from the master bedroom. I knew I would need to pay closer attention to these to make out who was actually in the room and what they were doing.

For the first two hours after I left on Monday, no one entered the room. Then there was a blur of activity.

I stopped the fast-forward and played the video at normal speed. I could see that Debbie had come home and was going between the bedroom and the bathroom, changing her shoes, fixing her hair, and redoing her makeup. She left the room, and there was no further activity until about nine that night.

Debbie and George entered the room at the same time, and they were doing the usual activities of a couple getting ready for bed. I was slightly relieved when both Debbie and George changed their clothes in the bathroom, and I didn't have to watch.

At about ten-thirty, Debbie turned off the TV, and the room was dark for the rest of the night. I watched them wake up on Tuesday morning at about six-thirty.

I fast-forwarded the video through the next two days, past the normal activities of George and Debbie getting dressed for the day and then getting ready for bed at night. I was eager to see what went on in the master bedroom yesterday afternoon.

My fingers were crossed that George would come back with his mistress and have a nice long romp. I was curious about who she was, of course, but I was more eager to be done with the assignment. Unfortunately, there was no activity in the room until Debbie came back from her charity events at about four-thirty.

Once again, I crossed my fingers as I watched the video of the master bedroom from earlier in the day today. Unfortunately, no one came into the room after Debbie and George left at about eight this morning.

Come on, George, have sex with the woman one more time so I can finish this.

I erased the videos from the cameras in the master bedroom and made the proper notations in my logbook. I then turned off my computer and went back up to the front offices.

Sophie was still working steadily away on her paperwork. She looked up as I walked closer. She gave me the once-over and looked concerned.

"You still look like crap," she said. "Is your head alright?"

"Actually, it's starting to feel better. I'm feeling a little glum because I was reviewing the video files from the George and Debbie Anson assignment. The one where the husband likes to cheat in the same bed he sleeps in every night with his wife."

"That's just wrong," Sophie said. "I can see sleeping with someone else and all, but not in the same bed. Debbie may suspect, but if she finds out for sure, it'll totally gross her out. She'll need to go out and buy a new bed."

"Well, I can't tell her without proof that'll stand up in court. I've done that before, and all it does is upset the client."

We heard the faint sound of the rear door opening. A minute later, Lenny came up to the front offices. He was swinging his briefcase and seemed to be in a good mood.

He went to his office door and turned to me. He used his index finger to give me a *come here* gesture and then disappeared into his office. Almost immediately, the clink of ice cubes falling into his glass rang out, so I knew the Jim

Beam couldn't be far behind.

"Good luck with Mr. Party Man," Sophie said.

I walked into the office, and Lenny was seated behind his desk, sipping his drink. He still had a big grin on his face.

"I've been at the police station talking to the detectives. It turns out there are a lot of Lester's fingerprints on the statue—way too many fingerprints. Like maybe Lester held it before he moved it Tuesday night to 'look-at-the-body'. The detectives will probably want to set up a meeting in a day or two to get some more information from him."

"So, he's now a suspect in the murder?"

"They're starting to form a case around him. You know, if we're lucky, they might even charge him in the next few days. The evidence so far is a bit sketchy, but I think they're trying to put together a plausible scenario that he killed the guy. If he's charged, it could generate some substantial work for us. Maybe we'll even get some decent press coverage for a change."

"Sophie found evidence Les took a cab from the hotel to the murder scene at around six-thirty. He then took the same cab back to the hotel at about seven-thirty on Tuesday night."

"Really? Well, if that's the case, they might not even wait to charge him. We might be able to get this rolling right away."

"About that."

"What? And why are you such a mess?"

"Les is missing. He left with a guy who seems to be from an organized crime outfit out of Chicago. Apparently, Les has been involved with them for several years."

"Left with a guy? Do you mean kidnapped? Crap. What happened?"

"We were in Lester's granddad's house when a guy walked in on us; he must have followed us in. The guy knocked me out and took Les."

"You know, the same thing happened when you were supposed to be watching Jackie Wade a couple of months ago. I'm starting to think you're bad luck."

"Hey!" I said. "It wasn't my fault."

"I was only making an observation. Did it seem like the guy wanted to kill Lester, or did he only need to get him alone for a while? Do you have a sense this is going to be a ransom situation?"

"The goon with the gun was called Magic. He told Les someone named Morningstar wanted to talk to him to explain how the situation had changed since Tuesday night. He also mentioned someone named Frankie. If Les was the person who killed the guy in the vault, it's likely the dead guy was also from the same Chicago gang."

"Well, that would explain why they're pissed at him. However, it could also suggest a self-defense strategy for our client. You didn't tell the police anything about this, did you?"

"No, I don't even know if he was really kidnapped or if he would have gone voluntarily. It seemed like Les and the goon were business associates. They certainly knew each other."

"I remember the mess we had with Jackie. The police and reporters only confused things, even if we did get some good press coverage. But now that Lester's a suspect, it'll look bad if he doesn't show up. We've been on the good side of the police ever since we tipped them off about that heroin shipment. I don't want things between us going to crap over something stupid like this."

As he was talking, Lenny opened his desk drawer, pulled out his pack of cigarettes, and lit one up. I got the feeling this would only be the first of many this afternoon.

"Alright," he said, "this might get ugly real fast. The police will remember the last time we had a client who became a murder suspect and then also 'disappeared.'"

"Okay," I said. "How should we handle it?"

"As of right now, nothing's more important than getting the client back. I want us to leave no stone unturned. There's a bond, maybe even a sacred trust, between an attorney and a client. Lester needs to know we're there for him and we'll never give up. Let's get everyone involved. Use Gina. Even use Sophie and Annie if you need to. Of course, let's also make sure to keep proper logbooks of our billable time and expenses. What do you think about the ransom angle?"

"I doubt it. Before he was kidnapped, Les confided to me that he was broke. The whole 'idle rich' thing he shows to the outside world is a sham. He doesn't have money to pay either you or the lawyer in Chicago. His only chance was to get us to help him find the jewelry."

"What? Les is broke? Are you serious?"

"Not only is he broke, but he already owes a lot of money to the same Chicago criminal outfit that snatched him. We'll be second in line to get paid, and they have guns."

Lenny sat perfectly still for almost two minutes, calmly smoking his cigarette and sipping his bourbon. He looked out the window and watched the shoppers as they walked up and down the sidewalk.

I've learned not to interrupt Lenny while he's thinking. Finally, he stubbed out his cigarette and put down his glass.

"Alright," he said. "Fuck it. We'll drop it now and cut our losses. Other than a day of time from you and Sophie, we're not out anything yet. I can't see us wasting any more time on a charity case, especially one that's being chased around by mobsters."

"What about the sacred trust between an attorney and his client?"

"That implies the client is able to reciprocate financially. If not, they aren't really a client, are they?"

"But we can't drop this," I said. "You're forgetting about the jewelry. There's twenty or thirty million dollars up for grabs."

"Oh, I haven't forgotten about that. But I don't see a reasonable way to get at it. This thing is starting to look like a big rat hole. Lester was our one avenue to the jewelry, and he's out of the picture. Hunting him down seems like a long shot. At the very least, it'll take both you and Gina, probably with a lot of support from Sophie. The way I see it, we *might* find the client, then he *might* get the jewelry, then we *might* be able to get a fee after the Chicago mafia's through with him. A lot of things would need to fall in line before we could even think about getting paid. I'm thinking we should simply report the kidnapping and wash our hands of the whole thing."

Lenny, think about the bigger picture.

"Look," I said, "Les wanted to split the jewelry with his sister. If we add up the jewelry, the house, and the real estate, we're talking fifteen to twenty million for each of them. Les may show up again on his own, but even if he doesn't, we're still representing him. Why don't we continue to look for the jewelry on his behalf?"

Lenny nodded thoughtfully, took a sip of his Beam, then twirled the first two fingers on his right hand to have me continue.

"We could also ask Elizabeth if she'll work with us," I said. "We'll help her find the jewelry on the condition that she splits the total with her brother. If Les has twenty million dollars in the bank, you should be able to get a nice cut of it, even if you aren't first in line."

Lenny lit another cigarette and thought about what I said.

"Do you think Elizabeth would go for that?" he asked. "From what you said, she doesn't even like her brother. Why would she do something to help him?"

"She seems like a reasonable person. Once she finds out her brother's in trouble, she might want to help him. If not, maybe I'll be able to convince her I have the only clues that'll lead to the treasure. She's stumbling around blindly, and by now, she knows she'll need some help."

"Yeah, okay, I like that. Use that as your new angle. Find Elizabeth and see if we can work with her. If not, we still look for the jewelry on our own. Keep an eye out for our client, but we'll go on with or without him. It also might be a good idea to contact the Feds who've been following him and see what their interest is in all of this. Maybe we can use them to help get our client back. At least they won't present us with a bill for their services."

"It wouldn't make sense for the Chicago guys to kill Les or even to hold him for long," I said. "They know he's looking for a big pile of jewelry, and if he doesn't get to it first, he gets nothing. It seems more reasonable they'll let him go to see if he can find it. Of course, once he has it, they'll probably come back and demand their piece of the treasure."

"I agree, and it all sounds reasonable from the comfort of our armchairs. But if Lester doesn't turn up by tomorrow afternoon, I'll need to talk to the detective in charge about our client and how he may be missing."

I got up and started to walk out the door.

"Hey," Lenny said. "Do you know you have a big hole in your pants? Half of your ass is hanging out. Good thing you're wearing underwear today."

Chapter Eight

I went back to the reception area. Sophie was still working on her reports.

"Well," she said. "How'd Lenny take the news that the client can't pay?"

"About like you'd expect. After he heard Les was broke, he almost gave up the whole thing. I convinced him there was a chance he could still get in on some of the money from the jewelry."

"And how are we going to get in on the jewelry? Lester's nowhere to be found."

"I'll talk to Elizabeth. I'll let her know her brother is missing, and he could be in danger."

"You really think that will work? You said they don't like each other."

"True, but I also have the only clue for finding the jewelry. By now, the police will have the entire contents of the vault somewhere in an evidence locker. It won't be released for months. Even when they do release it, Elizabeth won't know to go and look through it. She can only guess the jewelry is somewhere in the house, but she can't be sure. She has a day job back in Chicago and she most likely doesn't have the time or resources to spend months tearing apart the house. Even if she hires the job out to someone local, they wouldn't know where to look for it either."

"But the only clue you have is something about a coffin rock, and you don't even know what it means."

"True, but I also know for sure the treasure chest is definitely located somewhere in the house. At least, that's what the note in the vault said. That's more than Elizabeth has to go on. I'm sure we can work out a deal."

I went back to my cubicle and pulled out my phone. Fortunately, I'd gotten Elizabeth's cell number the night of the murder while we were in between interviews with the detectives.

When I called her number, the phone immediately went to voicemail. I then left a message and asked her to call me.

Curious about what I looked like, I went into the office bathroom and studied myself in the mirror. Sophie was right. I was a hot mess.

I hadn't realized how much dirt and grease had accumulated in the trunk of my car over the years. Now, much of it was plastered in my hair and on my shirt. Between the rip in my pants and the stains in my shirt, I agreed with Sophie that the entire outfit would probably be a total loss.

I went back up to reception, where Sophie was busily arranging piles of papers on her desk. She looked up at me and gave her head a little shake of frustration.

"See what happens whenever you find a dead body?" she grumbled. "I spend the next two days doing paperwork. Lenny not only wants me to document everything associated with you finding the corpse, but I also need to do full background checks on everyone associated with the murder. Next, I'll start up a full set of log sheets in case we eventually get to bill someone. I then have to get all the police reports associated with the murder, and those are sometimes hard to come by, even with our contacts. Lenny also has me scanning the news reports in case the murder has made it into the press."

"Hey, it's not my fault. It's not like I go out and look for them."

"Oh, I know," Sophie laughed. "Ignore what I'm saying. I'm just practicing my venting. I read on Yahoo this afternoon that constructive venting will help keep me centered and give me a calm and pleasant demeanor. The article said my overall stress levels would drop way down if I occasionally voiced my frustrations to a friend. You know, someone who'll understand the therapeutic benefits and won't take it personally."

"In that case, I can take it. Vent away."

"No, I'm good now. Besides, I'm ready to say screw it and go home."

I looked at the clock on Sophie's desk and saw it was already five-thirty. I needed to go home and clean up before my date with Reno.

"I'm out of here too," I said. "It's been a long crappy day."

"How are you feeling? Are you still getting together with Reno tonight?"

"The headache's gone, and the lump's already starting to go down. But I'm not sure about Reno. It depends on when Elizabeth calls me back."

"Reno would be a lot more fun than an angry sister of a kidnapped client. Especially one who can't pay his bills and won't be a client for long, even if he doesn't show up dead tomorrow."

"I'm supposed to meet Reno at Frankie Z's for dinner, but I also need to talk with Elizabeth. I left her a voicemail, but I'm not sure when she'll call back. After I go home and change, I might need to head to her hotel and see if I can catch her there."

"But didn't you say you and Reno had one of your 'discussions' Saturday night?"

"Yeah, but I talked with him Tuesday night, and we're good again."

"But the first date after a fight is when you get to have make-up sex. You can't pass that up. Make-up sex is the best. All you need to do is imply you're still a little upset and a little horny. Then, lay back and let him do all the work. He'll be glad to show you how sorry he is. There's nothing like a man wanting to please you with some quality make-up sex."

"Sure, that sounds great, but I don't think we'll have time for make-up sex tonight. I get the feeling this thing with Elizabeth and the jewelry is starting to ramp up."

"Seriously? I'm thinking you need to sort out your priorities. There'll always be another client, but good make-up sex is something you don't get but once or twice a year. Well, maybe more in your case, since you and Reno fight like once a month."

"We don't fight. We have discussions."

"Yeah, whatever. But still, don't pass up this opportunity. Otherwise, you'll be kicking yourself all week."

I drove back to my apartment, stripped off my clothes, and inspected the damage. The capris were a total loss. The hole I'd ripped to open the pocket had taken out the entire left side of the seat.

The T-shirt wasn't a lot better. In addition to the dirt and the black grease, there were several small holes that must've been caused by me thrashing around in the trunk.

I folded the clothes for one last time and walked over to my trashcan. I gently placed both the shirt and capris on top of the pile of garbage. I felt a brief pang of loss and regret as I retired two pieces of clothing that had served me well.

Feeling a little melancholy, I lingered in the shower and then had to hurry. I only had a quick fifteen minutes to fix my face and hair.

I'd just put on the last swipe of mascara when my phone rang. I looked at the caller ID and saw it was Elizabeth.

"Hey," I said. "Thanks for calling me back. I need to talk to you as soon as possible."

"Can we do this over the phone?"

"It'd be better in person. Where are you?"

"After everything that's happened the last few days, I didn't want to have anything to do with the jewelry or with Les. I got up early and drove up to the Grand Canyon. I've spent most of the afternoon at the overlooks around Grand Canyon Village, looking down into the canyon."

"What did you think about it?" I asked.

"It's so beautiful. I'd love to come back up sometime and spend a few days here. Maybe I'll even ride a mule down to the bottom. I saw a group of tourists start down the Bright Angel Trail, and it looked like a lot of fun."

"Where are you now? Will you have a few minutes to talk when you get back into Scottsdale?"

"I'm coming into Flagstaff. The sign I just passed said I'll be there in five miles."

"Perfect. You should be back at your hotel in about three

hours, so around ten o'clock. I'll meet you in the lounge in the main reception building. It's called the Center Stage Bar. It's a nice place to relax and talk."

"Is this about Les?"

"Yes."

"Did he do something stupid?"

"Um, maybe."

I heard her sigh. I could tell this wasn't the first time someone had told her Les had done something stupid.

"Okay, but I'm still on Chicago time, and I'm already worn out. I'll meet you at the bar for a drink, but then I'll need to go to sleep. Deal?"

"Deal."

I'd just pulled onto Miller Road when my phone rang. I looked at the screen and saw it was a 202 area code number. I answered, and there was a serious-sounding male voice on the other end.

"Miss Black, this is Special Agent McCoy. I'm with the FBI. My partner and I are investigating the movements and activities of Lester Murdock. I assume you know who I'm talking about?"

I wasn't surprised the FBI had my phone number. After having firsthand experience with the super-secret database, I knew a lot of things were possible.

"Are you the guys who've been following me around in the blue sedan all week?"

There was a pause. When he answered, he sounded

surprised. It was as if he couldn't understand how he'd been made.

"Miss Black, we have evidence that Lester Murdock is currently with members of a criminal organization based in Chicago. We'd like to discuss the circumstances of how he came to be with them."

"Sure, he was sort of kidnapped."

"Could you explain the 'sort of' part?"

"We were at Lester's granddad's house, and a guy came in with a gun. His name was Magic, and Les seemed to know him pretty well. Magic wanted Les to go with him to talk to somebody named Morningstar."

There was a pause, and I could tell that Special Agent McCoy was talking to somebody on his end.

"Miss Black, the FBI is asking for your help with an ongoing investigation. We'd like to meet with you and discuss this further. Would tomorrow morning be convenient?"

It figures. It's always one more thing.

"Sure. Tomorrow morning will probably work. You know I work for an attorney, right? Perhaps we should meet down at his office?"

"If you wish, Miss Black. However, we may be able to speak a little more openly if an attorney is not present during our interview."

I couldn't argue with that, especially since I knew he was probably right. At this point, the FBI knew more about this than I did, and I needed to learn all I could.

If Lenny was there, I wouldn't be able to get as much information. Lenny tends to put people in a bad mood.

"Okay," I said. "Where do you want to meet?"

"We're staying at the Scottsdale Blue Palms. I assume you know where that is?"

The thought of the FBI guys paying to stay in one of Tony DiCenzo's hotels brought a smile to my face.

"I know where it is. What time?"

"Let's say nine o'clock. We'll book a conference room where we can talk. I'll text you the location in the morning."

I pulled into the parking lot of Frankie Z's right at seven. Being on time was throwing me off a little since I'm typically a little bit late. I drove around looking for a parking space and finally had to park in the last row, against a hedge of tropical plants.

As I walked in, I took a deep breath and smiled. I caught the wonderful aromas of garlic, Italian sausage, and freshly baked bread.

It's funny, but I sometimes think that walking in and taking the first deep breath is the best part about going to Frankie's. It's almost as if the first whiff of garlic is the start of a great meal.

I saw Frankie at her usual place, at the hostess stand. She was wearing a long black dress, flat black shoes, and a single strand of pearls.

I don't think I've ever seen Frankie wearing anything else. She must have a closet full of long black dresses.

As always, her salt-and-pepper hair was pulled up in a tight bun, held in place with a black knitted hairnet. When she saw me, she smiled her warm motherly smile.

"Well, I'm glad you came back," she beamed at me. "It's

nice I can feed you again. You're still too skinny."

"Hi, Frankie," I said. "I love walking in the door. Everything always smells so great."

"That's because we make everything ourselves, right here. Nothing ever comes out of a can or from a freezer. I cook like they do back home, like my Mama and Papa cooked. Your cute boyfriend is already here. I put you two in the corner on the patio, underneath a fan. Very nice, very romantic."

She looked up and yelled, "Mario!"

Mario, one of Frankie's teenage grandsons, came scurrying up to the hostess stand. Frankie handed me off, and Mario led me through the lounge.

Over the sounds of people talking, I caught the background music, the soundtrack from *The Godfather*. Over the years, it seems to have become the standard background music for most Italian restaurants. I always find it to be somewhat ironic, given the plot of the movie.

Frankie's youngest son, Little Zappy, was working at his usual spot behind the bar. Little Zappy's in his mid-forties and weighs a good three hundred pounds. He looked up from pouring a beer and waved as he saw me walking through.

Mario then led me to the outdoor patio. Even though the night was warm, I still preferred to eat outside.

Here, the great aromas of the restaurant mingled with the delicate scent of fragrant jasmine vines that covered the red brick walls of the courtyard. Overhead sprayers were spraying a light cooling mist of water over the area.

As always, the patio was beautifully lit with dozens of strands of clear Christmas lights. I smiled as the *Love Theme* from *The Godfather* softly played in the background.

Reno was seated at the table, playing with his phone. I

was almost at the table before he looked up and saw me. He smiled his great smile and stood up, his arms out for a hug.

"You're early," he said as I walked closer. "I didn't expect you for at least another ten or fifteen minutes."

"Hey, I'm on time."

"I know, but on time's early for you."

"Jerk, give me a hug."

As I gave him a hug, I saw he had a fresh black eye and a nasty-looking scrape on his right forearm. It's not unheard of with Reno, but it's still a little unusual now that he generally leaves the actual takedowns to the younger officers. They find it exciting, and Reno requires fewer stitches.

Dominic, Frankie's middle son, came to take our drink order. We each ordered a scotch and started chatting.

As always, it felt great being next to Reno. Whenever I'm near him, my life seems to make sense, and my problems don't seem so big.

I feel like I don't have to be the leader and the problem solver. I can let someone I trust lead for a while. Plus, he's sexy as hell, and I love what he can do to me when we're alone.

"Did I hear you were locked in your trunk today?" he asked with a slight grin on his face.

Damn. It didn't take long for him to find out about that.

"Sort of. It was an accident."

Reno looked at me for several seconds with his blank-faced cop-stare, the one that seemed to read my thoughts. I find it sort of weird that both Max and Reno can do that to me.

"I'm glad Chugger was able to get you out," he said at

last. "That couldn't have been comfortable."

"Oh, it wasn't so bad. You know, one of those things."

"At least you had your phone with you and were able to call it in. How'd you get trapped in your trunk anyway?"

"Like I said, it was sort of an accident."

"Doesn't your car have an internal latch release? Couldn't you have pulled that to open the trunk?"

"Um, it's broken. I've been meaning to get it replaced."

Make sure to cut the latch release tonight.

Reno looked at me again with the cop-face for about ten seconds. I made an effort not to look down at my wrists where the cuffs had gouged into me.

Make sure to put makeup on the bruises.

"Well, I'm glad you're okay."

"I'm fine," I said. "Speaking of okay, how'd you get the shiner? It looks painful. The scrape on your arm also looks a little nasty."

"Oh, that? Um, well, it's no big deal. Actually, it was also sort of an accident. You know, goofing around with the guys."

"Really? There've been a lot of accidents in Scottsdale lately. But I'm glad you're okay."

Dominic brought out our scotches and set them on the table. We both sat in silence and slowly sipped them. Neither of us looked directly at the other for a minute.

Dominic helped us break our silence when he came back over and took our food orders. It didn't take long since we always order the same things.

"What are you working on this week?" Reno asked.

"The usual. One cheating spouse and one real investigation."

"What's the investigation?"

"The client's a guy who's in from Chicago. His granddad died a few weeks ago and left both him and his sister a fortune. The weird thing about the fortune is it's hidden somewhere in a big house up on Camelback Mountain. If either the brother or sister finds it first, they get to keep the whole thing. It's turned out to be a treasure hunt of sorts."

"Maybe Gina had it right," Reno said. "Maybe I should quit the force and go work for Lenny. Your cases sound more interesting than taking on the Mexican drug cartels."

"Not really. So far, it's been rather dull and routine."

Reno looked at me for several seconds.

"What?" I asked. "What's the look for?"

"I know what's routine for you. That's what always has me worried."

At least he hasn't found out about the latest dead body.

"So, what about you?" I asked. "What are you working on?"

"It's the usual for me too. The last few weeks have been all about drugs. I'm helping out with a team that's targeting some of the larger shipments coming into the city. The team made a big heroin bust a couple of months ago, and it got some good press coverage. I know, you were there too, but don't remind me. After that, the city gave them some additional funding. I've been assigned to help them out for a while. We're getting solid information from the Feds, and we've been able to make some good busts."

"I haven't heard anything on the news about it."

"So far, they've done a good job keeping it quiet. We

want to arrest as many as possible while the information from the Feds holds out. They must have someone deep undercover to get this kind of information. At least half of the tips they've been feeding us have led to arrests."

"Are you back to being directly involved with the busts, or are you still more in the background?"

Reno turned a little red and seemed to shift around in his seat. I saw him glance down at the forearm that had the fresh scrape on it.

"Well, mostly in the background. You know, it's mainly the younger detectives who like to go charging in. Sometimes I get caught up in things, but my job is mostly routine paperwork and reporting."

"Right, routine."

I held up my glass. "To our dull and routine jobs."

Reno smiled a somewhat knowing smile and clinked his glass against mine.

If I was being honest with myself, I really didn't want to know a lot more about Reno's assignments. There was always the possibility that the drug shipments he confiscated belonged to Tony or Carlos. Either way, the less I knew about the details, the happier I would be.

Dominic brought out our dinners, and we spent several minutes eating without a lot of talk. I didn't realize how hungry I was until I tasted the first bite.

Then I started eating and didn't want to stop. Dominic came out at regular intervals to give us more breadsticks and to bring out fresh drinks.

At last, I'd eaten to the point where I was full and feeling wonderful. Dominic then brought out two coffees. I poured cream in both of them. Reno stirred his coffee and looked up at me.

"I've been thinking," he said. "Since you left rather suddenly the other night, I was assuming you'd somehow want to make it up to me?"

"Like how?"

"Well…"

"What?" I asked. "You want *me* to give *you* make-up sex?"

"Well, it only seems fair."

"I'm not sure about that. You're the one who hurt my feelings. I'm thinking maybe I should get make-up sex from you. But even if I agree, what do I get out of it?"

"You'll get a sense of fulfillment by knowing that you made your boyfriend really happy."

"I can probably live without that. What else?"

"Well, if you do an extra good job, we could play with the toy. It's been a while, and I like the way it makes you wiggle and squirm."

Several months before, almost as a joke, Reno bought me a toy. It was sort of shaped like a saguaro cactus, and I know it was probably expensive. So far, we've only played with it a couple of times.

Partially, it's because Reno knows that when we start, the next hour will be all about me. I think it's also partially because he's a little jealous about what the toy can do to me.

"So, what do you say?" Reno asked, with a playful grin on his face. "Do you want to come over tonight and play?"

"Tonight? Um, I can't do it tonight. I'm meeting with the client's sister at the Hyatt Gainey Ranch at ten."

Reno's face fell. "Tonight? Are you seriously working tonight? Laura, you've got to organize your work schedule to include time for your boyfriend. I'm a healthy guy. I have needs."

"You have needs? You tease me about using the toy, then talk about *your* needs? What about me?"

"I'm working evenings for the next week, then I'm scheduled for three days off," Reno said, still a bit sad. "Let's plan for next Saturday. Let's schedule an actual sleepover and not just dinner. Maybe we can even spend a few days together. It's been a couple of weeks since we've had a weekend to ourselves."

"Okay, unless the world is coming to an end, I'll tell everyone I'm out Saturday night and all day Sunday. Mother in the hospital or something like that."

"So, what are we going to do until then?" he asked. "That's a week away."

"We could probably work in a lunch or two."

"Lunch is good," he said. "But I was hoping for something a little more personal."

I got a naughty thought and looked down at my watch.

"Walk me out to my car?"

"But you don't have to be at Gainey Ranch until ten." Reno looked at his watch. "You don't have to leave for almost an hour."

I lifted his hand, put his finger in my mouth, and gently sucked on it. Reno's eyes lit up, and he got a wide smile.

"So, you gonna walk me to my car?" I asked again. "I'm parked way in the back, where it's really dark and lonely."

I drove over to Gainey Ranch and pulled into the main parking lot at the Hyatt Regency Scottsdale. The hotel is huge, and it took a few minutes to walk through the parking lot, past the conference rooms, up the escalators, and through the lobby.

Fortunately, I'd timed it well. By five after ten, I was sitting at a table on the outdoor patio of the Center Stage Bar, waiting for Elizabeth.

I'd been to the lounge a few times over the years, and I'd always found it to be a great place to have drinks and conversations. Half of the bar was inside the main reception building, and half was outside on a patio surrounded by dozens of date palms. There were high ceilings and splashing fountains that made the lounge a very open and inviting place.

A performer was on a small stage singing love songs and playing an old acoustic guitar. He had a sweet voice that immediately put me in a good mood.

Although I'd made Reno extremely happy and relaxed, all it did for me was get me going. I was having some thoughts that had nothing to do with being hit in the head or being thrown into my trunk.

I was halfway through a twelve-dollar scotch when I saw Elizabeth at the hostess stand, looking around the bar. I waved, and she came over right away. A waitress came to the table, and Elizabeth ordered a glass of house chardonnay.

"How was the Grand Canyon?" I asked.

"It was amazing. I've seen it before in books and on TV, but there's nothing that can prepare you for how big it actually is. I hiked over to Maricopa Point and spent an hour standing on the edge. From there, the canyon's ten miles across and almost a mile deep. The scale is so massive your brain doesn't even know how to process it."

"I know what you mean," I said. "You can't really get a perspective on what big is until you see something like that."

"The size alone would make it remarkable, but then you add in the pure beauty of the place. I thought it would look like a dusty gray hole in the desert. I didn't expect to see a rainbow of colors. I would've loved to have stayed up there and watched the sunset, but I'm still beat from Tuesday night, and the time change isn't helping."

"It sounds like you had a nice time."

"I really did. You're so lucky to live here. I imagine you go up once or twice a year."

"Honestly, I've only been up to the canyon three times. Once, when I was a kid, the family took the train up to the park from a little town called Williams. Another time, I went up with some girls from college for a drunken weekend when I was twenty-one. And I went up once with Sophie. She's my best friend, and she also works at the law office."

The waitress brought Elizabeth her wine, and she sipped it in silence for a minute. I could see she was gathering her thoughts.

"You wanted to talk about Les?" she asked.

"Yes. First, you need to know that your brother was taken by a guy with a gun earlier this afternoon."

"You mean he was kidnapped?"

"Well, maybe. They seemed to know each other pretty well, and Les didn't seem surprised to see the guy."

"Oh my God. Are you going to call the police?"

"It might come to that, but right now, I'm not sure it would help. I think Les was already working with the guy and probably would have gone with him even without being forced to do so. Earlier in the day, your brother told me he'd been working with some organized crime members from a group out of Chicago. The guy with the gun seemed like he was from the same group. Les said he was trying to leave the group, but it was going to cost him a lot of money. With his half of the inheritance, he was going to buy himself out of trouble."

Elizabeth slowly shook her head and gave a small laugh.

"You know, that really doesn't surprise me. Les is always in some sort of trouble, and he's always trying to scam someone. In fact, it explains several things he's been doing for the last two or three years. He seemed to have a lot of money, but he didn't seem to have a job. He'd sometimes travel to Mexico, or Asia, or even South America on short notice. Sometimes, he'd be gone for two or three weeks at a time. I only knew this because I'm a Facebook friend, and I follow his tweets. Before Monday, we hadn't actually spoken to each other in several years."

"You should also know that the police suspect Les may have had more to do with the murder Tuesday night than he let on. The investigation's still in the early stages, but the evidence is starting to come together."

Elizabeth didn't answer. She sipped her wine and stared out over the people and the lights on the terrace. After not speaking for almost a minute, I saw she was crying.

"I want you to know I'll do my best to help," I said. "I mean, help both of you. If Les doesn't show up soon, we'll need to contact the police, and I'll need to start looking for him. We're also still representing him in this treasure hunt thing. Lenny, that's my boss, is convinced the treasure is part of the reason Les was taken. If we can find the jewelry, we'll have a better chance of clearing this whole thing up. I know Les wanted to split the jewelry with you. Would you like to work together on this? I think I might have some clues that could help find it."

"You'd still be willing to do that?" She took out a tissue and wiped her eyes. "I was sort of a bitch to you the other day. I'm sorry about that. It's the effect my brother has on me. I'll be honest, I don't have any idea where the jewelry is, and I can't spend more than a few days looking for it. I took vacation time to come here, and I'll need to get back home by the end of next week."

"Don't worry about the other day," I said. "I understand families can sometimes have some tension. What happened between you two?"

"Well, the latest round of issues started after Dad died. I agreed to let Les be the executor of the estate. We were to split about six million dollars in stock. I suggested we sell everything as soon as possible and put the cash into two bank accounts. One for him and one for me."

"That seems reasonable," I said.

"Les, of course, had a better idea. He was going to keep everything in stocks, and he set up three brokerage accounts for me and three for him. He said it would spread our risk, and we'd still keep making a lot of money. You have to remember, back then, the stock market was still going nuts."

"Okay. What was the problem?"

"Les didn't want to break up any of the blocks of stock, so he took some, and he gave me the others. Unfortunately, most of the stock he gave me was from a company that soon went bankrupt. When I first got it, the stock was over eighty dollars a share. But by the end of the year, it was worth less than a dollar a share."

"You couldn't sell the stock when you saw what was happening?"

"I tried to sell it, but the estate had been frozen in the final stages of probate, and I couldn't touch it. I then tried to work out a deal with Les to re-divide everything, but by then, he had dropped out of sight. I didn't know where he lived or how to get ahold of him. I tried to email him on his Facebook account, but he always ignored me. Meeting him at the lawyer's office this week was the first time we'd talked face to face in over ten years."

"Wow, I can see why this has stirred up some bad memories. I assume your granddad knew about the issues you and Les were having?"

"Yes, and I know he felt bad for both of us. He was always sending me presents. Two years ago, a new car showed up at my house from Granddad."

"Well, like I said, Lenny's representing Les in this jewelry treasure hunt thing. Why don't we have him write up a document that formally states how the jewelry is to be split, assuming we can find it? That way, you'll be sure to get your half this time."

"I would appreciate that. Honestly, I keep getting visions of helping Les find the jewelry and then having him take off with it. Having something that spells out what each of us will get would make me feel a lot better."

"I'll talk to Lenny tomorrow and have that taken care of."

Elizabeth drained the rest of her glass. "I need to go up to bed. Things are starting to spin."

"Would you like to get together tomorrow? We can start searching."

"Okay, but not too early. After the last couple of days, I think I need a morning to sleep in."

"That works with me. Maybe meet for lunch. Say eleven?"

"Perfect. I should be up and going by then. Text me when you get close. I'll meet you somewhere down here."

"Why don't we meet by that queen palm?" I said, pointing with my head toward a beautiful queen palm in the courtyard by the lobby.

She squinted and looked around. "Which one is that? The one next to the bar over there?"

"No, that's a Mexican fan palm. Those have the short and round fronds, like a hand with fingers. The queen palm is the one next to the fountain with the long feather fronds."

"Long feather fronds? You mean like the ones in the courtyard of Granddad's house?"

"Sort of, those are date palms. They're some of the most expensive palms in Scottsdale. All the best hotels and shopping malls have them. They're sort of like status symbols."

"Hey, I'm a tourist from Chicago. They all look alike to me. What about the coconut palms? Where are those?"

"We don't have those in Scottsdale. Even a light frost will kill them."

"You get frosts in Scottsdale?"

"Once or twice a year. Every few years, we even get an actual freeze."

"There's a difference between a frost and a freeze? It seems like they're the same thing."

"Most plants down here will tolerate a frost. A freeze will kill a lot of things."

"Well, what about the short palm over there, the one that looks like a pineapple?

"That's a younger Canary Island date palm. Those actually produce dates, which most people don't want to deal with. They're really messy, and they tend to attract ants and scorpions."

"Scorpions? Seriously? You have scorpions here?" She eyed the ground around her feet.

"Well, you won't see one here at the hotel, but you'll see them around sometimes. Don't try to pick them up. If you see one, just step on it."

Elizabeth got the most horrible look on her face.

"*Eeeewww,* yuck," she said. "The thought of stepping on a scorpion is so gross. And why would anyone try to pick one up? I tell you what. If I see one, I'll just start screaming, and I'll let you step on it."

"You get used to them. They're not so bad in the established neighborhoods. You almost never see a scorpion there. But in some of the newer neighborhoods, there can be a lot of them. The areas around the old orange groves are the worst. It's life in the desert. We don't have blizzards, tornados, or hurricanes. We have monsoons, rattlesnakes, and scorpions."

I walked out to my car in the parking lot. It was after eleven, and I knew Reno would probably be asleep.

I've called him a few times in the middle of the night to meet for a quickie, but it's usually better when we can take our time. Plus, after our escapades in Frankie's parking lot earlier in the evening, I knew he wouldn't be as receptive to being woken up. I instead decided to drive home.

Chapter Nine

I woke up to see my bedroom bathed in bright sunlight. But when I glanced over at the clock, I saw it was only six-fifteen.

I didn't have to be at the Blue Palms until nine, so the night before, I'd set the alarm for seven-thirty. I rolled over to go back to sleep, but then I started thinking about Max.

I tried to shut him out of my mind, but then my thoughts drifted to Reno. I was really starting to regret not being able to have make-up sex the night before.

After a half hour of rolling back and forth in bed, I got up and staggered into the bathroom for a long hot shower. It seemed to help. I then put on a pot of coffee and got ready for the day.

Since I'd be meeting with the Feds, I put on an outfit that was maybe a little nicer than I'd usually wear for an investigation. I didn't know if it would help, but I thought it couldn't hurt.

I wasn't sure what Elizabeth and I would end up doing for the day, but I suspected we'd be back up at South Mountain. I grabbed my cooler and put half a dozen cold water bottles in it. I then fed Marlowe and was out the door.

The drive up to the Blue Palms was beautiful. There's something about driving on Scottsdale Road that makes you appreciate what a great place Arizona is to live. I called up Sophie at work.

"Hey, Sophie. I met with Elizabeth last night, and she's going to work with us."

"That's good. Did you have make-up sex with Reno?"

"Well, not really. I needed to meet with Elizabeth."

"Didn't we talk about this?" she scolded. "Elizabeth could've waited. You could've met with her today or even tomorrow."

"Reno got make-up sex. Does that count?"

"Really? Did you do a parking lot thing on him again? You're such a bad girl. But still, passing up on make-up sex wasn't a good move. Next time you get together, it'll only be regular sex."

I sighed. Sophie was right. Missing out on make-up sex was starting to dominate my thoughts again. I could tell I was going to need Reno sometime soon, or else I'd start to get twitchy.

"I'm meeting with the FBI at the Blue Palms in a few minutes," I said. "I need to see if I can pump some information out of them."

"Good luck with that. They never seem like the friendly sorts."

"We'll also need to have Lenny write up an agreement for Elizabeth to split the treasure and real estate fifty-fifty with her brother. She's worried that Les is somehow going to screw her out of the jewelry, assuming we can find it."

"No problem. I already have something standard on file. I'll get it printed up."

"Let's make sure it's solid. The more I know about our client, the more questions I have. Let's make sure there isn't any wiggle room for him to get out of it."

As we were talking, I got a text from the 202 area code number that I now knew belonged to Special Agent McCoy. It said we would meet in the Boardroom at the Blue Palms at nine o'clock.

I'd expected more traffic, so I got to the hotel about fifteen minutes early. I parked in the visitor's lot and walked up the hill to the main reception hall. I checked the hotel directory and saw the Boardroom was a small conference room located down a long hallway from where I was.

I took a few minutes and looked around the lobby. I hadn't been here since investigating Alex Sternwood, six months before.

I walked over to the grand piano and stood on the spot where Alex had switched a bag full of diamonds for an empty bag from a distracted Russian mafia courier. The Russian had paid with his life for losing the diamonds, and Alex almost came to the same end.

I then wandered to the shops in the back lobby, going into the store that sold high-end dresses, purses, and shoes. As always, I wondered who would actually pay the outrageous prices at the hotel when the Scottsdale Fashion Square was a ten-minute ride by cab, and they could get the same things at half the price.

I saw there was still a display of Ferrucci bags against the back wall. I was slightly disappointed that the black Spy Bag wasn't being shown. The thought it might have been discontinued made me a little sad.

At nine o'clock, I made my way to the Boardroom. It was nestled in with several other offices near where the main ballrooms were. When I walked in, I saw there were two serious-looking men seated at the table. When I looked around the room, I couldn't help but smile.

Hanging on the wood paneling of the walls were half a dozen oil portraits of famous Arizona business and political leaders. What made me smile was the image I saw when I first walked into the room. On the wall directly behind the two federal agents was a formal oil portrait of Tony DiCenzo.

Both men stood when I entered the room and made their introductions. Now that I had a chance to look at them, they were about as I expected.

Both men were big and solid. They looked like they would fit in as detectives on almost any police force. Both had short military-style haircuts. Both were dressed in inexpensive blue suits.

The older of the two seemed to be the leader. He was a white guy in his late forties. We shook hands, and he introduced himself as Special Agent McCoy.

The other agent was an African-American guy in his thirties. He introduced himself as Special Agent Conquest.

"Miss Black," Agent McCoy said, "we know Lester Murdock has retained the legal services of your employer, Leonard Shapiro. We also know you've been assisting him since he came to Arizona on Monday night. Since you're a recognized member of the law firm, this gives you certain responsibilities regarding this matter. However, it also allows us to reveal certain information to you on a strictly confidential basis. We'd like to share this information with you on the condition you keep it strictly to yourself and share it with no one."

"Okay, I can do that."

Special Agent Conquest pulled out a document from a folder and handed it to me.

"This is an agreement to keep confidential anything we tell you concerning this case," Agent Conquest said. "There're severe criminal and civil penalties for violating the terms of this agreement."

I glanced over it, and it seemed straightforward. "Okay, where do I sign?"

I not only had to sign, I also had to hold up my hand and swear an oath. Both agents witnessed the document, and Agent Conquest slipped it back into his folder.

"Alright, Miss Black," Agent McCoy said, we'd like to talk to you about the activities of Lester Murdock. As you are apparently aware, we are keeping track of Mr. Murdock on behalf of the federal government. He's a material witness to the activities of a major criminal organization based in Illinois. We're not only here to monitor his activities. We're here to help keep him safe and out of trouble. We know of the terms of his grandfather's will and about Mr. Murdock's efforts to recover the property in his grandfather's estate, primarily consisting of antique and historic jewelry."

"What do you want to know?" I asked.

"What do you know about the Chicago organization and Lester's association with them?" Agent Conquest asked.

"Not a lot. The only one I met was a goon named Magic. He talked about somebody higher up called Morningstar. He also mentioned somebody named Frankie."

"Magic would be Vannier Magic," McCoy said. "He's hired muscle for the organization. Morningstar is Horace Morningstar. He's the top lieutenant. We have evidence that both are currently in the Scottsdale area along with Frankie

'Two Guns' Cantone, the man who was murdered Monday night."

"Has Morningstar contacted you yet?" Agent Conquest asked.

"Not yet," I said. "Tell me about him. What's he look like?"

"He's short, and he's fat. He's also a cold-blooded killer. He rapidly rose through the ranks by being the primary assassin for the group."

"What do you want with Lester?" I asked.

"As I said, we're only here to keep an eye on him," Agent McCoy said. "We want him to testify against the other members of his organization. We have evidence Lester Murdock was involved in several crimes that could easily net him several years in a federal prison. We've offered him immunity and a relocation package if he cooperates."

"I take it Lester hasn't decided if he's going to play along or not yet?"

"That's correct. We realize that as a member of the criminal organization, he's going to have dealings with them. We don't want to lose sight of him while he's making a decision. Plus, we worry that since he'd be testifying against both Morningstar and Magic, they may catch wind of what's happening and decide to eliminate him as a problem."

"Then you wouldn't have any testimony. Not to mention, my client would be dead."

"We'd rather that not happen."

"What do you know about the murder on Tuesday?" I asked.

"We know Mr. Murdock went to the house on Camelback Mountain by cab. We know Mr. Murdock then took the cab back to his hotel. We also know of the events later that night when you and Miss Elizabeth Murdock were with him."

"Do you know who killed the guy?"

"No. We've contacted the local police, and the physical evidence is pointing to Mr. Murdock, but nothing's definite yet. We've asked the police to contact us before they make an arrest."

"What do you want me to do?"

"Keep us informed of what you know. We want to know what's going on with Mr. Murdock, but we're also interested in Elizabeth Murdock, Horace Morningstar, and Vannier Magic."

"Anything else?"

"We would appreciate it if you did not attempt to lose us again," Agent Conquest said. "Don't make us go through the process of having tracking devices installed on your car. The paperwork on that takes all day."

"I hope you understand," I said, "my first duty's for my client. I can't do anything that isn't in his best interests."

"Miss Black," Agent McCoy said. "We understand your feelings toward your client. However, we hope you don't do anything to hinder our investigation. That would be a serious matter. There could be prison time involved."

"Fine, no need to get cranky. I'm just saying."

"As to your client, keep in mind there's a good possibility he's about to be charged with murder. If Mr. Murdock cooperates by testifying against his associates, having that charge removed could be part of the immunity package."

"Alright," I said. "I guess you'll be hearing from me."

I was due to meet with Elizabeth at eleven, which gave me about an hour to get up to the hotel. I decided to stop by my apartment first and change into something comfortable enough for poking around on South Mountain.

As I walked back out of my apartment and turned to lock the door, Grandma Peckham stepped out into the hallway. She was dressed to go shopping.

"Well, hello, Laura," Grandma said. "How's your week been?"

"Oh, you know. The usual."

"Well, dear, I hope you're being careful. I know how the usual is for you."

"How was the movie Tuesday night?" I asked. "Did Tom Cruise stop the bad guys?"

"Well, that movie wasn't showing anymore. For some reason, he wanted to see a movie about a group of vampires."

"I talked to him in the hall the other night. He said you told him you liked vampire movies."

"I told him I liked the Dracula movies when I was a kid. I hadn't watched a vampire movie since *House of Dracula.*"

"Well, how was this new vampire movie? Was it as good as Dracula?"

"Honestly, I don't understand the movies anymore. This film was about one group of teenage vampires having a fight with another group of vampires. After a while, they also started fighting with a bunch of teenage werewolves. For some reason, I think one of the vampires had fallen in love with one of the werewolves. But then she changed her mind and fell in love with another vampire. Then, one of the werewolves fell in love with a baby vampire. There were a few humans, but they only seemed to be in the way. The only time everyone stopped fighting was to have sex with each other."

"That sounds like some movie," I said.

"For about half an hour, there was a big battle with the good vampires and the werewolves on one side and some bad vampires on the other side. A lot of them died in all sorts of gruesome ways. I'm not exactly sure why they stopped fighting, but it seemed to involve some sort of time travel. When the fighting stopped, everyone who had died was now alive again. Honestly, it was a little confusing, but I think in the end, the werewolf married the baby vampire."

"Not the kind of vampire movies you remember?"

"Land sakes, not at all. Bela Lugosi lived in a coffin in a castle dungeon in Transylvania with dirt and cobwebs. But these vampires lived in a big house in Washington State with really nice bedrooms."

"I guess it would be harder for them to keep having sex with each other if they only slept in coffins," I said.

"My kind of vampires turned into skeletons and died if you drove a wooden stake through their heart or if they were exposed to sunlight. These vampires wore sunglasses and sparkled in the sunshine. They could only be killed by pulling off their heads and then setting them on fire."

"How was the guy? His name was Grandpa Bob, wasn't it?"

"Oh, he seems alright. Not so much of a stuffed shirt as some of the others."

"Well, hopefully, you'll remember what this one looks like when he asks you out again."

"I made sure this time. There was a booth at the movie theatre where they gave you a strip of pictures for five dollars. We went in and posed while the machine took our pictures. After the movie, we came to my apartment, and I put them on the Frigidaire with a magnet. He said it was sweet, but I only wanted to have a picture so I could remember what he looked like. There've been so many men lately I'm getting a little confused."

"You brought him back to the apartment? How'd that go?"

"Well," Grandma said as she bent close to me and lowered her voice. "Let's just say I'm glad you were out for the evening on Tuesday. With the thin walls of these apartments, you wouldn't have gotten a lot of sleep."

The drive up to Elizabeth's hotel went smoothly. I half expected to see either the FBI or some goon from Chicago following me. Even though I kept a constant lookout, I didn't see a thing.

I made it to the Hyatt and parked in the main lot. I then took the escalator up to the lobby and found Elizabeth waiting for me next to the queen palm.

"Good morning," I said. "How was your night?"

"It's the first time I've felt like myself since they read the will on Monday. After you left, I went to my room and fell asleep right away. I slept until almost ten this morning. I would have woken up even later, but the maid knocked on my door. It's a good thing she did since I hadn't set an alarm."

The lobby had several groupings of couches and chairs. I led Elizabeth to one of these, and we sat.

"We need to decide how we are going to go about this," I said.

I pulled out my phone, found the pictures I'd taken of the card in the vault, and sent them to Elizabeth. After she received them, we both looked at the pictures.

"According to the card," I said, "we need to look below the coffin rock as seen from Dobbins Lookout."

"Where's Dobbins Lookout?"

"It's in South Mountain Park. You can see it from your granddad's house."

"I assume you and Les were already there?"

"Yes, and we didn't find a thing. We also came back to the house and looked around again. I'm assuming the chest with the jewelry is in another hidden room. We just need the clue on how to find it."

"Well," Elizabeth said. Let's go to South Mountain Park and look around. Even if we don't find anything, it will help orient me as to what you've already done."

"That sounds good. Are you hungry?"

"Starving, I haven't eaten since Flagstaff last night."

"What are you in the mood for? A chain or something local?"

"Local, definitely local. Spicy is good, but not too spicy. I think it will take me a while to get accustomed to the food here."

"I know the perfect place," I said. "And while we're at it, maybe you could meet the women I work with."

We stepped out of the hotel and walked to my car. I'd noticed earlier that Les would flinch at the heat when he walked out of the air-conditioning, but Elizabeth seemed to enjoy it. When we walked into the parking lot, she sighed with contentment.

"I know you'll think I'm crazy," she said. "But I love how hot it is here."

I gave her a look that said her feelings were a bit unusual for a tourist.

"Look, you have to understand one thing about me. I live in Chicago, and I'm cold all the time. Winters are slow torture; it doesn't matter how many layers I wear.

"The heat here doesn't bother you?"

"Not so far. It's the first time I've been warm in years. This might sound crazy, but I'm finding the air-conditioning is set too low in the restaurants at the hotel. I've had to step outside a few times to warm up."

"As a kid, the worst part about summer was going out to restaurants. I could never figure out why they were so cold. We'd order our food, then Dad would let us go outside to warm up before our dinners came out."

We drove down Scottsdale Road and had just passed Jackrabbit when I got a text. I glanced down and saw it was from Les.

My adrenaline kicked in. I told myself not to get too excited. Just because the text had come from Lester's phone didn't necessarily mean it had come from Les.

"I got a text from your brother's phone."

"What's it say?"

I pulled into a parking lot and read the message. "It says he's okay, and he's decided to work with Morningstar for a few days to look for the jewelry. He'd like to meet with me tonight to see what I've learned. I can't be sure, but for now, I'll assume it actually was your brother who sent the text."

Elizabeth looked relieved but also confused.

"I'm glad he's okay, but who's Morningstar?" Elizabeth asked.

"He's one of the leaders of the criminal gang out of Chicago. He was the one who ordered a goon called Magic to get your brother the other day. I don't think either one of these guys can be trusted."

"Does it say when or where he wants to meet with you?"

"Nope. I guess I'll need to wait."

I texted him back that I'd be willing to meet. I also told him to let me know when and where the meeting was to take place.

I pulled out of the parking lot and drove down Scottsdale Road until we got to Old Town. I parked in my covered space at the law office. Sophie and Gina both had their cars parked there as well.

Elizabeth and I went in through the rear security door and then made our way up to the front reception area. Sophie was typing on her computer, and Gina was walking out of Lenny's office with a stack of folders.

"Ladies," I said. "This is Elizabeth Murdock, Lester's sister."

Everyone shook hands and started talking.

"Is Lenny in?" I asked. "We got a text from Les' phone. It says he's okay, and he'll be working with the hoods out of Chicago for a while. They want to meet with me tonight to go over what I've learned. Les will let me know later when and where we'll meet."

"Lenny's out for the morning," Sophie said. "He's back over at the Phoenix district station, seeing what he can find out about the murder."

"Let me think about how to approach this meeting," Gina said. "These aren't nice people you'll be dealing with. Call me before you go over there?"

"No problem," I said. "I'll want your advice on how to handle it."

There was a brief pause as everyone's thoughts lingered on Les and the gangsters. Gina looked at Elizabeth. "You've been through a lot this week. How are you holding up?"

Elizabeth thought about it for a second. "Well, on Monday, I took a day of vacation and went to a lawyer's office. He said Granddad had left a large estate, and Les and I were supposedly rich. So, on Monday night, I fly halfway across the country to get the jewelry. Of course, it's hidden somewhere, and I'm supposed to start a treasure hunt to find it. On Tuesday afternoon, I had the first real conversation I'd had with my brother in about fifteen years, and it was an argument. Tuesday night, we found a dead body and were interviewed by the police until two in the morning. Now, Les has been kidnapped and is supposedly working with criminals. So yeah, you could say I've had a difficult week."

Elizabeth again thought about it for a second and laughed. "And it's only Friday. I can't wait to see what happens next."

"I hate to tell you," Sophie said, "but it's par for the course around here."

"I was about to take Elizabeth to Dos Gringos," I said. "Have either of you had lunch yet?"

"That sounds like a great idea," Gina said. "It's been weeks since we've all been there."

"Oh yeah," Sophie said. "I was thinking it's almost lunchtime. And since this will be sort of a business meeting, I'll charge it to Lenny. I'm sure he won't mind buying everyone a nice lunch."

We headed out the front door, and Sophie locked up. We walked down the street and then crossed over. Five minutes later, we'd made it to Dos Gringos.

We asked Elizabeth if she wanted to eat inside or out, the inside having air conditioning. She said outside would be perfect. We found a great table in the shade underneath one of the overhanging trees on the front patio.

Everyone ordered a bottle of Corona, and we gave Elizabeth a chance to study the menu. Gina then chose the grilled chicken Caesar salad. I had the six-pack of carne asada street tacos. Sophie got the steak fajitas, and Elizabeth ordered a shredded chicken burro.

The waitress brought out the beers, a bowl of sliced limes, and some chips and salsa. We all started munching while we waited for our lunches to come out.

While we were sitting and chatting, I texted Agent McCoy to let him know Les was apparently alive and okay. I also told him I had a meeting set up that night with Horace Morningstar.

He texted back that he wanted all the details on when and where the meeting was to take place. He also wanted a phone call when it was over.

"What do you do in Chicago?" Gina asked.

"I work in marketing," Elizabeth said. "I handle television and internet advertising for three accounts. One's a car company, and two are retail."

"That must be exciting," Sophie said. "It beats what we do around here."

"I wouldn't call it exciting, but it pays the bills."

"Are you married?" Sophie asked.

"No, divorced. It's been five years."

"Way to go," Gina said as she held up her hand and gave Elizabeth a high-five. "It's the same with everyone here. I've been divorced for seven years, Sophie about five years, and how long has it been for you?" she asked me.

"It's been a little over three years," I said. "I joined the law firm not too long after it was final."

Sophie held up her Corona bottle. "Here's to freedom from annoying husbands." We all clinked our bottles together.

"Now then," Sophie said. "What about a boyfriend? Husbands are a pain to deal with, but everyone needs a boyfriend."

"I broke up with my last boyfriend about two months ago," Elizabeth said. "But honestly, I was only using him for sex. I'm trying the internet dating thing for something long-term, but so far, I haven't found a decent one yet."

"Don't tell me," Gina said. "The good-looking ones don't have jobs, and the ones with jobs look like trolls."

"You nailed it," Elizabeth said. "I hate to lower my standards too much, but I also hate spending Saturdays alone."

"Well," Sophie said. "Before you go back to Chicago, we'll need to take you out to the clubs. We'll show you what the men of Scottsdale are like."

"Although truthfully," Gina said with a laugh. "They probably aren't much different than the men in Chicago. But at least here, they all have tans."

"Oh, that would be wonderful," Elizabeth said. "I'd love to go out. Let's plan on it."

"Besides," Sophie said, "if we can't find you a boyfriend,

we can at least get you laid. Then you'll have a nice memory of your visit to Scottsdale when you're in Chicago, shoveling snow next winter."

Elizabeth blushed but then smiled. Sophie took that as a yes. She held up her bottle. "To finding Elizabeth a man. He doesn't have to be Mr. Right as long as he's Mr. Right Now." Everyone laughed, and we all clinked our bottles together.

"Can you imagine having that much jewelry?" Sophie asked. "I agonized for weeks before I bought a pair of gold hoops. I couldn't imagine how it would be to have a real treasure chest with dozens of big, sparkly pieces. Especially ones that are so old and famous. I heard about Elizabeth Taylor's engagement ring. Could you imagine going to a party with that on your finger?"

"That one's nice," Elizabeth said. "But my favorite is a necklace with an eagle surrounded by pearls and diamonds. Granddad got it in Germany. It's somewhat gaudy, but when I was a girl, he let me put it on, and I'd pretend I was a princess."

"What's your next step in hunting down the treasure?" Gina asked.

"We're going to head up to South Mountain," I said. "The card in the vault said it's where to go to find the coffin rock. Les and I didn't have any luck, but maybe having Elizabeth and a fresh pair of eyes will help."

"Maybe the treasure chest's hidden underneath some nasty old coffin buried on South Mountain, and you're supposed to dig it up?" Sophie asked. "You know, find the grave, grab a shovel, and keep going until you get the jewelry. It would sort of be like something from *Pirates of the Caribbean*, but instead of a tropical island with coconut palms, you'd be on a mountain in the desert with saguaro cactus."

"Didn't the clue read that Dobbins Lookout was only the place where you *could see* the coffin rock?" Gina said. "Maybe the coffin rock isn't at the overlook at all. Maybe you can only see it from there."

"I'm not sure where it is," I said. "Les and I looked both in the overlook and in the area surrounding it. But at this point, I'm willing to take any suggestions."

Our lunches came out, and conversation stopped for several minutes while we stuffed ourselves. Elizabeth seemed happy with her choice, and she eagerly attacked it.

"This is great," she said between bites. "Chicago has the best deep-dish pizza, plus a lot of fancy places, but they don't do Mexican like this. I can see why you come here so often."

"You know," Sophie said. "You're going to inherit a big fancy house. Why don't you move down here and live in it?"

"Well, don't laugh," Elizabeth said. "But I've thought about it. I'd love to live somewhere where it doesn't snow, and I could be warm all the time. Every time I scrape ice off my car, I imagine I'm lying in the warm sunshine next to a blue pool surrounded by palm trees. But the maintenance on a house that big would be more than I could ever afford, and that's assuming I could even find a job down here. Plus, I don't even get the whole house. I'd need to split it with Les."

She sighed and got a sad look on her face. "In the end, I imagine we'll sell it and go our separate ways."

After lunch, we walked back to the office and said our goodbyes. Elizabeth and I got into my car, and we drove down to South Mountain Park.

When we went through the main entrance to the park, we

went over a series of speed bumps in the road. As we did, I heard the thumping of my trunk lid against the car.

"What's that?" Elizabeth asked. "It sounds like your trunk is open."

"The latch is broken. It's tied down with a bungee cord."

Elizabeth looked at me with a slightly confused expression. "Oh."

We soon began to wind our way up the mountain. I thought it might be helpful to learn more about Elizabeth's family history.

"Tell me about your granddad and how he got to be so well off. Why'd your dad argue with him so much?"

"Sure, none of that's a secret. Granddad was a fighter pilot in the last few months of World War II. Right after the war, he was one of the Allied technical specialists who stayed in Germany to evaluate some equipment they found in a secret military research laboratory. He later returned to the US and almost immediately 'invented' improvements to modern air-conditioning. It was obvious to everyone where he got those ideas, and he spent the next fifteen years in court defending the patents."

"Okay," I said. "I can see where there may have been some shenanigans with the inventions. But why did that make your dad so angry?"

"Dad said it was Granddad's patents that made air-conditioning systems expensive to the point where only the wealthy could afford them, while the common man was left to bake in the heat. Dad would say that Scottsdale could have started to grow ten years earlier if air-conditioning had been cheap and more widely available. Dad thought Granddad should do something to give back to the community. But Granddad said he earned every dime, and Dad didn't know what he was talking about. It went on like that for years."

We pulled into the parking lot at Dobbins Lookout. As on Wednesday, the large lot had roughly a dozen cars spaced around it. The groups of women were here again, selling the same Native American jewelry.

We got out of my car, and Elizabeth broke out in a huge grin as she looked over the city vista. She wanted to go to the edge of the overlook right away.

I first made her stop and put on sunblock. I then pulled out two big sun hats I had in the back seat and gave her one.

Hat on her head, she rapidly walked to the stone ramada. She then stood in the window and took in the view of the city.

"This is beautiful!" she said when I caught up with her. "You can see the entire city from here." She pointed to Camelback Mountain. "Is that where Granddad's house is?"

"Yes, if you squint, you can see it from here. I have a pair of binoculars in the trunk if you'd like to search with those."

"Okay," she said. "Let's look for a coffin rock."

Chapter Ten

As I'd done with Les, Elizabeth and I searched for over an hour for anything that looked like a coffin. Unfortunately, we didn't find a thing.

While Elizabeth was looking in an area near the stone ramada, I went to my car and grabbed two bottles of water from the cooler in the back. I then went to the stone structure and called Elizabeth over.

We sat in the shade on one of the ledges, looking over the city, and sipped our cold bottles of water. Elizabeth looked flushed with the heat, but she seemed happy.

"Okay," she said as she fanned herself with her hand. "I do like the heat, but I think an hour in the sun is about my limit."

"Did you see any coffin rocks?"

"Not one. I even took Gina's advice and looked outside of the park. Of course, when you have a city of several million people stretched out in front of you, it's sort of hard to know where to look first."

"Let's look for another ten minutes and then call it quits for the day. It's almost a hundred and ten out here. I don't want you to lose your good feelings toward the heat."

We each did one more circuit of the trails around the lookout. Unfortunately, neither of us found a thing.

On the way back to the car, Elizabeth stopped to look at the jewelry that was spread out on several colorful blankets next to the parking lot. I went to my car, opened the windows to air it out, then walked back.

Elizabeth was still shopping and talking with the women seated next to the blankets. After about ten minutes of looking at the pieces, she bought a nice turquoise and silver ankle bracelet.

We walked back to the car and were both happy when the air-conditioning cranked up. We sat with the air blowing over our faces while we each sipped on another bottle of water.

"I like your ankle bracelet," I said. "Sophie has one that's similar."

"I hope you don't think I'm being silly. I mean, here we are, looking for millions of dollars in jewelry, and I stop to buy an ankle bracelet. I can't help it. I love jewelry, especially if it's unusual. I caught the bug from Granddad, of course. When you spend your childhood putting on antique gold rings and necklaces, it's hard not to fall in love with it."

"Tell me more about the jewelry. Do you have any idea why your granddad collected jewelry and not stamps or rare coins?"

"Well, he started collecting jewelry in Europe after the war. He was never shy in saying he got some great bargains by buying from people who were desperate for money. It always sounded a little unethical, but the government didn't ask a lot of questions about where the jewelry came from. Apparently, a lot of soldiers brought home war souvenirs."

"Les said the jewelry had full sales documentation and all of the historical paperwork."

"Well, yes. Everything except the original pieces from after the war. There's nothing to go along with those. To be honest, I think that's why Granddad continued his collection. After the war, he found himself with a lot of valuable jewelry that could never be sold. Having a large collection of legitimate jewelry helped disguise the fact that so many of the early pieces were obtained under questionable circumstances."

"You don't think any of the pieces were stolen from museums or anything, do you?"

"No, nothing like that. I only heard Granddad talk about it a couple of times, but from what he implied and from what I've been able to read in history books, a lot of people were desperate after the war. Granddad said whenever he was able to give out food and warm clothing to the refugees, they would often give him whatever they had in return. He said someone, who called himself a duke, traded him a necklace that had been in his family for six generations in exchange for twenty dollars and three cartons of cigarettes. That's the same eagle necklace Granddad let me wear as a kid. If nothing else, I hope to find that one. It has a lot of sentimental value."

My phone rang, and I saw it was Les.

"It's your brother," I said to Elizabeth. When I answered, the voice on the phone sounded tired but alert.

"Hey, Laura," Lester said. "Are you doing okay? I've been worried about you. I wasn't sure if you could get out of your trunk on your own the other day."

"Yeah, I'm alright," I grumbled, thinking about being stuffed in my trunk and almost dying in the heat. "I'm more worried about you. Are you with those guys voluntarily?"

"Yeah, for now anyway. They want a share of the jewelry. I told you the story. They want to stick close and help me look. They'd like to meet tonight over at the house to go over strategy. I was thinking the parlor would be the best place to do it. You already know where it is, and it's a good place to talk."

"What time?"

"Eight o'clock."

"I'll be there. I hate to bring this up, but the police are going to want to talk to you again about the murder. They have some evidence you were at the house earlier that night, and there are some extra fingerprints they can't explain."

"Well, I can explain that, but it will take a while," Les said.

"Do you want to get away from those guys? I can bring in the police."

"No. At the moment, all they want to do is help find the jewelry. After that, they'll take their cut and hopefully go away."

"I wouldn't trust them to stop at only taking some of the jewelry."

"I don't trust them either, but at the moment, I don't have a choice."

"Alright, I'll see you at eight."

I hung up and looked at Elizabeth. "Les seems to be okay. I'm meeting him and the Chicago thugs at the house later tonight. Hopefully, I can learn something."

We had a few hours until the meeting. I was tempted to go back to the house and look again. But without the clue, I got the feeling it would be pointless.

Plus, there was a possibility Les and the crooks from Chicago would be there. I'd rather have a talk with them first and set some ground rules before we randomly run into each other.

"I'm not sure where to go next," I said. "Les and I have

been through the house, twice. We've looked for secret rooms, lifted carpets, and looked behind paintings."

"I've done the same things," Elizabeth said. "I don't know why Granddad made this so difficult. If he wanted to keep the jewelry safe until we could pick it up, he could've left it in the vault and given the combination to his lawyer."

"I keep thinking the same thing. Maybe he thought you and Les would enjoy a treasure hunt?"

"I'm sure that was part of it. When we were kids, Granddad would always play hide and seek with Les and me. He probably thought we'd have fun playing hide-and-seek with him one last time to get his treasure."

"Why don't we call it a day? I'll drop you off at your hotel, and you can relax. It's only four-thirty. Spend some time by the pool and have a nice dinner. We'll get together tomorrow morning. Hopefully, I'll learn something tonight that'll be useful. If not, we'll keep going between the house and South Mountain until we figure it out."

"That sounds like a plan," she said.

I dropped Elizabeth off at her hotel. I still had over three hours until I had to be at the house. I parked under the shade of a cluster of fan palms, then pulled out my phone and called Reno.

"Hey," I said when he answered. "I know you're working nights this week, so what time do you start tonight?"

"I need to be there at six, so I need to be on the road by five-thirty. I won't even have time for a quick dinner with you tonight. Are you feeling neglected after you took care of me so well last night?"

"Yes, and I've been thinking about it all day. I don't think I can wait a week."

"Sorry, sweetheart, it can't be helped."

"Easy for you to say. After last night, you'll be all calm and relaxed for the next few days. I'm still ready to go."

"Well, you know the hours I'm working this week. Feel free to swing by my place sometime in the late afternoon. You can wake me up in that special way I love so much. It'd only be a quickie, but better than nothing."

"Oh, you know me. I prefer the romance that goes along with it. I love being with you for dinner. I love it when you tease and flirt with me. I love the handholding and the kissing. Then I love spending the entire night with you. It's the buildup that makes it so wonderful."

"So, a quickie next week is out?"

"I didn't say that. I only said I like it better when we can spend the entire night together."

"So, we're back to next Saturday?"

"It looks like it. But still, don't be surprised if you get woken up this week in an unusual way."

"I'll look forward to that," he laughed. "Talk to you soon."

I hung up and texted Agent McCoy to let him know when and where I was to meet with Lester. I then called Lenny to let him know what was going on. As usual, he wasn't in a good mood.

"You still haven't found the jewelry? You've been at this for four days already. When you meet with these guys tonight, make sure they're okay with you working with Elizabeth. Now that our broke client has thrown in with the gangsters, she's still our best path to getting paid. I can put off the detectives for another day or two, but they're going to want to talk to Lester soon. Make sure he's available when they need him. What about your cheating spouse? Do you have evidence of the affair yet?"

"I have five cameras going in George Anson's house, but so far nothing. I still need to review what happened today."

"Alright, you know what to do. Call me with some good news next time."

Lenny hung up. Out of frustration, I flipped off the phone. I know I shouldn't let him get to me, but you'd think after all this time he'd let me do my job.

Next, I called Gina and talked to her about the meeting.

"We're meeting at the house at eight o'clock. I think they want my help finding the treasure. I should be okay talking with them."

"I'm uneasy about you being with gangsters," she said, "even if you do suspect their motives tonight are clean." I'd like to go over to the house as backup, just in case."

"We're meeting in a room called the parlor. It has a big picture window, and it's clearly visible from the courtyard in front of the house. I imagine if you got there before I did, you could hide in the shadows and watch the entire thing."

"That sounds like a plan. You won't see me, but I'll show up fast if something happens. Plus, if something looks like it's about to go wrong, I'll call in the police to assist. Don't forget these are violent and dangerous criminals. Don't take any chances. Sophie looked up Horace Morningstar, and he's homicidal. From what happened to you yesterday, this Magic guy isn't any better."

Since I had some time before I needed to be back at the house on Camelback, I decided to go home and get some things done. I first tried to pay off some bills, but without money in the checking account, it was proving to be a hard thing to do.

I then tried to read another chapter of a romance novel I'd started. Unfortunately, it seemed like I'd forgotten everything I'd already read, and I didn't want to start from the beginning again.

My thoughts were on the meeting, and I couldn't concentrate on anything. I eventually gave up and started flipping channels.

At twenty minutes to eight, I went down to my car and took off. I found an old Pitbull CD I'd downloaded onto my phone and played it through the car audio system.

I found a song I liked, then turned it up loud. The pulsing music helped calm my nerves and helped me think as I drove to Camelback Mountain.

I parked in the courtyard, went in the front doors of the house, and then walked down to the parlor. I'd already been in the room several times during our previous searches of the house, so I knew it well.

It was a large formal room near the front entrance and seemed to be set up for meeting visitors. The room was dominated by a large picture window that looked onto the courtyard and then to the valley below. As always, the twinkling lights of the city were hypnotic.

I purposefully didn't spend time looking out the window. I knew Gina was somewhere in the shadows, watching what was going on in the room. Knowing I had a friend like her gave me a wonderful feeling. It helped cancel out some of the anxiety I was feeling by being in a room with gangsters.

Special Agent Conquest's description of Horace Morningstar had been accurate. He was short, no more than five foot six, and he must have weighed close to three hundred pounds.

Even with all the weight, he carried himself well, as if he was not affected by the extra load. He looked to be somewhere in his mid-fifties, had a receding hairline with short blond-grey hair, and had a chubby baby-like face. He was dressed in a nicely tailored white suit.

Les was seated alone in a leather chair, drinking a beer and staring out the large picture window. He looked drained of emotion, but I was glad he looked good physically. I walked over to where he sat.

"Are you okay?" I asked.

"Yeah, I hope you don't mind that I'm looking for the jewelry with these guys. You already know my situation with them. I guess as long as we find it before Elizabeth, that's all that matters."

I lowered my voice so the goons couldn't overhear, at least not clearly. "I've talked with her. She's willing to split everything, no matter who gets it first. Let's find it and then figure out what to do with these guys."

Vannier Magic was nervously pacing in front of the window, occasionally stopping to look out to the valley below. Seeing him again pissed me off, and I had to control my thoughts of going after him.

Memories of being pistol-whipped and waking up in the trunk of my car flashed through my head. It also made me nervous that he was looking out into the courtyard, but I didn't want to do anything to draw attention to it.

Morningstar walked up to me and warmly shook my hand as if we were good friends who hadn't seen each other in a while.

"Miss Black, it's truly good to meet you. Lester has already told me of your assistance in the recovery of the jewelry. We have much to discuss. What will you have to drink with me? Lester has already taken a beer, and I do not let Magic drink alcohol. However, I've noticed the service staff has kept the bar fully stocked with some excellent spirits. It'd be a true pity to waste such an endeavor."

"Scotch," I said, "one ice cube."

"Very good," Morningstar said with a laugh. "I like a woman who knows how to drink. It tells me you're not afraid alcohol will somehow make you weak or make you say things you're not supposed to say. I myself prefer brandy. Like scotch, it's a drink for the connoisseur. In fact, I have my eye on a bottle of Rémy Martin Extra Old. It's a brandy produced in the Cognac region of France and is therefore more properly called a Cognac. It's truly a rare spirit and should be consumed only by those who can appreciate its subtleties."

Morningstar went to the bar and pulled out two glasses. From the freezer, he took out what appeared to be a sealed bag of ice cubes.

As I watched him, I knew Gina would scold me for taking a drink from an enemy. Although I didn't think Morningstar would try to poison me, it was best not to take the chance.

I might have told Les I drank scotch, and he may have told Morningstar, who'd already grabbed a bottle of 18-year-old Macallan. Since I'd already searched the room multiple times over the past several days, I knew that next to the Macallan was a sealed bottle of Caribbean Cask Balvenie.

"Hey," I said. "Since we're both raiding the liquor cabinet, I'll take the bottle of Balvenie to your left."

"Excellent," Morningstar said as he switched bottles and broke the seal. "I like a woman who can freely discuss her wants and desires. I hope you'll continue to be frank with me, Miss Black, and in turn, I will be open and honest with you. I distrust a woman who's not open with her thoughts. It shows she's keeping secrets. In my business, secrets are the things that get people killed."

Morningstar took the drinks to one of the couches. He gave me a glass with three fingers of scotch and a small ice cube. In his other pudgy hand, he had a large snifter with four or five ounces of brandy in it.

I took a seat away from Morningstar, but one that gave me a good view of Magic. After what happened the day before, I wasn't going to let him get behind me again.

"One ice cube," Morningstar said. "The melting water serves to open up the flavors of the spirit in the nose and on the tongue. Similar in effect to letting a bottle of wine breathe before drinking. When I take a scotch, I prefer a few drops of room temperature spring water, but the effects are much the same."

He spent several seconds swirling the snifter, then brought it to his nose for a deep sniff. He loudly exhaled and looked at me. "As I said, a truly excellent Cognac." He then lifted his glass and drained about half of it in one massive swallow.

I brought my glass to my nose and inhaled, as Morningstar had. I was rewarded with the wonderful and complex aroma I've come to expect from a Balvenie.

Smelling the scotch gave me a pleasant memory of sitting next to a sparkling blue pool and talking with Muffy Sternwood. It seemed like a long time ago, although it had only been about six months. Thinking about her made me smile.

I brought the glass to my lips and took a small sip. I took in enough so I could physically detect the effects of any poison that might be there, but not enough to succumb to it. At least, that was the theory.

When I took the sip, my mind left all thoughts of poison behind. I was instead overcome with a sensation of warm pleasure that started in my mouth and slowly went all the way down.

Well, if I have to go, this is the way to do it.

Morningstar saw the look of joy that must've been on my face. "Outstanding," he said. "I like a woman who can appreciate a fine scotch. It tells me she knows the difference between the ordinary and the exceptional. But now, to business. Lester tells me you've been employed to assist him in locating a large and ornate wooden chest that belonged to his grandfather and is said to contain a substantial quantity of exceedingly valuable jewelry."

I looked over at Les. He was still sitting in his chair, sipping his beer and vacantly looking out the window. Magic was still pacing and occasionally giggling.

Like the others, I was learning to ignore it. I purposefully kept my eyes from the window, not wanting to draw attention to what was beyond.

"That's right," I said. "We've been looking for it since Tuesday."

"Yes, so I have gathered. Lester showed us all of the locations that had been searched in the house, and we went up together to South Mountain to look for a coffin rock. I assume you know what I'm speaking of."

"Yes. I went back there today but didn't find anything. I feel like I'm running in circles."

"As do I. However, we must both continue to persist. I've

given the matter much thought. I feel that to succeed, we should work in two physically separate groups. You'll pursue the clues you find. I'll follow up on the clues I uncover. You'll use all of your instincts to locate the chest using your own techniques. I'll do the same. We'll need to be in constant communication to share what we've learned, of course, but two groups working independently will have a greater chance of success than if we explore as a single pack."

"That makes sense," I said. "My employer is having me continue to look, even though Les is with you. We're contracted to help him locate the jewelry, and that's what I'm going to do."

"Excellent. I was thinking perhaps it would be helpful if I had Magic work with you. He's quite clever and an excellent problem solver."

I again got a vision of the way he'd pistol-whipped me and then left me to die in the trunk of my car. I did my best to maintain a steady voice, even as my anger started to rise.

"No, I can't work with him. He's the jerk that knocked me out and stuffed me in the trunk of my car. He then left me to die on the side of the road. I've still got a lump on the back of my head. If we were together, I'd be looking for an excuse to shoot him. Not a threat, just being open and honest."

Morningstar seemed surprised at this. He looked over at his subordinate. "Magic, did you do those things to this woman?"

Magic didn't say anything. He rapidly shifted his eyes between Morningstar and me. Panic showed on his face, and he let out a loud, nervous giggle.

"Very well," Morningstar said. "Perhaps it's best if Magic does not accompany you. It's true he's young and can act rashly at times. I hope there will not be any lingering feelings of ill will between us over the incident. However, it's still best that you have another person to help you. The saying that 'two heads are better than one' has withstood the test of time for a reason."

"I've been working with Lester's sister, Elizabeth. She has an interest in the outcome, and she'll be a good partner for me."

I saw Les look up at Elizabeth's name, but he remained silent.

"I can accept that," Morningstar said. "However, I expect you to report back to me on a regular basis. I also expect a phone call the moment you discover the location of the chest."

"Sounds good to me," I said, although I'd already mentally crossed my fingers on that promise.

Morningstar lifted his glass in a toast. "Well then, to a successful hunt."

I hadn't felt any ill effects from the first sip, and it seemed a shame to waste the outstanding scotch. I lifted my glass and took a longer sip. I was rewarded with another wave of warm pleasure.

As I drove east on Camelback Road, I got a call from Gina. I told her what had happened in the room and thanked her for watching over me.

I next called Agent McCoy and downloaded him on the meeting. I let him know Lester would be working separately with Morningstar and that both of us would be looking independently for the chest.

As Agent McCoy was talking, I heard road noise in the

background. I assumed that since I'd told them when and where the meeting was, the two agents were again following and keeping an eye on Les.

I hoped they'd do a better job of trailing Morningstar than they had done when following me. I'd noticed the tail right away.

I got back to my apartment building and took the elevator up to my floor. Since it wasn't even ten, Marlowe seemed surprised to see me.

He walked over and brushed against my leg. He then trotted into the kitchen and sat next to his food bowl. He looked up at me and let out a pathetic little squeak that's the best he can do for a meow.

Ignoring his food demands, I went into the bedroom, threw my clothes into the basket, and found a big T-shirt. As I climbed into bed, I thought I'd be awake for at least an hour, going over the facts in my head. That's the last thought I had before I was asleep.

I woke up Saturday morning to a bright room and my ringing phone. I picked up the phone and saw it was Elizabeth.

Please don't let this be anything horrible.

I answered the phone. Elizabeth was talking so fast I could barely make out what she was saying.

"I think I found it! It was right in front of us the entire time. It turns out we weren't reading the clue literally. Gina was right. When it says the next clue is below the coffin-shaped rock as seen from Dobbins Lookout, that's exactly what it means. You'll need to see this so we can figure out what to do next. I'll drive back to my hotel. Meet me in the lobby in an hour. I'll be by the queen palm. We can go up to the lookout together. Bring your binoculars. I'll show you what I found. Hurry up. I don't want the mafia guys to find it first."

"An hour?" My mind still wasn't taking everything in. "What time is it now?"

"Are you okay?" she asked. "You sound terrible. It's six-thirty. I've been up since three, thinking about Les and everything. Did you talk to him last night? Is he alright?"

"He's fine. I'll be there as soon as I can. But it might be more like an hour and a half."

"Okay, in that case, I'll be having breakfast in the restaurant. Come find me. I'll wait for you there. The sun just came up. It's a beautiful day in Arizona."

I slowly got up and almost fell over. I was having a hard time waking up. I stumbled into the shower and stood for twenty minutes under the hot water.

By the time I got out, I was feeling more like myself again. I went into the kitchen and put on a pot of coffee. Marlowe trotted into the kitchen beside me and again sat down next to his bowl.

I went to the cabinet and opened a can of Deluxe Turkey Supper, then plopped a big spoonful into his bowl. As always, he gobbled down the food as if there were five other cats trying to fight him for it.

Since it looked like I was still going to be hunting treasure, I went into the bedroom and put on a loose, comfortable outfit. I kept the makeup to a minimum and used a clip on my hair to keep it out of the way. Today, Elizabeth would need to take me as I am.

The drive to the hotel was pleasant. Since it was early on a Saturday morning, traffic was nonexistent, and I could see no one following me.

The temperature was still at the low for the day, a pleasant ninety-three degrees. I had my arm resting out of my open window as I drove up Hayden Road, listening to the latest pop song from Taylor Swift.

The parking lot at the hotel was only about half-full, and I got a good space. My car would be in the shade for at least half an hour.

I took the escalators up to the lobby level and found Elizabeth eating breakfast in the Southwest Bistro. I sat down and ordered a coffee and toast.

"I can't wait to show you what I found," she said.

"Well?"

"No, you have to see it for yourself. But I'm sure it's it. Did you bring your binoculars?"

"They're in the car. Okay, let's finish up, and we can head up there."

Twenty-five minutes later, we were in my car and headed east on Doubletree Ranch Road. Thirty minutes after that, we pulled into the Dobbins Lookout parking lot. I was surprised there were already a half dozen cars parked at the lookout.

"When I first got here," Elizabeth said, "there were a bunch of people waiting for the sun to come up. Some of them had binoculars to watch the birds. I borrowed one and started looking around. Come on, grab your binoculars, and I'll show you what I found."

She hopped out of the car and trotted down to the overlook. I grabbed my binoculars from the trunk and followed.

Elizabeth was standing next to the stone ramada and pointing toward Camelback Mountain. "Look at Granddad's house."

I raised the binoculars and trained them on the house. Even from a distance of almost ten miles, the details were sharp and clear. Living in the desert has its advantages.

I looked at the house for fifteen or twenty seconds. I saw the courtyard, the windows, the roof, the pool, and the terrace next to the library. I didn't see anything that looked like a coffin. "What am I looking for?"

"Look to the left a little. Look at the mountain right above and behind the swimming pool."

I moved the binoculars to the left and looked at the pool, then to Camelback Mountain behind it. When I did, I saw the rocks on the mountain come into focus in the shape of a coffin.

It was like seeing an optical illusion. Once you saw it, there was no way not to see the pattern. The bottom of the coffin shape was only a few feet above the back deck of the pool, right where Elizabeth's granddad had his statue.

"I see it!" I shouted. "Right above the pool deck."

"You see how the rocks form a coffin shape?" Elizabeth said excitedly. "I know it isn't one big rock shaped like a coffin. It's a bunch of smaller rocks and it's only because of the angle we're looking at it. But I don't see how it can be anything else."

"The bottom of the rock is right above where the bust of your granddad is," I said.

"I know," Elizabeth said as she laughed and clapped her hands together. "Let's go back to the house and get the jewelry."

We hurried back to my car and took off down the mountain. We'd gotten back on I-17 when my phone rang with Rihanna's song *"S & M,"* Sophie's ringtone. I answered, and it sounded like she'd just woken up.

"Hey," Sophie said with a yawn. "I wanted to remind you that Annie's graduation is at one and the reception's at four. She won't care if you miss the graduation, but you know you'll hurt her feelings if you don't make it to the party."

"I know, and I'll try, but no guarantees. Did you just wake up? How late were you out last night?"

"Oh, it wasn't too late, but this is the first time I've gotten to sleep in for days. How goes the treasure hunt?"

"We found the coffin rock, and we're off to the house to get the clue."

"No shit? You found the rock?"

"Elizabeth found it. When I see Gina next, I'll tell her she's a genius. She had the right idea all along."

"Well, I hope you find the treasure. Then be sure to come to the reception and tell me all about it. Wear some jewelry that belonged to the Queen of England or something."

I hung up with Sophie, and thirty seconds later, my phone rang again. This time, it was Morningstar.

"Miss Black, I wanted to remind you of your promise to keep me apprised of your movements. I was surprised I hadn't yet heard from you today."

"Hey, it's not even ten o'clock. Elizabeth and I are in the car heading over to the house on Camelback. We're going to spend the next couple of hours looking for the chest over there."

"Excellent," Morningstar said. "Magic, Lester, and I will travel back to South Mountain to more fully explore that part of the clue. To me, that seems the most promising. However, I'm glad we will not overlap our efforts for the next few hours. Be sure to call me if you happen to find anything of value."

"Sure," I said. "You do the same."

"Rest assured," he said. "You can count on it."

Chapter Eleven

In no time at all, we were winding our way up the street to the house on Camelback Mountain. As we got closer, I slowed to a crawl.

"If there's already another car there," I said, "let's keep going. I'd rather not have to explain to anyone what we're doing at the house."

Fortunately, the courtyard was empty. I parked, and we went in through the front door.

We quickly went through the house and out the side door to the pool. Elizabeth and I both looked up to see if we could see the coffin rock shape from the pool.

"Wow," she said. "From down here, it only looks like a hill full of big, flat rocks."

"You're right," I said. "Nothing looks even vaguely coffin-shaped. But I'm sure this is the right place. The card said the next clue was below the coffin-shaped rock. That ends about six feet up and directly over where your granddad has that small bust of himself."

We both walked over to the pedestal. It was positioned about three feet from the back wall, which was right against Camelback Mountain.

We'd looked at it before and knew there was nothing remarkable about it. The pedestal was about four feet tall and was bolted to the concrete decking of the pool.

A small bust of Elizabeth's grandfather sat on top. From what Les had told me when we'd first searched the pool area, it was a good likeness.

The bust was attached to the pedestal with a piece of wire, presumably to keep it from blowing off in the summer monsoons. A small brass plaque attached to the top of the pedestal read: *Wilbur Murdock, a pioneer in modern air-conditioning and refrigeration systems.*

"Your granddad had a bit of an ego," I said.

"Oh, Granddad didn't put it up. It was Dad. When he learned he was dying, Dad had it made. I think it was his way of telling Granddad he was sorry for the years of quibbling. Granddad's had it here ever since."

"One thing's puzzled me about it," I said. "Why are there two busts of your granddad?"

"Two?" Elizabeth asked, somewhat confused.

"Well, there is the statue here on the pedestal, and there is the same one upstairs on a bookshelf in the office next to your granddad's bedroom. I was going to ask Les about it, but it never seemed important."

"As far as I know, there's only one, and it's here."

"Before we get excited," I said, "let's go upstairs and see if I'm right. If I am, let's bring that statue down here. Then we'll see what we can find out about this one."

Elizabeth and I hurried into the house and up the stairs to the office, which was next door to the master bedroom. I saw there was still crime scene tape and forensics seals strung across the door of the bedroom.

We walked into the office, and on one of the upper bookshelves behind the desk was the exact same statue. It was about two feet tall, and it looked slightly weathered as if it had been exposed to the elements for several years.

"I'll be damned," Elizabeth said. "I've searched this room twice and didn't notice this statue was the same as the one by the pool. There're so many sculptures in the house, it didn't even register."

I reached up and slid the bust off the shelf. It was heavy, and it was all I could do to keep it from crashing down on the floor. I carefully set it down on a pad of paper on the desk.

"This looks like the original statue," Elizabeth said. "But if this is the original, what's sitting on the pedestal?"

"Well," I said. "There's only one way to find out."

We took turns carrying the heavy statue down to the pool. When we got to where the other sculpture was located, we were both a little winded.

"Okay," I said. "Let's get this one off the pedestal and find out why it's here."

I unwrapped the wire from the statue and lifted it up. I was surprised when it didn't seem to weigh nearly enough. I knocked on it with my knuckles, and I shook it.

I then walked over and rubbed the top of the statue against a rock that was part of the back wall. Where I'd rubbed, the statue was now a bright white.

"This one seems to be made of plaster," I said. "It sounds hollow, and there seems to be something rattling around in it."

Elizabeth was intently watching what I was doing. Her eyes suddenly got big, and she yelled out, "There's something written on the bottom!"

I turned the statue over. Written on the bottom of the statue in cursive writing were the words: *Smash Me!*

With my heart pounding, I thought about the best way to go about this.

"I don't want the Chicago thugs finding out about this," I said. "If you hear a car coming into the courtyard, sing out. We'll pretend we aren't doing what we're doing. We'll then calmly go back in the house and pretend to look in there until they go away again. Let's put the original statue from upstairs on the pedestal and put the wire back on. That way, even if Morningstar finds the coffin rock, he won't be able to get any further."

I set the fake plaster statue behind an oleander bush next to the pool. Elizabeth and I then spent several minutes wiring the real statue onto the pedestal. We laughed when we saw the original bust had holes drilled at the bottom, and these fit exactly with some bolt holes that had been previously drilled into the base of the pedestal.

"When this is over," I said, "We'll need to find the bolts and put this back on properly. I wouldn't want it to blow off in the next monsoon."

When we finished, I took a few steps back. With the wire, it looked exactly as before. Only now, the original statue was where the fake one had been.

"Where should we go to smash the fake?" Elizabeth asked.

"The basement," I said. "It's the only place in the house where no one will notice some extra dust."

We walked into the house and down into the basement. We found a corner that still had a clear section of concrete floor.

I lifted the statue over my head and was about to smash it down on the floor. Instead, I lowered it and gave it to Elizabeth.

"It's your fortune," I said.

Elizabeth raised the statue, then threw it down on the concrete. It shattered into a hundred pieces.

In the center of the pile of plaster shards and dust was a laminated card. It had the same cursive writing as on the note in the vault. Elizabeth picked up the card and read it out loud.

I congratulate you for coming this far. If you still can't find my jewelry, go to Prescott and look for Penelope. She'll show you where the jewelry is. But be aware, it will take the efforts of both of my grandchildren to take possession of my fortune.

"Is that all it says?" I asked.

"Yes," Elizabeth said, anger and frustration in her voice. "That's it. I was hoping the card would say to go to a specific bedroom and pull up some floorboards or something like that. But it's only another clue leading us on another hunt. This hide-and-seek nonsense is getting old."

I looked down at my watch. I wanted to get this over with as soon as possible, but I could tell Elizabeth had had enough treasure hunting for one day.

"Prescott's about an hour and a half away," I said. "Even if we left now, we wouldn't get there until almost three. Let's go tomorrow, and we can spend the whole day there if we need to. I'm supposed to go to a graduation reception in about three hours. You should come too. It'll be fun, and you already know Sophie and Gina. It will be a great way to take your mind off this."

Elizabeth blew out a long sigh and looked a little relieved. "That sounds nice, but how fancy is it? I didn't bring anything dressier than a skirt."

"No problem," I said. You're taller than I am, but we're about the same size. We can stop by my place, and I'll find you something."

We then spent several minutes cleaning up the mess from the broken statue. I was determined not to leave any evidence that anything unusual had happened in the basement. I found a plastic bag, put the pieces in, and then carried it to my car.

The drive to my apartment took about twenty minutes. When we parked, I took the plastic bag and tossed it in the apartment dumpster. I felt a sense of relief when the dumpster lid clanged shut.

We rode the elevator up to my floor, and I apologized for the mess when I unlocked the door. Marlowe was sleeping on the couch. When he saw someone new had come into the apartment, he quickly left through the cat door in the bedroom.

I showed Elizabeth the side of my closet where I kept the dresses and my nicer outfits. I told her to pick out anything that would fit.

It took her only three tries to pick out a pretty plumb-colored cocktail dress with wide black trim. I'd gotten it about a year before and had only worn it once when Reno took me to a party at a police captain's house.

Elizabeth looked at herself in the mirror. She was almost as skinny as I was, but she also had me by two cup sizes. Since most dresses are made with this body type in mind, she filled it out perfectly.

"I don't have any purple shoes," I said, "but I have tons of black. What size are you?"

"I'm a nine," Elizabeth said.

I started digging through the closet. "That's all right. I'm an eight, but I remember buying a pair of nines last year."

Elizabeth looked at me with a slightly puzzled look.

"They were cute and on clearance," I said with a shrug.

I started pulling boxes out of the closet and making a pile on the floor. I finally found the right box on the shelf in the back.

I took the shoes out and gave them to Elizabeth. They had an open toe and a wide four-inch heel.

She slipped them on and stood in front of the mirror. After looking at herself for about ten seconds, she giggled and then twirled around twice.

"Wow," I said. "You look better in that dress than I do. All right, you work on your hair and makeup while I figure out what I'm going to wear."

After four attempts, I found a short maroon sleeveless dress and a pair of workable black flats. Even though this was supposed to be a quiet reception, I knew better than to wear heels.

My bathroom counter had two sinks. Elizabeth and I each took one while we went through my collection of tools and makeup. We then traded the curling iron back and forth until we were both presentable.

Since I knew Jackie was going to be at the reception, I went into my hiding place and took out my small jewelry case. I removed the bracelet Jackie had given me and put it on.

"Wow, that's a beautiful bracelet," Elizabeth said as she came over to look closer at it.

"I know," I said as I turned my wrist and watched it sparkle. "I really love it. It's one of the two nice things I have."

Elizabeth took my wrist and slowly turned it while she bent over to look at the bracelet.

"The diamonds are beautiful, and the rubies are matched well. I've never seen a bracelet quite like it. Where'd you get it?"

"I got it from a friend. Her name is Jackie. She'll be at the reception today, and I'll introduce her to you. How I got it is a long story. Maybe I can tell you about it sometime."

The Scottsdale Saguaro Sky Resort and Spa is one of the newer resorts in north Scottsdale. It was built about ten years ago in the hilly foothills north of the McDowell Mountains.

I'd only had a chance to visit the resort a few times over the years, and this was the first time I'd been up here since Jackie had taken ownership. I was looking forward to seeing the hotel now that she was in charge.

The drive up to the resort was going to take half an hour, so Elizabeth and I left the apartment at about three-thirty. The invitation to the reception instructed us to use the valet at the main entrance, and I gladly did as I was told.

Valet is one of those nice things I never allow for myself. Mostly because I can never justify spending the money. But if the reception included valet parking, that was a completely different story.

Elizabeth and I had dropped off my car and were heading into the main lobby when we saw Sophie and Gina walking toward us from across the lobby. They were both dressed to impress.

"Wow," I said as we got together. "Everyone looks great today."

"Yeah," Sophie said. "Well, you never know who you're going to meet at a fancy reception at a nice hotel. We've been looking at the map to find the Hohokam Terrace. It's on the other side of the main pool."

"How goes the hunt for the treasure?" Gina asked.

"You said you found the coffin rock?" Sophie asked.

"Elizabeth found it," I said. "Gina, you were right. The rock was on Camelback Mountain, and it was only visible from the overlook.

The coffin rock led us back to the house, where we found the clue. It says we need to go to Prescott and find someone called Penelope. Apparently, she'll show us where to get the jewelry."

"Prescott is where Elizabeth's granddad owns a bar on Whiskey Row," Sophie said. She thought about it for a second. "It's called the Gilded Garter."

"So, that makes the second clue," Gina said. "I wonder how many there'll be before you can actually get the treasure?"

"It's so frustrating," Elizabeth said. "I know Granddad wanted to leave us his heirlooms, but all these clues are a little maddening. It would be so much simpler if he came out and told us where the jewelry was. I'm not sure why he's putting us through all of this nonsense."

"What?" Sophie asked, sounding a little annoyed. "Are you serious? You're on a treasure hunt to find a chest filled with millions of dollars worth of famous and historic jewelry. Your granddad thought enough about you and your brother to come up with an interesting way to find it. You're living out a story that'll be passed down for generations in your family, no matter if you find the chest or not. But if you do find it, you'll never have to work another day in your life. If you ask me, that doesn't sound so bad."

"You're right," Elizabeth said, now a little embarrassed. "And I'm grateful to my grandfather. But when you're in the middle of the whole thing, it really makes your head spin. We were so excited to find the clue, and all it did was tell us to find another one. Not to mention, I've found out my brother's working with gangsters, and that terrifies me."

"How is Les?" Gina asked me. "Did it appear he was being held against his will?"

"It's hard to say. He said no, but his associates were standing nearby at the time. It looks like they're in a relationship where the bad guys are only in it for the jewelry. Les wants to pay them off and then be done with them. At the moment, everything's at a stalemate."

"Well," Gina said. "Let me know if you'd like to get together and talk about this. I'd also like to ask you about the friends who were following you the other day and what happened with them."

"Friends?" Elizabeth asked.

"Yes," I said. "They turned out to be federal agents. But they're not directly related to the treasure hunt."

"This whole trip to Scottsdale keeps getting better and better," Elizabeth said as she shook her head.

We followed a couple of long hallways through the main building and eventually found the right room. The four of us walked in and looked around.

The space Jackie had picked out for the party was beautiful. Half of it was inside a fairytale ballroom, and half was outside on a tropical terrace.

An open bar had been set up against the left wall and had already attracted a crowd. A long buffet table was against the wall on the right side. Glancing at the food, I saw Annie wasn't kidding when she said we should come hungry.

A DJ booth was set up next to a dance floor in the back corner of the room. Instead of the dull music of a typical afternoon reception, the DJ was playing some seriously upbeat dance music. I noticed several people were already dancing to the pounding beat.

We found Annie talking with a group of people who'd just come in. We walked over, and each gave her a hug. I then introduced her to Elizabeth.

"I'm so glad you could make it," Annie said to all of us. "It means so much that you're here." She looked over at me. "I'm glad nothing came up. I know how things get when you're working on your assignments."

"Are you kidding?" I asked. "I wouldn't have missed it. You've been talking about this for months."

Annie took off to greet the new people as they came in. Gina, Sophie, and I walked Elizabeth around the room, introducing her to the people we knew.

We found Elle, Shannon, Pammy, and Cindy, each looking like a model on a catalog shoot. Although I always felt a little intimidated when I was around the girls, it also made me feel good to know I had such friends.

We'd each gotten another glass of champagne from a waitress with a silver tray when Jackie walked over. As always, Jackie was dressed to match the occasion.

The five of us formed a circle while I made introductions.

"Jackie, this is Elizabeth Bright-Murdock. We're helping her out with a few things that have come up. Elizabeth, this is Jackie Wade, our friend and the owner of the Scottsdale Saguaro Sky."

"You're lucky to have Laura, Gina, and Sophie on your side," Jackie said. "It's because of them that I now own this." She spread her arms wide and looked around at the beautiful resort. "They pulled me out of a mess that was way beyond what I could have gotten out of by myself."

Jackie got a sad look on her face and became quiet. I saw her looking at the diamond and ruby bracelet on my wrist— the bracelet she'd given to me as a token of our friendship.

I knew seeing it would bring back some powerful memories for her. Jackie then motioned Elizabeth to come closer and lowered her voice, so only our group could hear.

"You should know if it wasn't for Laura, I'd probably be dead. Not a lot of people know the full story, but she risked her life more than once to save mine. Don't ever make the mistake of looking at her and seeing a skinny, helpless woman. I'd put her up against any five guys you can find. If you want to know the truth, I've seen her take on a room full of hardened criminals and come out on top."

At this, I felt my face grow hot. It was sweet that Jackie said those nice things, but I certainly wasn't what she thought I was.

Plus, her words brought back a flood of horrible memories from a couple of months before, when Jackie and I really had faced a room full of criminals. Men who'd tried to kill us. My eyes started to tear up, and I did my best to shake off the memories.

"Thanks," I quietly said. "But don't believe everything Jackie says. She's being nice since it's her party."

Gina raised her glass. "To Jackie. I'm glad we met you. I'm glad we could help in our own small way. Mostly I'm glad we've made such a good friend."

We all raised our champagne and drank to Jackie. Each of us was lost in thoughts of how Jackie had indeed almost died but had instead become our friend.

After a moment, when no one said anything, Sophie looked up. "I don't know about anyone else, but I see some crab claws and shrimp that have my name on them. I'm going to see if I can put a dent in the buffet."

An hour later, we'd eaten until we were completely stuffed. The champagne had flowed freely, and we were in a good mood. The DJ was spinning his last set of records when Jackie and Elle stopped by our table.

"Everyone's heading out to the clubs tonight," Jackie said. "I hope you four can make it."

"Clubs?" Elizabeth asked.

"Sure," Elle said. "We'll go around to a few of the clubs in town and maybe dance a little. Sophie, Laura, and Gina often come with us. We'd love it if you came too. In fact, I insist."

Elizabeth looked at me, a little flustered.

"Of course, we'll go," Gina said for everyone. "Where shall we meet?"

"I was thinking tonight we'd start off at the lounge at Nexxus," Jackie said, "sometime around ten. It's a nice place to talk while everyone gathers. Then we'll probably go across the street to the Maya Day and Nightclub. They have a new

DJ, and he's really good."

After Jackie and Elle left, we agreed to drive to the office separately and then to Nexxus in one car.

Sophie looked over at me. "Are you going to make it this time?"

"Of course, I'll make it."

"You don't think something'll come up?"

"What can come up?" I asked.

"You know, I think I've heard you say that before. We'll probably leave the office to go to Nexxus at about ten. If you can't make it to the office by then, hopefully, you'll be able to meet us at the club."

"I'll make it."

After the reception, I dropped Elizabeth off at her hotel. She asked if it would be all right if she wore the dress out to the clubs later on.

I told her it would be a shame to waste a dress that fit so well. I also told her I'd meet her at the office at a little before ten.

I drove back to my apartment and took the elevator up to my floor. As I got out, I saw Grandma Peckham and Grandpa Bob walking down the hall towards the elevator, both dressed for a night on the town.

Grandpa was in the middle of telling some lively story, and Grandma Peckham was looking up at him and giggling.

"Hello," I said as I got closer.

"What's buzzin', cousin?" Grandpa Bob asked.

"I've been at a graduation reception for a woman from work. It was nice. Where are you two off to tonight?"

"Grandpa Bob and I are going to dinner at the Compass Arizona Grill," Grandma Peckham said. "That's the restaurant at the top of the Hyatt downtown. I haven't been there in years, but I love the views of the city as the restaurant slowly rotates."

"That's right," Grandpa Bob said. "It's hard to get a bad seat when the whole place is turning. Every seat has the same great view."

Grandma got a funny look. If I didn't know her better, I'd say she was slightly embarrassed. "Dear, are you staying in or going out tonight?"

"I only came home to do some stuff. I'm heading back out in a little while. I'll probably be back fairly late."

I saw that Grandma looked a little relieved.

"After dinner, Bob and I are planning to come back here to watch a movie." She lowered her voice and bent closer to me, "Thin walls." I swear she blushed a little bit.

"Oh," I said. "Not a problem. I'll probably be out until late."

I told Grandma and Grandpa goodbye and went into my apartment. The main thing I wanted to do was to stash Jackie's bracelet. It was no problem wearing it at a reception at a nice resort, but wearing it out to the clubs wouldn't be a good idea.

Marlowe got up from the couch and followed me into the bedroom. I put the bracelet away, went back to the living room, and sat on the couch.

I then picked up the remote and started flipping channels. Marlowe lay down in my lap and started to purr.

I had slowly flipped through every channel and was about to do it again when my phone rang. I saw it was Horace Morningstar.

"Miss Black," he said. "I would like to see you tonight. We need to discuss our efforts of today."

"What, now?"

"Why, yes, is this a problem? Perhaps you have something more important to do tonight?"

"Where do you want to meet?"

"We're now staying at the Scottsdale Tropical Paradise, as I wanted to be close to Lester. Let us meet at the lounge in the main building. It's called the Headhunter, and it should be adequate for our needs. It's a public place, but we should be able to talk there. By all means, bring Elizabeth along if she also wishes to come."

"It'll only be me tonight. What time?"

"Very good. I like a woman who gets straight to the point. It tells me you're still taking this matter seriously. Well then, let us say ten o'clock."

Ten o'clock. It figures.

I continued to slowly flip channels until nine-thirty when I took off. I decided not to change out of my dress from the reception. I was still planning on meeting everyone at Nexxus or Maya, and I didn't want to change clothes for the meeting with the hoodlums.

I parked in the main lot in front of the reception building at the Tropical Paradise and walked up the hill to the main valet entrance. It's always fun to see the collection of sports cars they arrange in the courtyard near the front.

Surprisingly, I was early. I walked into the lobby and spent a few minutes admiring the tropical rainforest and waterfalls that make the lobby of the Tropical Paradise so unique.

I told myself I shouldn't linger in the lobby for too long. Since this is where Tony DiCenzo had his main offices, I knew I was tempting fate by even being here.

I walked past the main reception desk and went down a hallway to the main casual lounge for the resort, the Headhunter. As with everything at the Paradise, the Headhunter had a tropical island theme.

Morningstar and Les hadn't arrived yet, so I took a seat at the bar. I looked behind the bar and saw several glass shelves full of high-end alcohol in front of a large mirror. Seeing the shelves and the bottles made me smile, thinking about an incident that had happened here about six months before.

A henchman by the name of Sonny Boy Muzzi had gone on a mini-rampage and had smashed up the lounge. At the time, he worked for Tony DiCenzo.

Since DiCenzo also happened to own the bar that was smashed, Tough Tony didn't take too kindly to Sonny's actions. I looked all around the bar, but I couldn't tell if anything was still missing or out of place from the previous time I'd been here.

Right at ten, Morningstar walked into the lounge with Les and Magic in tow. The hostess sat them at a large table, and I walked over to join them. A cocktail waitress came over, and we all ordered drinks.

"Well, Miss Black," Morningstar said. "I hope you've had a more productive day than we did."

"Not really. We went through the entire house again. I

keep thinking we'll find something that looks out of place, or if we pull on the right book on a bookshelf, it will open a secret door."

I am such a fibber.

"Very good," Morningstar said. "I see we're thinking along the same lines. What are your plans for tomorrow?"

"Well, in addition to the house on Camelback, Lester's granddad also owned four big tracts of land and a bar in Prescott. Elizabeth and I are thinking we'd go to Prescott tomorrow and then maybe go out to the parcels of land on Monday."

"What do you hope to find in Prescott?" Morningstar asked somewhat suspiciously.

"At this point, we're looking for anything unusual. We're hitting dead ends on South Mountain and at the house. Speaking of South Mountain, did you find anything up there today?"

Les perked up and was about to say something when Morningstar interrupted. "No, unfortunately, our efforts there were also fruitless. However, I think we'll concentrate our efforts on the house tomorrow. But tell me, I don't want us to duplicate our efforts. In which parts of the house did you look today?"

I noticed that Les was giving Morningstar a strange look.

"We looked all over the house," I said.

"Yes, but did you concentrate on any specific areas? Say, the pool perhaps, or um, the master bedroom? As I said, I don't want to duplicate your efforts."

Oh my God. He's found the coffin rock and wants to know if I know, too.

"Well, the master bedroom's still sealed, and it will be

hard to get in there without the police knowing. We've searched the pool twice so far, but there doesn't seem to be a lot out there. Mostly, it's lounge chairs and umbrellas. Certainly nothing big enough to hide a chest."

At this, Morningstar brightened up. "Excellent, yes, by all means, you should go up to Prescott tomorrow and see if you can find anything helpful. The three of us will be at the house searching, in vain, no doubt, but searching nonetheless. Remember, if you do find anything, I expect to be notified immediately. After all," he laughed a hollow laugh, "we're all partners in this little endeavor."

I'd made it out to my car and was about to pull out of the hotel parking lot when my phone rang. This time, it was Agent McCoy. I pulled the car back into a parking space and answered.

"Miss Black, this is Special Agent McCoy. I'm sorry to say we've lost track of Lester Murdock. Do you have any information as to his current location?"

"I just left him. He's with Morningstar and Magic at the Headhunter Lounge at the Scottsdale Tropical Paradise, Lester's hotel."

I heard Agent McCoy repeating everything I was saying to somebody, probably Agent Conquest.

"By the way, Morningstar and Magic have switched hotels and are now both at the Tropical Paradise too."

"We were not aware of that. Thank you for the information. Are you getting any closer to recovering the chest with the inheritance?"

"I'm making progress, but nothing's final yet. Elizabeth

and I are heading up to Prescott tomorrow for the day. That's a tourist town in the mountains. We think the next clue is up there with a woman named Penelope."

"Miss Black, I'll be as honest with you as I can be. We're growing concerned about Lester Murdock's safety. We need him to testify, and he can't do that if he's dead. We're considering bringing him in. Of course, it will end any credibility he has with his group, and we'd rather it not come to that. But we also can't take the chance Morningstar will suspect anything and overreact."

"I won't tell you how to do your job, but I'd hold off for a couple of days," I said. "They're all still looking for the treasure, and I don't think Les will be in any danger until they actually find it. Of course, once it's found, all bets are off."

"We understand, Miss Black. Please keep us apprised of your movements and discoveries."

Jeez, why can't anyone do their jobs by themselves?

"Alright," I said. "I'll let you know what's going on."

Chapter Twelve

The drive to Old Town was uneventful. Since it was almost eleven-thirty, I knew the girls would've moved on from Nexxus. I hoped they were still at the Maya.

I parked in a public lot and walked to the Maya Day and Nightclub. As always, there was a large knot of people at the front entrance. Since I wasn't with the Cougars, I had to wait several minutes until I could get in.

Once in the club, I walked out to the pool. Finding the girls was easy since they always had an area all their own.

I got to the circle of couches under a big canopy, and everyone said hello. Being late was not unusual for me, and no one was surprised.

Elle was talking to a younger guy who looked like he could have played football for ASU. Two new guys arrived with fresh drinks for Pam and Shannon.

I was somewhat surprised to see Elizabeth talking to a man roughly her own age. He was dressed nicely, and from the way he talked, he seemed to have an education. I slid in next to Sophie.

"Why are you so late?" she asked. "Are you having another shitty night?"

"Well, not exactly shitty, more like crappy."

Sophie stopped and looked me over. From the way she was swaying, I could tell she'd already had a few drinks.

"You didn't get tossed in your trunk or peed on by a dog again, did you?"

"Um, no."

"Okay then. Shut up about your crappy night, and let's have some hot men buy us drinks. You can pretend they're Max, or Reno, or whoever's at the top of your list at the moment. You can even take one home if you're still feeling frisky."

"I thought you said no more one-night stands?"

"Well, I told myself I wasn't going to hook up with anyone tonight, but I can already feel my resolve weakening. It's because I've been drinking, and these men smell so good. It's not my fault. Besides, who knows? Maybe this is the way I'm supposed to find my Mr. Right."

I stayed in the club for a little over an hour. At one point, a guy bought me a drink, but I was distracted with thoughts of work and after a few minutes of conversation, the guy went away.

Sophie had her arms wrapped around a good-looking guy who appeared to be four or five years younger than she was. The pink glow on her cheeks showed that the guy was in for a long night.

By about twelve-thirty, Sophie and the guy, Justin, were getting ready to leave. I also decided to call it a night.

Elizabeth had been talking to the same guy all night. When I looked, they were holding hands and sitting close. I got up and walked around to where they were sitting.

"Don't forget I'm picking you up tomorrow morning."

"What time?" she asked.

"Nine? By the queen palm?"

Elizabeth looked over at the guy and then back at me. "I'm not sure when the club closes, but let's make it ten."

I woke up Sunday morning to the alarm going off. I opened one eye and saw it was only eight.

That seemed too early, so I hit the snooze. Nine minutes later, I hit it again. I kept hitting the snooze until it was eight thirty-six, and I was going to have to rush to get to Elizabeth's hotel by ten o'clock.

I pulled into the parking lot of the Hyatt a few minutes after ten. By ten after ten, I was in the lobby by the queen palm.

I looked around, but Elizabeth wasn't anywhere. For some reason, this annoyed me a little.

I guess when you're always the person who's late, you expect the other people to be waiting for you. When they're even later, it somehow seems sort of rude.

At twenty-five after ten, Elizabeth came walking through the lobby. She looked happy, but I could tell she hadn't gotten a lot of sleep.

"Sorry I'm late," she said. "I couldn't get up this morning. I'm not used to staying out all night."

"You didn't go home with that guy, did you?"

Elizabeth blushed bright red and giggled. "No, but to be

honest, when I woke up this morning, I was a little disappointed I hadn't."

"Well, the Cougars go out a couple of times a week. I'm sure they'd like to have you come along again. Maybe you can find another one?"

"Maybe, but I like the one from last night."

"It'll be hard to find him again. It seems like there's always a different group of guys every night."

"Actually, it won't be too hard to find this one," Elizabeth said as she pulled out a business card.

"Oh, you bad girl," I said. She handed me the card, and I read it out loud. "Jeremy Mathews, Director of Strategy at Glick, Goldberg, & Edwards."

I looked up at Elizabeth. "I've heard of them. They're a big brokerage firm downtown that services the old-money people in Scottsdale and Paradise Valley. Are you going to call him?"

"Probably, it depends on what I'm going to end up doing with myself. I need to make some decisions about my future. I already have a life in Chicago, but to be honest, it might be time for a change."

There are several small towns in the mountains north of Scottsdale, with Payson, Sedona, Prescott, Pine-Strawberry, and Jerome being some of the most popular. On any given day in June, you can be assured the temperature in the mountains will be fifteen or twenty degrees cooler than down in Scottsdale.

Prescott's a town with tons of charm and loads of history.

It's about an hour and a half up Interstate-17 from Scottsdale.

The center of the town is called the Plaza. The old courthouse, which sits in the middle of a large, green city park, is the central feature of the Plaza.

Whiskey Row is along the west side of the Plaza. After the Civil War, almost twenty saloons crowded this one block, making it the center of social activity in the young Arizona Territory.

Over the years, I'd taken many people to Prescott for a bar crawl. Heading up to Whiskey Row and having a beer in each of the saloons was on the must-do list of many first-time Arizona tourists.

As we drove into downtown Prescott, signs and banners along the road announced that the town was having an annual arts festival. The park in front of the courthouse was filled with dozens of tents jammed with paintings, ceramics, sculptures, and crafts.

There were at least a dozen food trucks and a large stage with a band. We parked and joined the crowd as they headed to the festival.

The first thing I noticed when I stepped out of my car was that the air was cool and smelled like pine trees. The band was playing classic rock, which made a nice soundtrack while we wandered through the gallery tents.

As we walked past the food trucks, I could smell grilling meat wafting out from several of them. I decided Lenny could spring for a snack for each of us.

I went to a truck featuring both carne asada and chicken street tacos. I got each of us a three-pack, along with a Diet Pepsi for me and a Coke for Elizabeth.

We took our lunches and sat in front of the stage at one of several picnic tables. The tacos were delicious and seemed to go perfectly with the fun atmosphere created by the music and the talking and laughing of the people sitting around us.

"Do you have any idea how we're going to find Penelope?" Elizabeth asked between bites.

"No idea," I said. "I did a Google search, and I couldn't find anyone named Penelope who lives in Prescott. The saloon your granddad owns is over on Whiskey Row." I gestured with my hand holding the Diet Pepsi to the saloons lining the other side of the street. "Let's head over there and see what we can find out."

After we finished our tacos, we walked to the bars. First, we went to the Bird Cage, then to Jersey Lilly, a bar with a great view from a second-floor balcony. Next, we walked to the Palace Saloon.

There's something special about being in a saloon that's been serving at the same spot for over a hundred and fifty years. Each bar was filled with a good-sized afternoon crowd of people.

At each place, we asked the bartenders and waitresses if they knew of anyone named Penelope. One bartender at the Bird Cage said he'd dated a woman named Penelope in college but didn't know of one living in Prescott.

We finally ended up at the Gilded Garter, the bar Elizabeth's granddad owned. It was slightly bigger than the other bars on the Row and was decorated as it had been in the 1880s.

There was a band on a small stage, and the crowd seemed a little larger and rowdier than at the previous places. The band's rock-n-roll sounded a little out of place in a saloon that seemed like it should have someone playing an old-fashioned song from an out-of-tune piano.

Elizabeth and I found a couple of empty stools in the

middle of the bar. Behind the bar was a large painting of a plus-sized nude woman with tightly curled dark hair and a Cleopatra-style headpiece.

She was lying on a red velvet chaise lounge with a piece of sheer white cloth artfully draped over her meaty thighs. Other than the headpiece, all she had on was a necklace and a ruby ring.

Attached to the wall on either side of the painting were what appeared to be genuine Native American eagle feather headdresses. A busy bartender served us two beers and then hurried away before we could ask him about Penelope.

I was getting frustrated by my lack of progress in finding both the jewelry and Penelope. It sometimes helped to go over things. Sometimes, saying what I know out loud seemed to put things in their proper place and helped me see connections.

"Okay," I said, half to myself. "So, what do we know?"

"Um, we know we're looking for Penelope?" Elizabeth asked.

"Yes, but in the broader sense, we know your granddad died and set up this treasure hunt for you and Les to run all around Arizona looking for his jewelry. We can't be sure why he did that. Perhaps he had a strange sense of humor, but I'm thinking he maybe wanted to force the two of you to work together and maybe patch things up. We know your granddad wants us to find the jewelry since he keeps leaving us clues. And we think the jewelry is somewhere in the house because everything your granddad told us has turned out to be true, at least so far."

"We know Les is involved with some pretty rough guys out of Chicago," Elizabeth said.

"We know a guy was killed. And we know a woman in

Prescott named Penelope has our next clue."

After that, Elizabeth became quiet and slowly sipped her beer. I could tell her thoughts were going out to her brother, and I didn't want to intrude.

After about five minutes, she was almost through with her beer and happened to glance up at the picture behind the bar. For some reason, the antique painting of the woman seemed to interest her. I could see her intently staring at the canvas, and I knew she was trying to make a connection.

"It's funny," she said slowly, "but the necklace on the woman in the painting is exactly the same as the one Granddad has. Remember, I told you about the necklace he got after the war from someone who said he was a duke? I said Granddad traded it for twenty dollars and three cartons of cigarettes. I used to wear it and pretend I was a princess. I swear it's the same necklace."

"How could it be the same one?" I asked. "Everything in this bar is an antique. Well, except for the beer signs. That painting looks really old, at least back to the eighteen-hundreds. Your granddad got the necklace about seventy or eighty years ago. It can't be the same one."

"But look," Elizabeth said. "In the center of the chains that hang down is a gold and black eagle with a green eye. And there are two black pearls and a big diamond on either side of the eagle. Do you see? I'm serious. It's the same one I would wear as a little girl. It's my princess necklace."

Elizabeth looked at the painting for almost two minutes without speaking. Her eyes were glazed over with a faraway look. It was as if she was looking at the painting but seeing something else entirely.

"You know," she finally said, "the ring on the woman's hand also looks familiar."

Elizabeth's voice had risen to a higher pitch, and she was getting excited. She knew she'd made an important connection. "Do you see the center stone's a big ruby surrounded by a bunch of smaller diamonds and rubies? I'm sure that's one of the rings Granddad got after the war. I've held that one in my hand as well. Both Les and I have."

The bartender came over and asked if we wanted another round. We asked him about the painting and the necklace on the woman.

"Interesting story about that," he said. "An old guy came in six or seven months ago. He was with a younger girl. Turned out she was an artist. He said he wanted the girl to paint a necklace and a ring on the painting. I told him he was crazy. That painting is over a hundred and fifty years old and has been in Prescott ever since the Civil War. It's been hanging over the bar here ever since they rebuilt the place after the big fire in nineteen hundred. I told him the painting was part of the history of the place, and he couldn't deface it."

"What happened?" I asked.

"Well, the manager was in that day, and I saw her rushing through the crowd to come over to us. I thought she'd also be pissed about what the old guy wanted to do. Instead, she was shaking the old guy's hand and doing everything but bending over to kiss his wrinkled ass. Turns out the old guy owned the place."

"So, it looks like he was able to add the necklace to the painting," I said.

"Yeah, but even though the old guy owned the place, I gotta tell you I was still pissed about him wanting to deface her. I've worked here for almost fifteen years, and the bar is sort of known for this painting. She's called Penelope of Prescott, and men have lusted over her for a hundred and fifty years. I've seen grown men get drunk and have long conversations with Penelope. I didn't want to see anything happen to her."

"It looks like the necklace and ring are part of the original painting," I said. "You can't tell they were added on."

"Well, you're right about that. It's the damnedest thing. It turns out the artist he brought with him was from the Phoenix Art Museum. I got to talking with her, and she specializes in restoring old masterpieces that have been damaged or vandalized. It took her about two weeks, but she painted on the necklace and the ring, and it's as if they were part of the original painting. Actually, I think it's great that Penelope has some classy jewelry now. She doesn't look so much like a cheap tramp any more. The part that confused me was why the artist girl also painted the Greek statue. I'm getting used to it, but it still seems a little out of place. Penelope has the Egyptian Cleopatra thing going on. I think an Egyptian statue would have looked better."

"What Greek statue?" I asked.

"The one behind Penelope and to the left," he said. "It's sort of in the background, but you can still make it out."

"The one that looks like a naked guy throwing a discus?" Elizabeth asked.

"That's the one."

Elizabeth got a faraway look in her eyes, and I could tell that, once again, she was thinking about something.

"You know," she said at last. "That looks like a statue in Granddad's house. I'm sure you've seen it too. It's in an alcove in the library."

"It does look familiar," I said. "Is it on the bottom level? On the wall against the side of the mountain, in a little recess?"

"That's the one. But why would Granddad have an artist paint a picture of a naked Greek throwing a discus behind Penelope of Prescott?" Elizabeth asked. "It doesn't make a lot of sense."

"I don't know," I said. "But it somehow ties into the jewelry. Let's go back to the house and take a look at it."

We drove back down Interstate-17 and only encountered one traffic slowdown, right before we reached Loop-101. We finally made it to Camelback Mountain at about five-thirty.

I drove up to the house and was about to pull into the courtyard when Elizabeth stopped me. "There's a white car in the driveway."

I turned the wheel hard and pulled back out onto the road.

"Thanks," I said. "Well, unless Morningstar was watching the courtyard, I don't think he could've spotted us. Let's see if he calls to ask what we're doing."

"If he does call, what should we say?"

"I don't know, but we'll think of something. Are you hungry? We can have dinner, then come back and see if they're gone."

"I'm starved. The tacos were good, but that was hours ago."

"Are you up for Mexican again?"

"Sure, if it's good and not too spicy."

"I know a great place."

We drove west on Camelback and made our way over to 12th Street and Mohave.

Elizabeth looked around the neighborhood. "Um, where are you taking me?"

"It's called Carolina's Mexican. It's not fancy, and it's in sort of a mixed neighborhood, but the food's some of the best in town."

"Okay, as long as you know what you're doing."

We pulled into Carolina's parking lot. It's a south-central Phoenix landmark.

The restaurant is housed in a building that had previously been a grocery store and a coin-operated laundromat. As usual, two police cars and a fire truck were parked nearby on the street. Carolina's is one of the favorite places of the working people in this part of town.

We walked into the restaurant, and Elizabeth looked around. Apprehension was written all over her face.

"Like I said, it's not the fanciest place in town. But in Arizona, don't judge a book by its cover. I've found that the nicer a Mexican place looks on the outside, the worse the food is on the inside. Not everywhere, of course, but more often than not. Let's go stand in line and figure out what you want. We'll order, then find a place to sit."

There was a long counter with a menu printed overhead. Behind the counter, three people were taking orders. Back in the kitchen, we could see at least a dozen people working on getting the food out. We got in the shortest of the three lines and made our way up to the counter.

"What are you having?" Elizabeth asked.

"I'm having the foot-long machaca burro, enchilada-style with green sauce and a beef taco."

"That sounds good, but is it spicy?"

"A little, but only enough. Carolina's is more about

flavors than heat. Go ahead and try it. If it's too much, we can always stop by the McDonald's on 7th Street."

We placed our orders, then went to the pop machine and got our drinks. We found a place to sit while we waited for our number to be called out.

"Wait here," I told Elizabeth. I went over to the dispensers and loaded up several cups of fragrant red salsa. When I got back to the booth, Elizabeth suspiciously eyed the cups.

"I love the food here, and they've won awards for having the best tortillas in town," I said. "But truthfully, I come here for the salsa. I'm not sure what there is about it, but it's easily the best in the city."

Elizabeth started to ask something. "And no," I said. "It's not too spicy."

Within five minutes, they called our number. I got our dinners and brought them back to the table.

Elizabeth eyed the Styrofoam containers and the plastic silverware. When I dumped three cups of salsa on the burro, she again looked at me.

Bowing to the inevitable and not wanting to seem rude, she cut off a small piece of her burro and delicately put it in her mouth. After a few seconds, her eyes opened wide. She cut off a bigger piece and stuffed it into her mouth.

"This is really good," she said before she put the next bite in. "You're right. It's not too spicy but has tons of flavors."

"Try some salsa," I suggested.

She took the next bite of burro, dipped a corner in the salsa, and then tasted it. Again, she seemed to like the flavor, so she dumped the rest of the cup on her burro.

We then spent the next fifteen minutes eating and getting

drink refills. I even had to go up and get more salsa. Elizabeth took everything I hadn't already used, and we needed more for the tacos.

Finally, we were using our plastic forks to scrape the last of the green sauce and salsa from the bottom of our containers.

"Okay," Elizabeth said. "I misjudged this place. Are there more little restaurants like this around town?"

"Sure," I said. "I'll be glad to take you to all of them."

After Carolina's, we drove back up to the house on Camelback. Since it was getting dark, I switched off my lights as we glided by the entrance of the courtyard.

We saw that Les, Morningstar, and Magic were in the pool area, which was brightly lit. It looked like Les and Magic were holding shovels. It also appeared they'd moved the statue, pried up a slab of concrete decking, and were digging a hole underneath.

We continued along the road. "It looks like they'll be there all night," I said. "We'll need to wait until they aren't here. Let's try again tomorrow morning."

"I have a monthly staff meeting tomorrow at one o'clock Chicago time. Even though I'm on vacation, I can't miss it. But it should be over with by two o'clock Arizona time."

"Alright," I said. We'll meet by the queen palm at two."

I dropped Elizabeth off at her hotel and then drove down to the office. It'd been a couple of days since I'd reviewed the videos of the bedrooms at George Anson's house, and I started to feel like I was neglecting the assignment.

I parked in the back and went in through the security door. After I turned on my computer, I saw I had a new collection of video files starting on Thursday afternoon.

Since this was Sunday night, I had three days' worth of videos from five different cameras to review. I went to the break room fridge and pulled out a bottle of Diet Pepsi.

I went through each of the video files, starting with the spare bedrooms and ending up at the master. Unfortunately, none of the cameras showed any evidence that George Anson was having an affair. Feeling a little dejected, I erased each file and made the proper notations in my logbook.

If I didn't get anything on video during the upcoming week, I'd need to change tactics and start tracking George. I was hoping it wouldn't come to that. I've done it that way before, and it usually means a week or two of frustration as I follow some guy around the city.

Half the time, I'm spotted, and the other half, the only evidence I can get is a video of the subject leaving a hotel room with his mistress. Sure, this is compelling evidence, but certainly not as conclusive as having an hour of high-definition video of the couple engaged in the act.

While reviewing the videos, I noticed the signal from one of the spare bedroom cameras was starting to pixelate. This usually means the battery is getting weak. I decided I would need to make time in the morning to go back to George and Debbie's house and change the batteries.

The drive back to my apartment was uneventful, and it felt strange to be home before ten o'clock. When I walked in the door, Marlowe hopped off the couch and rubbed against my leg. I think he was also surprised that I was home again so early.

I crawled into bed and checked emails until about eleven. I then rolled over and fell asleep.

I woke up to the sound of my alarm and I reached over and hit the clock until it stopped. I'd left it set for eight, not because I had anywhere I needed to be, but because I didn't want to waste a morning when I could be productive.

I texted Debbie Anson and said I needed to stop by the house and check on things. I needed to know when the house would be empty so I could change the batteries in the cameras.

Her answer came back that George was going to be at his dealership in Mesa for the day. Debbie also said she had a charity function and would be out of the house from nine-thirty until three-thirty. That gave me several hours to replace the batteries without the client hovering over me.

Although it might sound like a good idea to have the client help with the cameras, it never works out in practice. As soon as the client learns where the cameras are located, they become overly shy or turn into an exhibitionist. Either way, the subject of the investigation tends to notice something is amiss and become suspicious.

I then called Horace Morningstar. I didn't want to tell him everything I knew, and I also didn't want to tell him my real plans for finding the treasure.

But I felt I needed to feed him progress reports that made sense and were at least somewhat accurate. If not, I risked losing the working relationship.

"Miss Black," he said as he answered. "I'd hoped I would've heard from you last night. What news do you have from Prescott?"

I mentally crossed my fingers and hoped I wouldn't go to

hell for lying.

"We didn't find a thing. The property Lester's granddad owned is a bar on Whiskey Row. We talked to fifteen or twenty people up there yesterday, but the only ones who even knew Lester's grandfather were a bartender and the manager of the saloon. When we talked to her, we found out Lester's granddad only came up to Prescott occasionally and had nothing to do with the day-to-day operations."

"Yes," Morningstar said. "That's what I would have expected. However, it's proper to be diligent and methodical. Until the chest is recovered, we must leave no stone unturned, quite literally in some cases."

"Today, I'll be going over to the other properties he owned," I said. "There are four tracts of undeveloped land scattered through the Valley. There's one northwest of the McDowell Mountains, one on Scottsdale Road at Jomax, one in Carefree, and one in the town of Queen Creek. Depending on what's there, it'll probably take all day and maybe a good part of tomorrow. Elizabeth has a work meeting this morning, but then she'll look with me."

"Very well," he said. "We may return to South Mountain at some point, but I am beginning to feel that may be somewhat of a dead end."

Of course, you do. You already know the coffin rock points straight at the pool.

"More than likely, we'll be here at the house all day," he said.

Damn, how are we going to get to the jewelry if you're always there?

"For some reason," Morningstar continued, "Magic has convinced himself that the clue may have something to do with the pool, or at least the area around the pool. I'm afraid he's been quite busy out there, digging holes and breaking things. I've left him to continue tilting at windmills since we ourselves are no farther along in the rest of the mansion. I will confess that I may have snuck into the master bedroom and looked through the vault. But alas, like Magic, I've been able to go no further in my quest."

After I promised to be better about checking in with my progress reports, I disconnected the phone and tossed it on my kitchen table in frustration.

If Les, Morningstar, and Magic were going to be at the house all day, it'd be hard to go in and start poking around at a sculpture in the library. Worse, there was always the chance they might randomly go into the library and discover the statue on their own.

Since there was nothing else to do until I could figure out a way to get the crooks out of the house, I took a long, hot shower. By the time I got out, I was starting to feel better but still had no real game plan.

Well, I thought, first things first. Change the batteries in the cameras at George Anson's and then figure out how to get the treasure.

It'd been a week since I had installed the spy cameras in George's house. Each camera ran off a small battery, which provided enough power for it to transmit to a repeater I'd installed in the garage.

The repeater then took the video signals and sent them over the Internet to the computers back at the office, where they were recorded and stored. The cameras' batteries were good, but seven or eight days was about all I could get out of them before they needed to be replaced. Since one camera was already starting to fade, I knew the rest of them would soon follow.

I pulled into George Anson's neighborhood at ten o'clock and parked two houses down the block. By ten-thirty, I'd replaced the batteries in the three cameras in the master bedroom.

I was in the process of replacing the batteries in the first guest bedroom when I heard the familiar sound of the front door opening. I then heard George's voice talking to a woman as they both came up the stairs.

Crap, not again.

I quietly closed the door to the guest bedroom and turned the ceiling fan to the lowest setting. The fan was a higher-end model, and it made no noise as the blades sent a cooling breeze throughout the room.

Fortunately, the cameras in the master bedroom were now fully functional. All I had to do was wait for them to finish.

I was glad this time I didn't need to listen to every sound George and his mistress made as they spent the next two hours down the hall in the master bedroom. With the exception of about a dozen times when the woman's moaning penetrated the thin walls of the bedroom, it was completely silent and peaceful as I lay on the bed, watching the blades of the ceiling fan slowly spin.

I suppose there are worse ways to make a living.

After I heard the front door closing and heard the car pulling out of the driveway, I replaced the batteries in the cameras in both guest bedrooms. Now that I wasn't in a rush, I walked down the stairway and took time to look at some of the pictures on the wall.

Most of these were of Debbie, George, and their kids on vacation over the years. There were the obligatory pictures of

Disneyland, the Grand Canyon, and the beach at Rocky Point.

There was also one taken in Paris in front of the Eiffel Tower. They really did look like a nice family.

I'd almost gotten to the bottom of the stairs when a picture caught my eye. It was a family gathering with Debbie and her kids, along with Debbie's younger sister Connie and her kids.

Debbie and her children were wearing matching green shirts, while Connie and her kids were wearing matching blue shirts. As I looked closer, it suddenly hit me.

Oh, shit.

I knew George's mistress had looked familiar. Debbie's sister had the same body type and brunette hair as Debbie, but she also had a Cindy Crawford mole on the side of her mouth.

Even though I'd only seen her briefly, when I'd opened the closet door, there was no mistake. George was having an affair with Debbie's sister, Connie.

A feeling of sadness and frustration washed over me. Sometimes, when I think I've seen it all, something new comes along, and I totally need to rethink what I know and what I don't know about the world.

Chapter Thirteen

The drive back to the office didn't take very long, but I was still upset thinking about George Anson, Connie, and Debbie.

Why do people do this to themselves?

I parked in my covered space and went in through the back door. I then walked up to the front reception area and collapsed into one of the big red leather chairs.

Lenny's door was closed. Sophie and Gina were having a lively discussion about a married guy named Shawn Phillips. Sophie had dated him several months back but had broken up with him when he canceled three dates in a row to be with his wife.

Sophie was relating story after story about how dating a married guy was more of a hassle than it was worth. After about five minutes of talking and waving her arms, Sophie stopped her stories and looked over at me.

"Hey," she said. "Why are you sitting there looking so glum?"

Gina looked over at me. I saw her eyes give me the police detective's once-over.

"Did something happen?" Gina asked. "You do look a little shaken."

"Are you having another shitty day?" Sophie asked. A crease of concern was on her forehead. "Did you get smacked in the head again?"

"I got the video evidence in the George and Debbie Anson assignment," I said.

"So, why aren't you happy?" Sophie asked. "You should be all bubbly and dancing around. You should be saying things like, 'I can eat real food and not have to survive on chicken ramen for the next two weeks' and stuff."

"Did something happen?" Gina asked. "Did someone get hurt?"

"No, nothing like that," I said. "The woman George Anson's been having his affair with is Debbie's sister, Connie."

"Oh no," Gina said.

"Her sister?" Sophie asked. "Holy crap."

"How are you going to handle that?" Gina asked.

"Well, Debbie's already going to divorce the creep," I said. "So, that part's done. But we also need to find a way to break up the affair. Marrying a jerk is something we all can do, but sisters are forever. If Debbie ever finds out, they'll never speak to each other again."

"Is that a bad thing?" Sophie asked. "After all, she's been nailing Debbie's husband for years."

"Of course, it's a bad thing," Gina said.

"Everyone makes a mistake from time to time," I said. "From what I heard, Connie isn't getting what she needs at home. Maybe she latched onto the first guy who was sympathetic toward her."

"It's happened before," Gina said.

"So, what are you going to do?" Sophie asked.

"I don't know yet. But we need to think of something. Divorces happen every day, but I don't want to see Debbie's life get ruined in the process. When will Lenny schedule the conference with George and the opposing council?"

"If you have the video evidence, it'll probably be tomorrow morning," Sophie said. "Both Lenny and opposing council are eager to wrap this up. George hasn't budged on any of his positions, and it's even frustrating for his own attorney. Lenny will use the videos to force a quick settlement."

"Okay, I have an idea," I said. "But we'll need to work fast. After seeing the videos, I've learned that George has a small personal problem. I think I know how we can make this work for Debbie."

I sent a text to Elizabeth to have her call me after she got out of her meeting. She texted back that she'd be done relatively soon.

We set up a small editing studio in the main conference room so Sophie could see if a client walked in off the street or get to her desk phone if it rang. We then worked on the videos for about an hour and a half.

We had the original videos in raw form. We would submit these to the court as evidence in case they were ever needed at a hearing.

Lenny came out of his office and walked into the conference room. "What are you three doing in here?"

"Laura got the video evidence of George Anson's affair," Gina said. "We're making copies so we can submit the originals to the court."

"Beautiful," he said, now with a wide grin. "Do the videos clearly show George Anson committing adultery in the marital bed?"

"We have two hours from three different camera angles," I said. "Everything's in focus and in frame. As instructed, Debbie left a copy of today's newspaper out where it would be visible. There's also a calendar on a dresser showing today's date."

"Perfect," Lenny said. "What about the woman? Do we know who she is? Is she someone who's prominent in the community? If we threaten to leak the name, it sometimes brings the other side around a little faster. Can we get any leverage off of her?"

"No," all three of us answered at once.

Lenny gave us a look that showed he thought we were up to something, but he ignored it. "Sophie, call opposing council and see if they can make a meeting over here tomorrow morning. Tell him we have conclusive video evidence of George's affair. Also, tell him if he comes over tomorrow, we'll make an offer of settlement before we show the videos to our client. That should rattle his cage."

Sophie saluted and then went to her desk to make the call.

"Now then," Lenny said, "where are you on the treasure hunt? Is Elizabeth still happy? We should approach taking her on as a formal client to keep the paperwork trail clean."

I downloaded Lenny on what'd happened so far.

"So, you found a clue, and that led to another clue, and that led to a painting, and that in itself was a clue. Jeez, this could go on for weeks. Now, it's not that I don't appreciate you accumulating all of these billable hours, but we'll have a much better chance of collecting the fee if you recover the jewelry. Can you concentrate on that?"

"I'll try," I said, desperately wanting to smack him. "What about Les and the police? When's his next interview? I'll need to get him away from the Chicago hoods."

"I haven't heard a thing," Lenny said. "Which typically means they're building a case around him based on the physical evidence."

Lenny got a smile, and he let out a little chuckle. "I need you to find the jewelry soon. It wouldn't surprise me if he were arrested when we go in. It'll get busy around here, and I need the client to have the funds to pay the fee."

Still chuckling, Lenny went back into his office and closed the door. I sighed with frustration.

"I so want to choke him," I said.

"Yup, he's annoying," Gina said. "And I don't think he'll ever change."

Gina and I stayed in the conference room and continued making our special edit of the video. After the phone call, Sophie came back, and then we all worked on it.

At about one thirty, Elizabeth called. I told her Morningstar was still at the house today and that we'd need to wait until later in the evening to sneak over there. We made plans to meet after dinner at the queen palm in the hotel lobby.

We finished the video by four o'clock. This left me free until I picked up Elizabeth at eight.

I started to think about Reno and his offer to go to his place and wake him up before he had to go to work. The more I thought about it, the better the idea sounded.

I got to his place at about four-twenty. Since I knew he had to be on the road by five-thirty, it would barely give us half an hour before he had to get up and get ready.

Oh well, a quickie is better than nothing.

I used my key and let myself into his place. I walked into his bedroom, quietly calling out his name. I've learned it's not a good idea to startle him awake.

"Jackson," I quietly called out. "Jackson Reno."

Reno stirred and opened an eye. He initially stiffened but relaxed when he saw who it was. He relaxed further when I crawled into bed with him.

"You do know my alarm's about to go off," he said.

"So, shut up and make me happy, quickly."

Five minutes after eight, I was in the Hyatt lobby waiting for Elizabeth. Although being with Reno had been wonderful, it wasn't the same as being with him for the entire night.

Before he left for work, we'd reconfirmed our date for Saturday night. Reno made me promise I'd be there, even if a giant meteorite destroyed all of downtown Scottsdale.

Elizabeth showed up at about ten after eight. She seemed to be in a great mood.

"Hey," I said. "Looks like you've had a good day."

"Well, you told me to keep myself busy until eight, so that's what I did. I'm really starting to love Arizona. Let's go get the jewelry."

Before we left, we grabbed a couple of chairs in a corner of the lobby, and I called Morningstar. When he answered, he sounded tired and discouraged.

"Yes, Miss Black. I hope you've made more progress

today than we have."

"Not really. We checked out four of the properties, and there isn't a thing but open desert at any of them. We looked for anything that could be a clue or indicate where one was buried. So far, we have nothing. Elizabeth and I are back at her hotel. I think we're going to call it a night."

As I said that, I saw Elizabeth cock her head to the side, and one of her eyebrows went up.

"We've also finished for the day," Morningstar said. "So far, we've found nothing. Magic has dug up a good portion of the pool, and there are several new holes in the walls of the manor, but there is no treasure."

"We'll check out the remaining property tomorrow morning," I said. "I'm not sure where to go after that. Maybe up to South Mountain again."

"Yes, well, call me immediately if you find anything of note."

I said I would, then hung up.

"We're done for the night?" Elizabeth asked.

"Not by a longshot. But I'm going to tell the crooks as little as possible. They don't know about Penelope or the statue of the discus thrower. I'd like to keep it that way as long as possible."

We drove to the house on Camelback. When we got to the driveway of the courtyard, we didn't see any other cars, and the house seemed dark.

We went in through the front door and looked around to see what progress Lester, Magic, and Morningstar had made.

The first place we went was the pool.

The concrete decking towards the back wall had mostly been removed, and holes had been dug in several places. The marble pedestal lay off to one side, and the bust of Elizabeth's granddad bust was nowhere to be seen.

We went back into the house, and everywhere we looked, there was a mess. As Morningstar had said, we saw holes in the walls and the floor.

"Wow," Elizabeth said. "They've really torn the place up."

"Come on," I said. "Let's go to the library."

We walked into the library expecting to see the same level of destruction as in the rest of the house. But when we walked in, the mess was minimal. One of the bookshelves on the upper level, next to the terrace windows, had all the books removed and the shelves pulled down, but that was it.

We walked over and looked at the statue of the Greek throwing a discus. The statue was maybe two feet high and was sitting on top of a marble pedestal. There was a small brass plaque screwed into the base of the statue. It read *Discobolus of Myron.*

The statue and pedestal were in a small recess between the bookshelves. It was the middle of three alcoves against the back wall, the same wall that was built directly against Camelback Mountain. Each alcove was about five feet across and lined with heavy wooden paneling.

"I've looked at this statue a dozen times," Elizabeth said. "But I didn't see what it could do with the treasure."

"Same with me," I said. "Well, let's look at it again."

The statue was of a guy in the classical pose for throwing a discus. He was bent over at the waist and had his left hand on his right knee. His right arm was high over his head, and he was clutching a discus tightly.

After looking at the statue for a minute, we grabbed it and tried to lift it off. We quickly found it was bolted to the pedestal, which in turn seemed to be bolted to the floor.

"Well?" Elizabeth asked.

"We can't move it. I don't see a seam where the arm meets the body," I said. "But let's try the obvious anyway."

I grabbed the arm holding the discus and pulled.

Nothing happened for a second, but then the arm slowly moved forward about three inches. We heard a loud metallic click and the whir of motors starting up from behind the wall and under the floor.

The wooden panel in the alcove behind the statue slid up into the bookshelves on the upper level. At the same time, the statue and the pedestal slowly sank. When it had completely disappeared below the floor, a small wooden panel slid shut to cover the opening.

Where the rear paneling had been, there was now a white marble face with a large stainless-steel vault door. The door didn't have a combination dial, only a steel handle.

There were also two small glass screens in the middle of the door, each about one by two inches. Above each screen were green and red lights.

The red lights above each of the glass panels were lit. Below the left screen was the word *Elizabeth*. Below the right screen was the word *Lester*.

"Well, damn," Elizabeth said. "I take back what I said about Penelope giving us a crappy clue. I think we're about to get the jewelry."

Elizabeth went to the vault door and pulled on the handle. Nothing happened.

"I think the door is controlled by the glass panels," I said. "They look like touchscreens."

"How do they work?"

"I'm not sure, but they remind me of the thumb scanner on my phone. Give it a try."

Elizabeth put her thumb on the glass panel above her name. The panel lit up for about three seconds, then the red light turned off, and the green one turned on. There was a loud metallic click from inside the vault door.

"Okay," she said. "Let's see if that did it."

She pulled on the handle, but again nothing happened.

"Okay," she said. "What am I doing wrong?"

"I was afraid that would happen," I said. "Do you remember what the clue from the pool said? It would take both you and Lester to get the treasure. There are two locks on this door. I think both you and your brother need to be here at the same time to open the vault."

"Well, that sucks. How are we going to get Les away from the crooks long enough to get the jewelry?"

"I don't know, but we'll find a way."

We tried the door a couple more times, but it soon became obvious that Les also needed to be there to get the vault open. After about twenty minutes of trying, there was nothing else to do.

There was a red button next to the vault door that was labeled *Reset*. I told Elizabeth to stand back, and I pushed it.

Motors whirred from the wall and under the floor. The wooden paneling slid down, and the statue slowly rose back into place. When everything was back where it should be, the motors shut off, and there was a loud click.

I went to the statue and looked at the arm. A seam was now visible where it connected with the body.

There also seemed to be some sort of metallic clay that had been disturbed when I'd moved the arm. I smoothed out the clay with my finger, and the seam again disappeared.

"Well," I said, "at least we know there's no way they can get into the vault without you, even if they do happen to find it. Let me get you back to your hotel, and I'll figure out how to work this out."

I dropped Elizabeth off and told her I'd call her in the morning. Then, I started driving randomly around the city.

I've done this before when I needed to solve a problem. Sometimes, it works, and sometimes, it doesn't. As I drove, I went over the facts in my head.

Lester was deeply involved with some Chicago gangsters. He wanted out, but it was going to take a lot of money.

Elizabeth didn't need the money as much, but she seemed like a nice person, and I wanted to help them both. On the positive side, I now knew where the jewelry was and how to get to it.

My first problem was Morningstar and Magic. They weren't going to let Les hunt around for the treasure on his own. I knew if they were there, they would simply take the jewelry and leave.

My second problem was the dead guy we'd found in the vault. It was looking like Les was involved, and he perhaps even committed the murder himself. The police were building a case against him, and it was possible that after they interviewed him, they'd arrest him.

My last problem was with the FBI. They wanted Les to testify against his fellow criminals. I knew they weren't simply going to let him go.

As I thought about the FBI, I started to get the seed of an idea. Both the Chicago hoods and the FBI were causing me problems. Could I use one group against the other?

I drove around Scottsdale for another half an hour and sorted out my thoughts. I then called Special Agent McCoy.

I woke up Tuesday to the alarm clock chirping away. I looked over and remembered I'd set it for seven-thirty.

I sat up but felt groggy. I walked to the kitchen to make coffee and then to the shower, still feeling fuzzyheaded. I hadn't gotten much sleep the night before, and I knew I was going to have a busy day.

I called Morningstar on the way to the office. Since he already knew about the coffin rock, South Mountain was about the only place I knew he wouldn't be this morning.

When he answered, he sounded a bit surly. "Yes, Miss Black, what do you want?"

"I'm only checking in. I'll be looking up at South Mountain today."

"South Mountain? What's to be gained at South Mountain?"

"The last clue said South Mountain is where we could find the coffin rock, which would lead us to the treasure. Since you aren't having any luck at the house, I thought I'd try South Mountain one last time. If I can find the clue up there, it might keep you from digging random holes at the house."

"Very well, keep me informed."

I told him that I would, then I hung up.

I then texted Les and asked him to call me when he was alone.

The conference between Lenny, George Anson, and George's council had been going on for about half an hour when Lenny called me into the conference room. Once there, Lenny introduced me as the investigator who'd placed the cameras at the request of our client, Debbie Anson.

I then went on to explain at length when I had placed them, where they were located within the various rooms, and how the videos were reviewed for evidence. Lenny then went over the procedures for deleting any files that were not relevant to the investigation.

All in all, it went on like this for another half an hour. To me, it was all very dry and routine. For the attorneys, it meant racking up billable hours. For George, it meant his costs were rapidly going up.

After several more minutes of going over the procedural aspects of the videos, Lenny got to the meat of the matter.

"No one has seen these videos except for my investigators and myself," he said. "To this point, I've hesitated showing them to my client, even though, considering the circumstances, she has a perfect right to see them.:

"Now, to be completely honest," Lenny said with a straight face, "I would hate to have to introduce these videos into evidence. Once I do that, they'll become a public record. Anyone will be able to go to the courthouse and request a copy. There'd be nothing to stop these videos from, say, being posted anonymously to the internet. It's my sincere hope that you and Mrs. Anson can work out a settlement."

Lenny and opposing council then asked for a few minutes alone so they could negotiate the details of the settlement. As George Anson came out into reception, Sophie asked if he would follow her into the back break room.

He seemed somewhat confused that Sophie wanted him to go somewhere, but he followed willingly enough. When Sophie smiles at a guy, they usually do what she asks. Gina and I trailed behind as we all went into the back offices.

On the table in the break room, I'd set up a laptop computer. When we all had sat down, I started talking.

"We know you're about to get divorced. And we know Lenny and your lawyer are currently arguing about how much you are going to pay Debbie a month in support. But what we care about is that you've been having an affair with Debbie's sister, Connie. We like Debbie, even if you don't. Yes, we want you to give your wife an overly generous spousal support, but we also want you to cut off the affair immediately. Never talk to Connie again, never see her again, never text her, and never email her."

"And why would I want to stop seeing her?" George snorted, anger rising in his voice. "After I'm divorced, I can do whatever I want with whomever I want. You know, I don't take too kindly to people who try to tell me my business. Especially not three little girls."

George stood up and was about to walk back to the front offices when Gina spoke.

"Yes, but in your line of work, people often decide to shop with you or not based on your reputation. People already have a low opinion of auto dealers. You know this better than anyone does."

"Yeah," Sophie said. "Isn't that why you've been calling yourself 'Honest George Anson' in your commercials for all these years? Isn't that why you always make sure to show the anchor tattoo on your arm? To show how honest and trustworthy you are?"

"What of it," he snapped. "My reputation is solid, and I'll sue the ass off anyone who tries to fuck with it."

"If you don't end your affair with Connie immediately," Gina said, "we have a video ready to go to the internet. Before we release it, we'll come up with an excuse to have Lenny introduce all the videos we recorded into evidence at a hearing. Then, they'll be public records. I imagine we won't be the only ones who request a copy."

"Yeah," Sophie said. "So much for suing our asses off. We call our video, *The Man Behind the Anchor, The Truth Revealed.*"

George sat back down, but I could see he was still angry and not in the mood to listen to what we were saying. I hit the play button, and the video started.

It showed George lying naked on a bed with a woman on top riding him Cowgirl. We'd chosen angles that clearly showed not only George's face but also the anchor tattoo on his arm.

We'd been careful not to include Connie's face or anything that could be used to identify who she was. We wanted to make sure George was the center of attention.

I looked over and could see George had gone from angry to slightly concerned. He was shifting in his chair, and his eyes were getting a slightly unfocused look, as if he was thinking rapidly.

He knew that anyone who'd grown up in Arizona would recognize him by the tattoo. He was starting to get the idea that we were serious and that his reputation could be in some amount of jeopardy.

"Since, by law," Gina said, "we weren't allowed to record sound in the video, we supplied our own soundtrack."

I reached over to the computer and hit the sound button. As the volume came up, we heard a cheesy music soundtrack that gave the video the feel of a cheap porno movie.

We also heard a woman's voice, a woman who sounded suspiciously like Sophie, telling George over and over: "Come on honey, you can do it, at least try."

As the video went on, I again looked at George. His forehead had started to sweat, and he looked more than a little nervous. I could also see that he was still thinking about how to handle this situation.

After almost a minute of watching the video, George decided to challenge us. "That's enough. Turn it off. This is disgusting. I won't put up with your blackmail attempts." His voice was probably supposed to be loud and angry, but it instead came out as little more than a high wobbly squeak.

"But we can't turn it off now," Sophie said with a devious smile. "My favorite part's coming up."

After another few seconds, the woman told George, "That's it. I give up. You're pathetic. You'll never satisfy a woman."

The woman in the video rolled off to reveal George in all his glory. Unfortunately, the video clearly showed that, even excited, George was not much bigger than Sophie's index finger.

The picture on the screen froze at the moment when George's undersized manhood was the most clearly visible.

The music then switched from sleazy porn music to the screeching violin sounds of the shower scene from the old Alfred Hitchcock movie, *Psycho*.

"Oh, jeez," George said weakly. His face had flushed red with shame and embarrassment.

The three of us tried our best to remain serious, but then Sophie started to giggle. She tried to hold it in, but that only made it worse.

She clamped her hand over her mouth, but the giggles came out even harder, and she started to shake with laughter. Now that Sophie had lost control, I couldn't help it.

I started laughing, and I couldn't stop. I laughed so hard I couldn't breathe, and tears started rolling down my face.

Even Gina gave a small chuckle as she smiled and shook her head. George started to shake with emotion and then hid his face in his hands.

"Dude," Sophie said between giggles. "It looks like you never went through puberty. What's up with that? Were you in some sort of industrial accident? Maybe something happened to you on a farm? Were you kicked by a horse or something?"

George was quiet for almost thirty seconds before he lifted his head. When he finally spoke, it was barely above a whisper.

"The doctors found out about my hormone imbalance when I graduated from high school, and I still hadn't shown any signs of developing. I've been on hormone replacement therapy for years, but they weren't ever able to fix – that." He then pointed to the picture of his tiny member on the computer screen and hung his head down again.

He then let out a deep sigh of defeat. "Alright, you win. What do you want me to do?"

An hour later, George Anson left the conference room with his sulking attorney. They both quickly left the office through the front door. A minute later, Lenny came striding out of the conference room, beaming with happiness.

"It went well?" Gina asked.

"It went like I expected it would," Lenny said, a little boastful. "I told George that not only was he going to give his wife the standard formula spousal support, but I said he needed to add an additional thirty percent for having an affair in the same bed his wife slept in."

"It sounds like you really put the screws to him," Sophie said.

"Yeah," Lenny said. "He really didn't stand a chance. It turns out I didn't even need to show them the videos of the affair. George admitted it and said he didn't need to see the evidence. I pressed him on the support, and he caved. Opposing council still wanted to play hardball, but George said he only wanted it to be settled. He even agreed to pay my fee. He gave me everything I wanted and then some."

"Congratulations," Gina said. "Debbie's lucky to have you as her attorney."

Sophie snorted a short laugh. She then turned red and clamped her hand over her mouth. Her eyes were wide with embarrassment. Gina looked at her with a disappointed expression and shook her head.

"You know," Lenny said, "I don't care why you're laughing or what you're up to this time. Everyone did good work, and the client will be delighted. We've accumulated some good billings on this. I'd be happy if every case went as smoothly as this one."

Lenny walked back into his office, and ten seconds later, my phone rang. I saw it was Lester Murdock.

"Hey," he said when I answered. "I have a few minutes to myself. How's Elizabeth doing? She must really be freaked out by all of this."

"She's doing okay. She's a lot stronger than you think. Listen, I'm going to try and get Morningstar and Magic out of the house soon, like within an hour or so. I'll need you to stay there."

"How should I do that?" he asked.

"Let Morningstar know you're starting to feel sick. Tell them you need to throw up or something. Maybe you could even ask to lie down and sleep. That way you can stay at the house when they leave. I need you to really sell it so they don't get suspicious."

"Okay," he said. "I can do that."

I hung up with Les and made another two phone calls. I then went up front to find Gina. I really needed her final advice on what I was about to do.

"It still sounds risky," she said after I told her the last of the details. "But it also sounds like it's gone too far to stop. My only advice for you is to stay strong. You have two other people counting on you to get them out of this in one piece."

Chapter Fourteen

I got into my car and drove to the Hyatt to get Elizabeth. When I went up to the lobby, I found her standing next to her palm tree.

"Well," she said. "If nothing else, I've learned what a queen palm is."

We walked down to my car in the parking lot and then drove to the base of Camelback Mountain. I parked in a deserted area that would have the right background noises. I waited until exactly noon, then called Horace Morningstar.

"I'm at South Mountain," I said, excitement in my voice. "I think I found something. I need to show you what I'm seeing. There is a coffin shape on the side of Camelback Mountain next to the house. How soon can you get here?"

Morningstar had been claiming ignorance about finding the coffin rock for three days. I knew he'd have to either come up to Dobbins Lookout or admit he'd known about it the entire time and had been lying to me.

"Well," he said with a hollow laugh. "That is good news. Perhaps you should come to the house and tell me about it. I'll want to know all the details."

"It isn't anything I can describe. You'll need to see it. Besides, we've been looking for the damn thing for a week. I'd think you'd want to see it for yourself. You still aren't getting anywhere at the house, are you?"

He then paused for several seconds. I could tell he was rapidly thinking.

"Very well," he said at last. "We'll be there in half an hour. But I hope you really have found the coffin rock. I've been to the top of that dusty pile of rocks so many times that it sickens my soul."

Morningstar hung up. I then drove my car to a place where I could see his car as it drove down Camelback Mountain.

My first fear was that Morningstar would insist that Les go with them. That would ruin everything.

My second fear was that Magic would stay at the house to watch over things while Morningstar was gone. That would be almost as bad.

Five minutes later, I breathed a sigh of relief as I saw the gangster's car drive down the mountain. Magic was at the wheel, and Morningstar was beside him. No one was in the back seat.

I took in a deep breath and sent two text messages.

"Okay," I said. "Let's go do this."

We drove up the hill, and I parked my car on the side of the road, about a hundred yards further up Camelback from the mansion.

The road curved on this part of the mountain so that no one could see it from the house. I didn't think Morningstar would be looking for it in any case.

Elizabeth and I hurried down the road and then into the house. Les was waiting for us inside the front entrance.

"I got your text. What's going on?" he asked. "I'm not sure where Morningstar went or how long he'll be gone."

"I needed to get him out of the way for a little bit so we could get the jewelry," I said. "Come on. It's in the library."

As the three of us hurried through the house, I explained to Les what we'd found. Les opened the big wooden library doors, and Elizabeth and I rushed in behind him.

We walked to the middle of the three alcoves on the wall against Camelback Mountain and looked at the discus statue on its marble pedestal. It looked as if it hadn't been disturbed from the night before. I took a step back and swept out my arm.

"Elizabeth, would you do the honors? Quickly, we don't know how long we have."

Elizabeth pulled on the statue's arm. It again moved slowly forward until there was a click and then the whirring sound of motors.

The wooden panel in the rear of the alcove again slid upward, and the sculpture and pedestal slowly sank under the floor. Les walked over and looked at the touch panels.

"I see what you mean," he said. "These appear to be scanners. From the size and placement on the vault door, I would assume they're thumbprint readers. You said you tried them, and nothing happened?"

"When I put my thumb on my side," Elizabeth said, "the red light above my scanner went off, and the green one came on. The red light over yours didn't change."

"It makes sense we'd need to do it at the same time if Granddad wanted us to work together on this," Les said. "Maybe he was trying to get us back together after all. I wonder how he got our thumbprints. It's been a while since I've been here, but I don't remember Granddad doing anything obvious to get it."

"He could have given you a clean glass and then lifted the

print off that," I said. "He probably did it with both of you."

"Granddad went through a lot of trouble to make sure we'd need to work together to get the jewelry," Elizabeth said. "You're right. I think he was trying to help."

"Okay," I said. "Hurry up. Both of you put your thumbs on the readers at the same time, and let's see what happens."

Elizabeth walked over and put her thumb on the glass panel. As had happened the night before, the red light above her scanner switched to green.

Les then put his thumb on his reader, and his red light also turned green. We waited several seconds, but nothing happened. We all looked at each other.

"This is so lame," Les said, now angry. "What's next, another clue that'll lead to yet another dead end?"

"Something should happen," Elizabeth said, a touch of panic in her voice. "Last night, there was a click."

From inside the door, we heard two loud metallic snaps, one after the other. Neither Les nor Elizabeth moved.

They were both mesmerized, staring at the door. I reached out and pulled on the vault's handle.

With the sound of several metallic pops and creaks, it swung open. What lay beyond was a brightly lit passageway seven feet high and six feet wide, with a brilliant white marble floor and walls.

Les went first, Elizabeth went next, and I followed behind. The passageway was about twenty feet long and gently curved to the right.

From the house's location, I knew it was going deep into the solid rock of Camelback Mountain. The passageway ended in a room about the size of my living room at home.

The floor and walls were the same smooth white marble.

There were only two objects in the room.

The first was a small polished dark wood table. Sitting on the table, and made of the same dark wood, was a large and ornate chest.

"Granddad's treasure chest!" Elizabeth squealed out. "I'd forgotten how beautiful it is."

"Well," Les said. "I honestly never thought we'd see this again."

We formed a circle around the box, our fingers lightly touching the wood. It was beautifully made.

The chest's surfaces were intricately carved with a delicate flower, leaf, and vine pattern. The flowers had hundreds of tiny mother-of-pearl inlays, and the vines appeared to be made of solid silver.

I could see it'd taken a master woodworker months, if not years, to make it. The chest was something you'd expect to see in a museum, not in somebody's house.

We saw there was a card lying on top of the box. It appeared to be the same neat cursive writing as the previous notes. Elizabeth picked up the card and read:

I congratulate both of my grandchildren on finding my treasure. When you wear these pieces of art and history, think of me. If you will allow me to give you both some words of advice from beyond the grave – I lost years of time when I could've been friends with your father. I don't want that happening between the two of you. I hope that through the process of going through my little treasure hunt, you two have begun to grow close once again. I urge you both to find ways to overcome your differences and to remember you two are all that is left of our family.

May you both have lives filled with peace and happiness.

I love you both dearly, Granddad.

I looked over and saw that a tear was running down Elizabeth's cheek. Lester walked over to his sister and gave her a long hug.

"Well," I said. "Let's open it up and see what's inside."

We heard movement behind us, and we turned to see Morningstar standing in the passageway. Magic was next to him, and both of them were holding pistols.

"Did you seriously think I was fooled by your feeble attempts to deceive me?" Morningstar asked with a chuckle. "As I correctly deduced, you had discovered the location of the chest and were merely trying to lure me out of the house so you could swoop in and remove it. Well, this makes things simple, for everyone."

Morningstar glanced around the room. I saw the look of greed on his face as his eyes focused on the chest.

He wanted to open the box and hold the pieces of jewelry as much as we did. I also saw him looking at the cramped space of the vault.

"Come out into the library," he said. "I'm not going to go into such a tight space. It would be too tempting for one of you to grab my gun. Come out now, or I'll have Magic shoot you where you stand."

Magic walked around behind us, motioning that we should follow Morningstar out.

We walked down the passageway, stepped back out into the library, and gathered in front of the alcove. Magic took several steps to one side. His pistol was still pointed in our direction. He then let out a loud and excited giggle.

I looked over and saw Morningstar had a strange, twisted look on his face. I was about to ask him about it when he turned and casually shot Magic twice in the chest. In the enclosed space of the library, the sounds of the twin gunshots were deafening.

Magic's eyes opened wide with surprise. He then fell in slow motion to his knees. His gun slipped from his fingers and clattered to the floor. As he fell, I saw him trying to speak, but no words came out.

Elizabeth screamed, and Les stiffened. After the initial shock settled in for about three heartbeats, I got really angry.

"Why did you do that?" I shouted to Morningstar. "He didn't do anything to you."

"In the room behind you is upwards of thirty million dollars of historic and extraordinary jewelry," Morningstar said. "I didn't trust Magic to keep his head. It might have been too big of a temptation for him to resist. There's nothing worse than a maniac with a gun. I'll be frank with you, Miss Black. I have the jewels, and soon, you three will also die. I'm not the kind of man who shares, nor am I the kind of man who leaves loose ends."

It was as if a light went on in my head.

"Les didn't kill Frankie Two Guns in the vault Tuesday night. You did."

"Clever girl," Morningstar said. "Yes, that's true. After I saw you, Lester, and Elizabeth leave the house on Tuesday afternoon, Frankie and I broke in. We waited in a room down the hall from the master bedroom. Lester had previously told me about the vault, and it wasn't hard to find the right bedroom. I assumed Lester already had the combination and was merely waiting to open the vault when his sister was not present. I knew he'd be back as soon as possible to take possession of the treasure. We were simply going to wait down the hall and pick up the jewels after he got them."

Morningstar looked over at Les.

"I was a little surprised when you showed up again, and you didn't have your shadow with you," he motioned with the pistol, clearly indicating that he was talking about me.

"I couldn't wait," Les said quietly. "The vault was supposed to be empty, but I didn't want to take the chance that the jewelry was in there. Elizabeth could have come back and found everything first. It was something of a race, you see."

"So, Frankie and I waited," Morningstar continued. "Sure enough, about an hour later, Lester shows up and opens the vault. We simply followed him in. Along the way, I grabbed the little statue off the table. After all, if the jewels were in there, I didn't actually *need* Lester anymore."

"Well?" I asked. "What happened?"

"Unfortunately, when Frankie found out he had waited for an hour and it had been for nothing more than a wild goose chase, he rather lost his self-control. Frankie began to shout and wave his gun in Lester's face. I was afraid things would start to get out of hand, and I didn't want Lester dead. At least, not before he found the jewelry. I used that little statue to put an end to Frankie and his shouting. But, truth be known, he was a vicious man, and the world is a better place without him."

"How could you kill your own man?" I asked.

"I already had Magic to help me find the chest. I didn't need two men to do that. Plus, to be completely honest, I think Frankie Two Guns was mainly down here as a spy to keep an eye on me. I don't think my boss fully trusted me with thirty million dollars worth of jewelry."

Morningstar gave a small chuckle. "Well, since I'm about to kill the three of you and disappear with the jewels, maybe he had a point."

"But why the deception about who killed Frankie?" I asked. "That doesn't make sense."

Morningstar gave me a look that showed he was disappointed I hadn't worked out his plan.

"Really? I thought that was the best part," he said, now looking at Les. "I know you saw me wiping down the statue. You might have thought I was wiping away the blood. But I was only wiping away my fingerprints. That's why I had you put the statue under Frankie. I knew the police would find your prints on the murder weapon, and they'd finger you for the crime. Since I was ultimately going to kill you and leave with the jewels, I thought it would be best if the police thought you were simply a mob killer who was avenged by one of Frankie's associates. That would make it simple for them, and they wouldn't put a lot of effort into finding the killer."

"You implicated Les just to fool the police?" I asked.

"Not only the police. I also needed to convince my boss that Lester was the one who killed his boy, Frankie Two Guns. Otherwise, he could've made it rough on me. I was covering my tracks. I'm not the kind of man who leaves things like that to chance."

"What about Magic?" I asked. "How will you explain him?"

"Lester grabbed my gun and shot poor Magic. Luckily, I was able to get my gun back before I executed him."

"Look, you didn't need the deception," Les said. "I know how to keep my mouth shut."

"Yes, maybe you do," Morningstar said. "But, in the end, I decided that you needed to be the fall guy for Frankie. I made sure you took your cab back to your hotel so there'd be a record of you being at the murder scene at the time of death.

I was careful not to leave any traces, so even if you told the police what actually happened, they'd never believe you."

"But that's nuts," I said. "There's like thirty million dollars in jewelry sitting in there." I pointed to the stone passageway where the jewelry chest lay. "Go get a pillowcase, grab five or ten million dollars worth of jewelry, and take off. We won't even tell the police you have it. It's only money. Take what you want and go."

"I'm sorry," Morningstar said. "But I'm getting rather tired of listening to you talk. Do you know how annoying you are? I can see why you're still single. Move back against the bookcase, all of you."

The three of us slowly backed up against a stack of books until there was nowhere left to go. I glanced around for something I could use to defend myself.

I could pick up a book and throw it at him, but all that would do is get me shot sooner. I looked around for something to use as a shield, but again, there was nothing.

Being a trained killer, Morningstar had taken a position fifteen feet from us. There was no way any of us could try for the gun without being shot.

Morningstar raised his gun, pointed it at Lester's head, and smiled. "Well, Lester, who's the stupid fat man now?" I could tell that Morningstar was savoring the moment. I knew he was thinking of all the things Les had ever done to upset him.

Les didn't try to run. I saw he also looked around for something to defend himself with and had come to the same conclusion as I had. I could also see he was mentally preparing himself for what was about to happen.

I became overwhelmed with a sudden and deep sense of frustration and failure. Elizabeth and Lester had entrusted their safety to me, and now they were about to be murdered.

I glanced at Elizabeth. She was staring at Morningstar in naked terror. Her body was visibly trembling.

I reached my hand over to hers. When they touched, Elizabeth grabbed onto it with a tight death grip.

Hurry up, hurry up.

"Don't worry, Lester," Morningstar said as the smile broadened. "I'll make it quick. One to the head should do it. I'll tell you what. Stand still, and I'll make it a clean shot. You won't even suffer, too much."

I closed my eyes, held my breath, and waited for the explosion from the gun. I knew Les would take the first bullet. I also knew I would probably take the second, and Elizabeth would take the third.

Anytime now.

"FBI!" came a loud shout from the door to the library. I recognized the voice as Special Agent McCoy. "Morningstar, drop your gun. Do it. Do it now!"

"Drop it, Morningstar!" yelled a second voice I knew was Special Agent Conquest.

Time went into slow motion as I watched Morningstar's eyes. He first looked down at Magic, now lifeless on the library floor.

Morningstar knew he'd be charged with the murder. I then saw a look of thoughtful expression as he realized he'd also confessed to the murder of Frankie Two Guns.

Morningstar's face got the same strange, twisted look I'd noticed just before he killed Magic. He raised his pistol and pointed it at Lester's chest. I then saw his finger start to tighten around the trigger.

Mainly through instinct, I began to run at Morningstar.

My only thought was to knock the gun out of his hand.

I'd made it two steps when he suddenly turned and fired off three quick shots at the FBI agents standing in the doorway. These were quickly answered by two shots fired simultaneously from Agents McCoy and Conquest.

Morningstar staggered. He tried to take a step towards the agents, but his knees buckled. His fingers relaxed, and his gun clattered to the floor. Like a great tree that'd been chopped down with an axe, Horace Morningstar slowly fell, face-first onto the floor.

The room became quiet as the sound of the gunshots rang in our ears. Agents McCoy and Conquest ran into the room.

Agent Conquest went to Morningstar, handcuffed his hands behind his back, and then rolled him over. From what I saw, Morningstar had taken a slug to the upper leg and one to the shoulder. Neither wound looked life-threatening, but there was still plenty of blood.

"Damn it," I yelled as Agent McCoy walked over to us. "You both cut it pretty fricking close. That jerk had already killed Magic and was about to start pulling the trigger on us. Don't you think you could have maybe made it down the hall a little sooner?"

"We needed to get all of Morningstar's confession," McCoy calmly said. "We have the murder of Vannier Magic on video. Once he confessed to the murder of Frankie Cantone, we came in right away."

"What? You knew the FBI was watching the whole thing?" Elizabeth shouted as she turned toward me. Her face was contorted with confusion and anger.

"How could you do something like that? We were almost killed." Les shouted, anger also rising in his voice.

"Don't blame Miss Black," Special Agent McCoy said.

"We spent most of last night installing cameras and microphones in this room, but I instructed her to keep you in the dark. People who know they're being recorded tend to play to the camera. Morningstar would have picked up on that in an instant. As it is, Lester, you're cleared of the murder of Frankie Cantone. Miss Bright-Murdock, both you and your brother have become very wealthy."

Agent Conquest applied first aid to a semi-conscious Morningstar while Agent McCoy called in the shooting and the murder. McCoy then went over to Lester.

"Mr. Murdock," Agent McCoy said. "You'll need to decide what to do about your future. As you know, Morningstar has already informed his superiors that you killed Frankie Cantone. Now, you'll also be viewed by the group as being responsible for the deaths of Vannier Magic and the arrest of Horace Morningstar. They'll come after you. I repeat my offer of immunity and witness protection if you agree to testify against the group. It might even be possible for you to testify as a confidential informant. If that's the case, we'll let it leak out that you were killed today along with Magic. The gang won't even think to look for you or to come after your sister."

Les looked over at Agent McCoy and nodded his head. "I've been thinking about this for a while. Yes, I'll testify. The only thing I ask is that you put me somewhere warm, preferably with a beach and palm trees."

He then looked over at Elizabeth. "I'm sorry," he told her. "It looks like we won't be able to be together again after all. But know that I love you, and I'll always have the best memories of us growing up together."

When he was done talking to Les, I walked over to Agent McCoy.

"I know the police and EMS will be here in a few

minutes to take care of Morningstar and Magic," I said. "But you know all about the treasure and what we've been through to get it. If the police find out about the jewelry, there's a good chance they'll want to impound it. Since this is a murder case with a federal connection, there's no telling when they'll choose to release it. It could be months or even years."

"I understand, Miss Black," Agent McCoy said with a smile. "And you're probably right about them wanting to impound the jewelry. But I'll be fair. You helped us in our investigation. We'll help you with yours."

Special Agent McCoy and Les went into the vault and then came out again, carrying the heavy jewelry chest between them. I led the way out into the hallway and then three doors down the hall to a small storage closet.

The men placed the chest on the floor, and I covered it with a blanket that had been sitting on a shelf. As soon as the police finished their investigation, Elizabeth could come by and pick up the jewelry.

I heard the first patrol car and the ambulance pull into the courtyard. I knew it would only be a matter of a minute or two before EMS came into the library.

I grabbed a book off a shelf, opened the vault door, and wedged the book in, so it wouldn't lock. I then hit the red button. The motors whirred, the statue rose, and the panel slid back into position. We then stepped back, and it looked exactly as it had.

I knew Lester would need to leave with the special agents, and he would want some time alone with his sister before he left. But there were a couple of things I needed to understand before he disappeared forever.

"Why didn't you tell us that Morningstar killed Frankie Two Guns?" I asked. "It put your life in danger with the goons from Chicago, and it almost got you prison time in

Arizona."

"Morningstar said if I didn't take the fall for Frankie, he'd kill Elizabeth. After everything that's happened, I believed him. I knew I'd be in jail for a while, but when I got out, I'd still have half the money. Well, that's assuming Elizabeth would still have wanted to split it with me."

Elizabeth walked over to Les. "Little brother, it was never about the money. I only wanted you to be my friend and not someone you played. As Granddad said, you're the only family I have left."

Lester looked at Elizabeth. "I'm going to miss you, sis. Wherever I end up, I won't be able to contact you directly, but hopefully, we can still write. I don't want to lose contact with you again."

Elizabeth held out her arms and hugged her brother. I couldn't help but see they were both crying.

The rest of Tuesday afternoon and the entire day on Wednesday was a blur of paperwork, answering questions, and swearing out statements. The library was sealed by the police, but Agent McCoy helped us again by getting the master bedroom released as a crime scene.

Lenny was thrilled when we called to tell him the jewelry had been found. With their new fortune, Lester and Elizabeth agreed to pay Lenny his full fee for helping them find the chest.

Although Lenny tried to hide it, I could tell he was disappointed they hadn't charged Les with murder. A rich client with a hopeless case is what Lenny lives for.

On Thursday morning, Sophie, Gina, and I brought over a dolly and helped Elizabeth move the jewelry to the safe in the master bedroom. When the treasure chest was safely in the vault, Elizabeth spent an hour going through all the drawers and explaining to us what she knew about each of the pieces.

When Elizabeth found the eagle necklace that had been painted on Penelope of Prescott, she burst into tears. I put the necklace on her, and she again looked like a princess.

We then had great fun trying everything on. Sophie took a picture of me wearing a crown that once belonged to the Queen of Sweden.

Elizabeth took pictures of Sophie, who had fallen in love with a necklace that once belonged to Raquel Welch. I took a picture of Gina wearing a ring that had belonged to Audrey Hepburn.

Then, to top it off, Elizabeth took a group picture of everyone wearing at least a million dollars worth of jewelry. It was like being in the middle of a fairytale.

On Friday morning, the three of us were back in the office. Danica's wedding was later that afternoon, and it became the main subject of the day, even edging out a treasure chest full of jewelry.

Lenny came by to tell everybody what a good job we'd done. He said I could have Monday and Tuesday off to make up for the days I'd missed over the past two weeks. It wasn't as good as a bonus, but I took what I could get.

Lenny disappeared back into his office and closed the door. Five minutes later, the front door to the street opened. We looked up to see Elizabeth come in. I wasn't surprised to see she was still wearing the eagle and diamond necklace.

"I'm glad everyone's here," she said. "I'm heading to Sky Harbor in a few minutes to catch a plane back to Chicago. I wanted to stop by first and thank you again for everything you three did for my brother and me."

"How's Les doing?" Gina asked.

"They've already started the process of changing his identity and relocating him." She pulled out a folded document from her bag. "Les signed a power of attorney for me to handle his financial affairs while he's away. The lawyer in Chicago is going to file it. The FBI agents gave me an address in Washington, DC, where I can write to him."

"Are you still going to auction off the jewelry?" I asked.

"I've already started talks with both Sotheby's and Christie's about an auction. Once I narrow down which one I'm going to use, the process will take about a year. There'll first be formal appraisals on all the pieces. Then, they'll photograph everything and create a catalog, both an online and a print version. I didn't realize how elaborate the entire process was going to be."

"Are you still selling everything?" Gina asked.

"Well," she said as she patted her necklace, "I'm going to keep a few pieces that remind me of Granddad, but other than that, everything will go. Christie's had one of their local appraisers look at the collection yesterday afternoon after you three left. She confirmed I couldn't sell any of the pieces Granddad collected without documentation, but everything else is good. Nothing's official yet, but she estimated the value of the collection to be put up for auction at between forty and forty-five million dollars."

"Holy crap," Sophie said.

The three of us clapped, yelled, and then congratulated

her. It was wonderful that things had worked out so well.

"What about the house, the bar, and the land?" I asked.

"Well, the land will go. I called the lawyer back in Chicago yesterday about that. He said Granddad was holding onto it until he found the right buyer. The parcels are rather large, and Granddad apparently didn't want to divide them up. But I'll sell them now rather than hold out for years to get top dollar. Once they're turned into cash, I can send most of that to Les. He'll need some money to get set up, wherever he is. I imagine the government is rather stingy on the lifestyle they choose for the people they relocate."

"We might know somebody who would be interested in the real estate," I said. "He's a developer who builds golf resorts. If you'd like, send me the information on the properties. I'll find out if he's interested."

"Thanks, I'd appreciate that. I think I'll keep the saloon on Whiskey Row. I drove up to Prescott after the appraiser left yesterday afternoon. I had a long talk with the woman who manages the bar. She showed me the books, and the place has made a nice profit every year for the last sixteen years. I told her I didn't see any reason why she couldn't keep running the bar as she had been. Granddad never was active in the day-to-day operations, so nothing will really change. Besides, I think it would be fun being able to say I own a real western saloon."

"And the house?" I asked.

"I'm going to keep the house," Elizabeth said with a big smile on her face. "It's beautiful, and it has so many wonderful memories for me. I'd hate to see someone else living in it. When I go back to Chicago, I'll begin the process of settling my affairs there. I'll need to sell the house I have in Northbrook, quit my job, and then I'll move down here."

"You'll be here full-time?" Gina asked.

"Yup," Elizabeth answered. "Give me a few months, and I'll be a full-time Arizona resident."

Sophie squealed and clapped her hands. Gina and I joined Sophie in smiling and clapping. A random thought suddenly ran through my head.

"You didn't happen to call Jeremy, that guy from the club the other night, did you?"

At that, Elizabeth blushed bright pink and got a huge smile. "Um, yes. As a matter of fact, I've already seen him three times this week. He's flying out to Chicago next weekend. It turns out that he grew up in Oak Brook. That's in the suburbs southwest of Chicago. He still has family out there, and we've already talked about me meeting some of them."

"What?" Sophie asked. "You've only been here two weeks, and you already have a potentially serious boyfriend. How does that happen?"

"Congratulations on finding someone," said Gina. "I hope he works out."

"Before I go," Elizabeth said, "I wanted to give each of you something."

She opened her bag and brought out three small, wrapped boxes. She then gave one to each of us.

Gina opened hers first, and the box contained a stunning pair of gold and diamond earrings. Each had a hanging pear-shaped diamond that was at least three carats, surrounded at the top by a cluster of several smaller diamonds.

"Oh my God," Gina said as she put them on. "They're beautiful. Thank you."

Sophie then opened her box. She squealed when she saw it contained a gold rope necklace with a huge diamond and emerald pendant. It was the one she'd tried on the day before and had fallen in love with.

Sophie tried to remove it from the box, but her hands were trembling to the point she couldn't do it. Elizabeth had to take it out of the box and put it around her neck.

"You're giving me Raquel Welch's necklace? I've never had anything this beautiful in my life." Sophie started to cry and laugh at the same time. She looked up at Elizabeth, and tears rolled down her face. "Thank you so much."

When I opened my box, I saw it was a gold ring with a ruby the size of a cough drop as the center stone. Surrounding the center ruby were a dozen smaller diamonds and rubies.

I suddenly realized what the ring was, and I looked up at Elizabeth. "Isn't this the ring in the painting? The same ring that's on Penelope of Prescott?"

"That's right. I know you have that beautiful diamond and ruby bracelet. Penelope's ring will go perfectly with it." She patted her eagle necklace again. "I'll keep the necklace from the painting, and you'll have the ring. Think of me and our adventures together whenever you wear it. I know I will."

As Sophie had done, I started to cry as well. I knew these were good tears. I also knew that in Elizabeth, I had made another real friend, someone I could always count on, no matter what. Elizabeth held out her arms, and we each gave her a long hug.

Over Lenny's grumbling objections, we all took off at noon to get ready for the wedding. Sophie, Gina, and I all got to the church at about the same time, and we went in together as a group. It was great to see both Gina and Sophie in heels and dressed up again.

Gina wore a mid-length yellow pleated dress with a plunging sweetheart neckline. It went great with her long, dark hair, which she had let down. She also had on her new earrings and a pair of heels with golden flowers on the toes.

Sophie looked beautiful in a bright-purple beaded crinkle chiffon cocktail dress with four-inch black heels. She also had on her new emerald necklace. The green and gold in the pendant made a beautiful contrast with the purple dress.

"I love the dress," I said. "It goes great with the necklace."

"It should. I spent the afternoon shopping for an outfit that would go with it. I got the dress and the shoes. I was also going to get a matching bag, but I ran out of time. I had to bring an old black clutch."

Sophie then stepped back and gave me the once over. "Hey, Gina," Sophie said. "Would you look at Laura? She's decked out like one of the Cougars."

I knew exactly what Sophie meant. I noticed the same thing as I had gotten dressed for the wedding.

In addition to Penelope's ring, I wore Jackie's bracelet and my diamond pendant. Although I knew I shouldn't tempt fate by wearing everything at once, I felt a little glamorous.

I can honestly say it was the first time in my adult life I'd felt that emotion. It was a great feeling.

Chapter Fifteen

Everything at the church was beautifully set up, with flowers and lace seemingly everywhere. We hesitated when they asked if we were friends of the bride or the groom since we'd been so deeply involved with both of them. But we eventually went in as friends of the bride and were escorted to our seats.

Looking around, I saw Muffy Sternwood in the front row, surrounded by several of her friends. As I looked at her, I squinted and tried to peel back the years. I saw she must have been quite beautiful as a younger woman.

Tony DiCenzo was also there. I was somewhat surprised at this, even though I knew he and Muffy had a long relationship going back to the days when Tony first moved to Arizona.

I noticed his group had carved out a corner of the church near the back. Sitting next to Tony was Max and seeing him again made my heart flutter. Johnny Scarpazzi and Milo were in the row behind and to either side of Tony.

I looked around and found Gabriella. She was standing off to the side in a position that gave her a wide view of the entire church. She'd ditched the black leather jumper and instead wore a red pantsuit with a cream button-down blouse.

Over her shoulder hung her large black bag. I knew it

contained her Uzi. As usual, I wondered what other weapons of mass destruction were in there.

As I was looking at her, I saw her eyes lock onto mine. Even with our growing understanding as of late, her stare was more than a little disconcerting.

Surprisingly, as she looked at me, her eyes softened, just for a second. I even saw the slightest trace of a smile flash across the corner of her mouth. Then the moment was gone, and she was again the ice warrior guarding over her charges.

The wedding ceremony was both formal and moving. During the exchanging of vows, Danica and Alex cried the entire time, which I always take as a good sign.

The reception was held in the grand ballroom at the Scottsdale Blue Palms, which was no doubt Tony's gift to the bride and groom. I noticed that Tony's bodyguards were not closely surrounding him, unlike at the church, and he had more freedom to circulate throughout the room.

But I also noticed a beefy waiter standing next to each of the ballroom entrances, and I remembered a couple of extra waiters standing in the hallways on the way in.

It made me a little sad to think Tony always had to be in a bubble of security. It only reinforced that his lifestyle was not one I wanted to join voluntarily.

After about half an hour, most of the crowd had gone through the reception line. Everyone was gathering around the bar for drinks and starting to organize for dinner.

In the corner of the ballroom, a DJ was playing pop tunes and dancing along with the music. The songs were lively and, fortunately, not too loud. Every few minutes, the DJ invited people out to dance, but so far, people were in more of a drinking and eating mood.

The three of us found a table halfway between the dance floor and the dessert table. We then circulated through the crowd, talking to old friends and meeting new people.

I talked for several minutes with Muffy Sternwood. She was as bright and lively as ever.

She was excited that construction on the new resort was due to start soon. She beamed with pride when she told me Alex was going to manage the hotel portion of the resort.

I thanked her again for the fifty-year-old bottle of scotch she had sent me a couple of months earlier. I told her everyone in the office was waiting for a special occasion to open it up.

I then walked over to where Tony DiCenzo stood. A knot of several people had surrounded him, and he had the start of a small reception line of his own.

It reminded me of a scene from *The Godfather*, with everyone gathering around to pay the Don their respects. But honestly, I suppose that was what I was doing there as well.

When it was my turn, Tony shook my hand and greeted me warmly.

"Laura Black, it's good to see you again," he said in his raspy Brooklyn accent. "I hear you've been keeping yourself busy with the affairs of Lenny's law office. I also hear from Max that you've offered to help him with a couple of issues he's been trying to resolve."

I noticed he paused for a moment while he studied the diamond hanging from the gold chain around my neck. When he looked up at me, I could see he now had a slight smile.

"I'm sorry our paths haven't crossed in the past couple of months," he continued, "for I do enjoy your company. As you can imagine, business has been rather busy as of late. Please stop by Junior Baker's Blues Club sometime soon as my guest. Or, if you'd prefer, I'd be glad to have you join me for a few holes of golf. As I told you the last time we played, your fundamentals are sound. In time, I believe you could become a very good golfer. Either way, feel free to set up a convenient time with Max."

I glanced over and saw Max was looking right at me. Up to this point, I'd avoided making eye contact with him. As soon as I saw him looking at me, an electric tingle traveled through my body, and I felt my heart start to pound.

How can he do that to me?

"Thank you, Tony. I'll take you up on that."

"That's wonderful. I look forward to seeing you again when we have a better chance to talk."

We shook hands one more time. I then stepped aside to let the next person in line pay their respects.

I quickly walked back to the table. Gina and Sophie were both seated and watched me return from the crowd gathered around Tony.

"Well?" Sophie asked.

"Well, what?"

"Did you go over there to talk to Tough Tony or just to get a better sniff at Max?"

"Don't deny it," Gina said with a smile. "We both saw the look that passed between you two."

"I don't know what you think you saw," I said. "You've both had too much champagne. I already have a boyfriend, and Max is only a happy memory."

Gina looked at Sophie.

"Denial?" Gina asked.

"Yup," Sophie said. "Total denial."

After dinner, Gina, Sophie, and I sat at our table, sipping champagne and chatting.

"I could use a piece of cake soon," I said. "I hope they don't make us wait too long."

"I love wedding cake," Sophie said. "Something about eating cake at a wedding makes it taste better than normal cake. Wedding cake is right up there with birthday cake."

"Well, make sure to get a piece early," Gina said. "I looked at the cake earlier, and it looks like someone in the back must have dropped the top layer. It looks a little mashed, and I think there were fingerprints on it."

"Yuck," I said.

Sophie held up her glass of champagne. "Get your wedding cake early. That could be my new motto."

Danica stopped by to chat, still in her wedding gown. She was beaming and couldn't stop smiling. As she was talking with us, she paused, and then suddenly burst into tears.

"I'm so glad you could make it," she said between sniffles. "I don't mean to cry, but I owe you all so much, and I've never really gotten a chance to thank you. You saved Alex's life, and you saved my life too."

She then paused and took a breath. I got the feeling she'd been waiting to get us alone so she could talk about what had happened. I also got the feeling that talking about it was going to help clear her memory of that shitty day that happened almost six months earlier.

"You have no idea how frightened I was when I was handcuffed to the bed in that old factory," Danica said. "I knew when those men came back, they'd kill me. Well, eventually, they'd kill me. The one guy made it pretty clear what he was going to do to me first. When I heard the noise of someone coming back into the room, I promised myself I wouldn't cry, no matter what they did to me."

Gina reached over and took her hand. Danica looked up at her.

"When I saw you'd come to rescue me, I suddenly felt better and more alive than I ever had before. I told myself I'd start to appreciate how wonderful my life is. Things have been better ever since the day you found me. I owe you so much for that."

At the memory of the bed, the handcuffs, and the torture chamber that was the abandoned print shop, I was also on the verge of tears. Danica then looked over at Sophie and me.

"Thank you both again for rescuing Alex. He doesn't talk about it very often, but I know he sometimes still has nightmares about what they did to him. If you two hadn't worked so hard to free him, I know he would've been killed."

Danica looked at Sophie and reached out her other hand. Sophie took Danica's hand and squeezed it.

"Alex talks about how you stayed with him when he was set free," Danica said to Sophie. "He was so scared and in so much pain that it really helped to have someone with him when he got to the hospital. He says you were very kind to him. You told him over and over that everything would be okay. He says you helped him more than anything the doctors did."

Sophie sniffed back a tear, and we all spent several seconds lost in our memories of that horrible day six months before. We then looked up at each other, everyone trying to hold back their emotions.

There was a pause of about three beats, and then Danica started laughing. Within seconds, everyone was laughing.

We laughed so hard the tears started, but this time from being happy and from feeling loved. Yes, that day had been terrible, but in Danica, we'd made a true friend. Plus, we'd been able to help two people who really needed it. It somehow all seemed worth it.

After dinner, a band set up and started playing romantic dance music. Danica and Alex had their first dance as man and wife. For the third song, the one where the parents traditionally dance together, I saw Tony ask Muffy Sternwood to the dance floor.

After the formal dances were over and the photographer faded back into the crowd, the band began playing the typical wedding mix of oldies and modern dance tunes. The bar was doing a steady business, and everyone at our table was now working on their fourth or fifth glass of champagne.

The ballroom was in near darkness. The only light in the room came from the candles on each of the tables and the swirling lights of the giant mirror ball hanging above the center of the dance floor.

Milo came over to our table and sheepishly asked Sophie if she wanted to dance. Sophie glanced up and gave him a dirty look.

Milo's face fell, and he stood there, looking like a big, sad puppy. Sophie glanced back up at him and saw the look on Milo's face.

She sighed and slowly shook her head. Without looking

at him, she slowly lifted her hand. Milo eagerly took it and led her to the dance floor.

By the end of the first song, I noticed Sophie had her arms tightly wrapped around him. Her face was pressed against his chest, and her eyes were tightly closed.

Even in the dim light of the ballroom, I could see the soft pink glow on her face, the glow she always gets when she mixes alcohol and men. Milo had a huge smile that showed off his gold tooth. From the smile, I'm pretty sure Milo also knew what that pink glow meant.

As I watched Sophie dance with Milo, I heard Gina clearing her throat. I looked around and saw Max standing next to me. My heart did a quick flip-flop, and for a moment, I couldn't speak.

"Laura, would you like to dance?" Max asked with his usual deep and confident voice.

Damn.

"Um, are you sure that's a good idea?"

"It's a wedding. Dancing is required by at least some of the people."

"Jerk, that's not what I meant."

"I know, but dance with me anyway."

I'm so going to regret this.

I stood up, and Max led me to the dance floor. We ended up in the back corner, away from Sophie and Milo. Unfortunately, we were also away from most of the light from the candles on the tables.

A slow romantic song was playing, and we started dancing. I deliberately kept my distance with my arms outstretched and my hands only lightly holding Max.

I did my best to stay calm. It's okay, I thought. I was committed to Reno, and I knew I could be mature enough to dance with Max. Besides, I again thought, nothing bad can happen if you aren't dancing too close to the man.

Even if he does smell great.

"How've you been?" Max asked. "Last time we were together, all we talked about was business."

"I've been busy. Mostly the usual. I've been abducted, pistol-whipped, harassed, almost shot, and was left to die in my trunk. But we were also able to help some people. How about you?"

"Things are quiet. Tony thinks it's only the calm before the storm. But I guess we'll see. Nice pendant, by the way. I'm glad to see you put the diamond to good use."

"Well, it turns out it will be overly suspicious to sell a diamond this big for a few years. But you're right. It does make a great necklace. What about you? Have you started seeing anyone yet?"

Oh God, why did I ask that?

Max gave a small chuckle. "No, not yet. As you know, starting a long-term romance is difficult between the hours I keep and my, um, unusual profession."

Yes! Oops, why did that make me so happy?

"You sound like a difficult person to date. I can see where romance would be a challenge."

"I've missed you," Max said as we slowly swayed back and forth to the soft music. "I assume you and your police detective are still getting along well. I'm happy for you, and I hope things continue to go well. But I wanted you to know that I've missed you."

Damn. It's okay, be cool about it.

"I've missed you too," I quietly said.

We danced for another minute in silence when I noticed that, somehow, I was now only inches from him, and his arm was gently encircling my waist. I slowly looked up into his eyes and noticed our lips were almost touching.

Without thinking, I stretched up and kissed him. My lips had taken on a will of their own, and I was instantly lost in the sensations.

As the kiss deepened, I reached up and ran my fingers through his hair while my other arm tightly wrapped around his waist. I felt myself desperately clutching him, not wanting to let him go ever again.

It wasn't only the waves of physical pleasure washing over me. I was feeling a surge of powerful emotions as well.

I felt like I was flying. I was filled with insane happiness. I was a flower in the desert soaking up a cool rain. Nothing in the world could ever hurt me again. I was safe, protected, and free...

What am I thinking?

I pushed myself away and shook my head to clear it. My face was glowing hot, and I could feel my breathing coming in short gulps.

Damn it.

I looked over and saw Sophie had stopped dancing and was staring at me, open-mouthed. I then looked back to our table. By the glow of the candle, I could see Gina shaking her head and giving me a look of motherly disapproval.

The dance ended, and the lights came up. The singer said that the band was going to take a break while Danica and Alex cut the cake.

"I shouldn't have done that," I said, looking up into

Max's eyes. I took a step back, and I could feel my face growing even hotter.

"I wasn't complaining," Max said as he took a step closer to me. "In fact, it's a shame our kisses always end so quickly. Do you still think of you and me together? From the way you kissed me, it seems like maybe you have."

"Of course, I think about it. I think about you more than I should, but you know that it's complicated."

"It doesn't seem so complicated from my end. Why don't I give you a call in a couple of days, and let's get together? For dinner, this time. I'm sure we can work out any complications you are feeling."

I just bet you could.

I closed my eyes, but I could still feel him looking at me. In that one moment, a feeling of desperation and panic came over me.

I opened my eyes and looked up at Max. In that moment, I realized I desperately wanted to be with him.

I'm so going to regret this.

"You go back to bodyguard duty, and let me think about it," I said. "Call me in a few days. Okay?"

"Okay, you think about it, and I'll give you a call."

I walked back to the table, feeling somewhat like a criminal on the news doing the perp-walk of shame. Sophie had just gotten there, and Gina was looking at both of us with a look of concern. I did my best to ignore it.

"Cake time," I said, trying to sound cheerful while also trying to ignore the fact my face was, no doubt, still bright red.

"Why were you kissing Max?" Sophie asked. "Are things with him still complicated?"

"Complicated doesn't even begin to cover it," I said. "It's like I'm okay with not being with Max and never seeing him again. I remind myself that having Reno in my life is good for me, and we're happy. Well, relatively happy anyway. But then, when I do get together with Max, I lose all control. It's as if Reno doesn't even exist. All I want to do is wrap myself around Max. Besides, why were you hugging Milo?"

"Well, it's nothing complicated on my end. I've been drinking, I'm horny, and I want to get laid. Milo volunteered to help me out."

"If you want my advice, both of you should run while you still can," Gina said in her big-sister tone. "If you're not careful, you'll both get sucked into their world of crime."

"I'll be careful, and I'm not going to get sucked into anything," I said. "Now, as soon as they are done with the pictures, I need a piece of cake."

"About time they cut the cake," Sophie said. "It's getting late. I'm going to have a piece of cake, and then I'm outta here. Milo's coming over after the reception, and I need to clean my apartment. I've sort of let it go over the past couple of weeks."

"Do you really think Milo will care what your apartment looks like?" Gina asked.

"Gina's right," I said. "Put on something suggestive. If you open the door wearing a negligée, Milo wouldn't notice if there's a dead body on the floor."

From across the room, we saw the wedding party, which was gathered around the cake for pictures. We got a good laugh when Danica delicately smashed a piece of cake in Alex's face.

When the pictures were done, a line for cake started to form. Gina and Sophie stood up and began to drift over, still chatting about Milo.

Off to one side, I saw Tony watching the festivities. Max was again close to Tony, acting as his unofficial bodyguard.

Gabriella hovered off to the side, keeping watch over the entire crowd. I noticed how well she blended in with the crowd, the sign of a true professional.

If I hadn't known who she was, I wouldn't have noticed anything unusual about her. She would have looked like an athletic wedding guest with a big shoulder bag.

Looking back at Max brought on a wave of confusion and sadness. Suddenly, I couldn't look at him anymore.

My eyes filled with tears, and I walked to the back of the ballroom. I wanted to be alone with my thoughts, and I didn't want Sophie or Gina to see me crying.

It was a mistake to have danced with Max. When he calls, I'll agree to be his friend, but nothing more. We won't go out—not for drinks, not for dinner, and definitely not anywhere we are totally alone.

Like my apartment? Yum!

Most of the guests had drifted over to where Danica and Alex were handing out pieces of cake. In my corner in the back of the ballroom, it was almost completely dark. The only light was a few faint circles on the floor from the dimmed overhead lights.

As I was composing myself, I noticed one of the security guards doing doorway duty had pulled out his cell phone. In my melancholy state, I silently hoped Tony or Max didn't catch him doing that.

I'm not sure what rules hoodlums have while on duty, but I was pretty sure checking Facebook while you're supposed to be guarding the perimeter isn't allowed. I looked over to where the crowd was still gathered around Danica and saw that Tony was next in line to get a piece of cake.

I looked back at the guard. Apparently, his phone wasn't working because it wasn't giving off the telltale glow, and I saw he was still messing with it. There was a spot of dim light on the floor about ten feet from the door he was guarding, and I watched as he casually walked over to the light.

My feelings of goodwill for the guard faded as I watched him do something stupid, like leaving his post to check his phone. I started to feel a little vindictive, and now I sort of wanted someone to see what he was doing so that I could hear his supervisor yelling at him.

My, I'm suddenly in a bitchy mood.

As I watched him get to the light, I saw he didn't look like one of Tony's typical henchmen. This guy was short and skinny.

Now that he was in the dim light, I saw he wasn't holding a cell phone but a cellphone-sized black box with only a couple of buttons on it and an old-fashioned rubber antenna sticking out of the top. He was angling it in the faint light to be able to see the buttons.

I slowly walked closer as the guy fiddled with the device. He looked up, gazing at the crowd gathered around the cake. The guy must have sensed movement because he looked over at me.

The man had a thin mustache, and the right side of his face was discolored. I looked into his small, squinty eyes, and there was instant recognition by both of us.

This was the same guy who'd tried to kill me a few months before. The same guy who'd thrown a hatchet at my car after I sprayed him in the face with a can of wasp killer. This guy was a soldier for Carlos the Butcher.

Time went into slow motion as my mind began to race. I

looked at the box the guy was holding and at the antenna sticking out of the top.

Crap!

I desperately looked around. Danica and Tony were chatting as she handed him a plate.

Directly behind them was the tower of the cake. Everything came together in an instant.

Gina said the top layer of the cake looked mashed and had fingerprints on it. In my mind, the top of the cake now seemed as though it had a spotlight on it.

"Bomb!" I shouted. "The cake! Everyone out!"

Without thinking, I took off running towards the guy. My only thought was to take down this creep while he was still fiddling with the black box.

I vaguely heard people screaming, people running, and then the start of a general panic. In four steps, I crashed into the guy. But even as we collided, I saw his thumb close on a red button in the center of the box.

There was a blinding flash and the deafening sound of an explosion. Both the creepy guy and I were thrown against the back wall of the ballroom.

I couldn't see anything but bright dots, and my ears rang loudly. I was stunned and shook my head, trying to clear it.

Then, the guy was on top of me, trying to punch my face while I was trying to block his blows. In the background, I heard more screaming and people running.

Something hard crashed against the side of my head, and hot pain radiated from behind my ear. I again shook my head and tried to clear it, but I was rapidly losing the fight.

I felt myself starting to float, and the world faded into darkness.

Chapter Sixteen

When I woke up, I was in a hospital room, and the room seemed to be very bright. There were a lot of machines, and I could tell it was a room in an intensive care unit.

I wondered how long I'd been unconscious. I had vague memories of being awake several times during the night, but those memories were already fading.

I carefully turned my head and saw Gabriella standing at the door, still in her outfit from the night before. I turned my head slowly to the other side and saw Tony DiCenzo, who was looking out of the window.

I'd been in this clinic before. It was located off Shea Boulevard at the base of the McDowell Mountains.

I also knew Tony was seeing a stunning view of Scottsdale, which was almost on par with the view from the Dobbins Lookout. At one glance, you could take in the entire city.

I started to panic. Why was I in the hospital? My head was pounding, but otherwise, I felt uninjured. Tony must've heard me moving around because he turned and looked at me.

"I see you're with us again. Before you speak, please don't concern yourself about being in an intensive care unit. The doctor will be in shortly, but he's already told me you're in no danger. The concussion you have is mild. They gave you a sedative and some pain medication when you came in last night. The doctors have assured me that by now, you will have slept off most of the ill effects of the blow you took."

I reached up and gently felt the new bump on my head. As I did, I pulled a small piece of wedding cake out of my hair.

"What happened?" I asked. I was still groggy, and my words were coming out as if they were a series of mumbles. "How'd I get hurt?"

"It was the man you were fighting with. He hit you with a metal box he was holding, presumably the transmitter he used to set off the bomb."

It was then that I looked over and saw Max lying unconscious on the other bed. For some reason, I hadn't recognized him before now.

In my dazed state, I'd assumed I was in a hospital room with a stranger. There was a respirator tube going into his mouth, and he was connected to a dozen machines with tubes and wires.

Oh my God!

The worst part was his face. It was a pasty-grey color that instantly made me choke up. It was the color of someone about to die. Tony saw where I was looking, and he walked over to Max's bed.

"Max placed his body between the bomb and me," he said with a curious mix of sadness and reverence in his voice. "Unfortunately, he took most of the explosion."

"Tony, he's going to be okay, isn't he?"

"Honestly, it's too soon to tell. He was in surgery for over three hours last night. The doctors who worked on him are the best, but they say the next twelve hours will be critical. They say he'll either show signs of improvement or his condition will deteriorate, perhaps rapidly. That's why I had you brought into the ICU last night. I wanted to explain to you personally what happened, but I also don't want to leave this room until I know about Maximilian, one way or the other."

"Was anyone else hurt?"

"Max was the only one sent to the hospital, excluding yourself. When I say he placed himself between the bomb and me, it would be more accurate to say that he threw himself at the table and tackled the cake. By doing so, he knocked it away from the crowd that had gathered around it. He then used his body as a shield to protect not only me but also everyone else in the room."

"My God."

"It was only your warning and Max's actions that prevented many more people in the room from being injured, or worse. From what we've been able to piece together, I was the intended target of the bomb. The explosive was at head level, and the bomber was apparently waiting until I was standing directly next to the cake. Once again, it appears you've saved me. I thank you for that, and again, I owe you."

"Tony, is Muffy okay? What about Danica and Alex? Sophie and Gina?"

"Danica and Alex are fine, although they'll have an interesting wedding story to tell their children. Like most of the people in the room, Margaret Sternwood was knocked on her ass by the blast, but she's otherwise uninjured. However, she's madder than I've ever seen her. As you know, I've had a longstanding business relationship with both her and her late husband. Because of this, I'm free to discuss certain facts with her that I could not discuss with an outsider. She was here until late last night, and it was all I could do to keep her from going after Carlos herself."

Despite everything, I still managed a small laugh.

"Muffy still has it going on, doesn't she? I imagine she was quite a force when she was younger. What about Sophie and Gina?"

"Your co-workers, Miss Rodriguez and Miss Rondinelli were both here with you last night. They're both fine, and they both know you're in no danger from your injuries. In fact, I believe Miss Rodriguez has already returned this morning and is in the waiting area. Hopefully, she isn't distracting Milo too much. He's supposed to be on guard duty."

"Tony, thank you for watching over me last night."

Tony absentmindedly waved his hand as if the gratitude was mildly insulting.

Worried I'd done something to upset Tony, I looked closer at him. My head was starting to clear, and for the first time, he was truly in focus.

My God.

He looked terrible. It was not only that he'd been up all night. It was something deeper. The look on his face was a mixture of shame, anger, and regret. It was the look of a man who'd failed.

"Tony, are you okay?"

"No, Laura Black, I'm not okay. This whole fucked up situation is my fault. My response to Carlos the Butcher was too weak, too slow, and I've paid the price. Carlos hit me at a wedding in a secure ballroom at my top resort. My guys tell me the bomb was a simple device that only contained a crude black powder explosive. It was a device meant to maim, but not to kill. If it had been encased in metal, there would have been flying shrapnel. Many more people would have been injured, and some would have no doubt been killed. Carlos was sending me a message that he could hit me anytime and anywhere. I believe this was just his way of telling me to fuck-off."

I lay there for a moment and tried to think.

"There isn't a way to hide the fact that someone tried to kill you with a bomb," I said. "There were almost a hundred people in the room. A lot of people are going to know what happened."

"We've already put out stories to the media that the explosion was caused by some pyrotechnics that went off prematurely. Since the explosive was a mixture of black powder rather than C4, it'll help corroborate the story. Some of the people heard you yell out that there was a bomb, so there may be some confusion about that. But most of the people there didn't hear a thing. In fact, once we put out the story of some fireworks shooting off, people came forward and gave vivid stories about the event that closely matched what we put out as a bogus cover story. People are funny that way."

"You don't think anyone there will cause a fuss about what happened?"

"Fortunately, the people who could've made it difficult for us, members of the city council, the mayor's staff, and the other resort owners, left immediately after dinner. Those who were still at the reception were mostly the family and friends of the bride and groom. I don't see that the media will treat it as more than a curiosity at a wedding. The police may have their suspicions, of course, but we'll make sure those suspicions don't lead anywhere."

"Were you able to get the guy that set off the bomb? He was the same jerk that threw a hatchet at me a few months ago. I owe him some serious payback."

"I was curious how you'd identified the man. I assumed it was by his actions with the detonator. Unfortunately, in the confusion after the blast, the man you fought with got away. The other two weren't so lucky."

"Should I ask?"

"Carlos wanted to send me a message with his bomb. Well, I've sent him a message, too. I've reminded him that we live in the middle of the Sonoran Desert. It's a big, empty place with lots of holes in the dirt. His guys just filled up two of them."

As Tony said this, I saw Gabriella turn. Until this point, she'd been looking out into the hallway, not moving.

When she turned, I saw she had a small half-smile. Her face and her chest were flushing a bright-red, as if she were reliving a powerful erotic memory.

Oh, um, of course, sure.

"I thought security last night was air-tight," Tony continued. "However, in light of the current situation, I should've been even more vigilant. They came at my guys while three of them were out on a smoke break. With the current workplace health and safety rules, the smoking area was outside of the security perimeter we'd established. Of course, that's a hole in security that has been corrected. Fortunately, they only roughed up the three guys and then stole their uniforms and ID badges. Again, Carlos didn't seem to want deaths in the open like that. It was all part of sending me his message."

A nurse came in and spent about three minutes checking all the instruments attached to Max. She then typed some information into a tablet computer and left.

"Laura Black, I'll be honest with you," Tony said. He was starting to lose the look of shame and regret. It was slowly being replaced with thoughtfulness and determination. "I need your help with this. You're under no obligation to do so. In fact, I'm already deeply in your debt. But I'd sincerely appreciate your assistance. Last night, you were able to identify the triggerman as one of Carlos' associates, which is something my guys completely failed to do. You have a good head on your shoulders, and you don't panic when the shit gets stirred up. Plus," he said with a small chuckle, "I've observed that whenever something happens, you always seem to be in the middle of it anyway."

Damn, I always knew it would come to this.

I looked over at Max. It was the first time I'd ever seen him this helpless and vulnerable.

I got a protective surge and knew what I had to do. I've never been a mother, but I can imagine this is the same feeling a mother gets when one of her children is threatened.

"Okay, Tony. For this one, and I mean for this one only, I'm on the team."

Sophie and I walked out of the clinic to the parking lot where she had her yellow Volkswagen. As soon as we stepped outside, we were met with a sizzling blast of Arizona desert heat.

I saw Sophie wince from the temperature and quickly walk towards her car. I walked more slowly as a strange sense of empowerment came over me.

"Are you coming?" Sophie turned to me and asked. "I need air-conditioning."

"Go ahead and start the car. I'll be there in a minute."

I walked over to a small mound in the landscaping, where the best view of Scottsdale was. I stopped to take in the view and enjoy the heat.

As I watched, Sophie gingerly opened her car door and stepped back from the rush of heat. I then heard her curse as she sat in the hot car seat and again as she tried to buckle the searing hot seat belt.

I realized all at once that instead of disliking the heat, as Sophie did, I seemed to draw strength from it. I think I'd always instinctively known this, but this was the first time I'd put it together as a complete thought.

The desert had tried to kill me several times over the last few years, but I always came out stronger. Somehow, I knew I always would.

From here in the parking lot, the view of Scottsdale was the same as the view Tough Tony had been seeing a few minutes earlier. From where I was standing, I could see where I'd grown up in the Granite Reef section of south Scottsdale.

I could see the bustling arts, nightclubs, and shopping districts of Old Town Scottsdale. I could see the mature resorts along Scottsdale Road and then up to the new resorts and high-end housing of north Scottsdale. I looked out and saw Camelback Mountain, Mummy Mountain, and Paradise Valley lying in between.

Looking down at the city, I realized I was looking at nearly everyone I've ever loved or cared about. I got an overwhelming desire to watch over and protect them.

It was like what I felt looking at Max earlier, like a mother needing to protect her children, but in a sense, it was more powerful. These weren't only my children. These were everyone's children.

At first, I felt overwhelmed by the size of the task, but then I understood I wasn't alone in my fight. As long as Sophie, Gina, and all my friends were fighting at my side, how could I ever lose?

I walked down to Sophie's car and climbed in. I felt wonderful that I was still alive after another close call and was terrified at the task I'd promised to do for Tough Tony.

I slowly shook my head as I marveled at how I kept finding myself in these situations. Well, as Gina had promised when I first started, the job wasn't boring.

"Are you done worshiping the sun god?" Sophie asked. "I sometimes think these concussions are starting to affect your brain."

Sophie drove me down to the Blue Palms, where my car was still parked from the night before. She told me to have a good time on my mini-vacation, and she'd see me on Wednesday. She then drove home to get ready for a date with Milo, assuming he could still get away from work.

I drove back to my apartment. When I walked in, Marlowe ran in from the bedroom and rubbed against my legs.

Since I wasn't sure if Grandma Peckham had fed him or not, I walked into the kitchen and plopped a spoonful of Seafood Deluxe Dinner in his bowl. He quickly sucked down his food and then walked to the back of the kitchen so he could throw up on his spot in the corner.

I went back to the living room and collapsed on the couch. I began to reflect on what a long two weeks it'd been.

Yes, it had sucked, and I had gotten myself a little banged up. But we'd been able to help Elizabeth, and, in a way, we'd even been able to help Lester.

If I looked at the bigger picture, it had been a good two weeks. The only real dark spot was Max. Seeing him in that hospital bed was horrible.

I hoped he would be all right. Tony said he'd call as soon

as he knew something. I would have to wait.

As if on cue, my phone rang. I was sure it was Tony with news of Max, but I was surprised to see it was Reno. I quickly composed myself so he wouldn't notice my melancholy mood.

"Hey," I said. "You aren't calling to back out on me tonight, are you?"

"I wouldn't think of it. I heard there was some excitement at the wedding last night. Are you alright?"

"I'm fine. Honestly, I wasn't anywhere near the fireworks when they went off."

The phone went quiet. I knew what Reno was thinking.

"Okay," he said. "I have reservations at Frankie's. Seven o'clock. Does that still work for you?"

"Frankie's at seven sounds perfect. Are you still off until Wednesday?"

"Yup. I got off late last night, and my next shift isn't until next Wednesday at eight in the morning. Why? When do you need to be back to work?"

"Not until Wednesday."

"Really? I'll need to think of some way to celebrate."

"You do that," I said. "I'll see you tonight at Frankie's at seven."

I hung around the apartment for the rest of the afternoon and didn't do much. My mind was filled with thoughts of Max, Tony, and Reno.

Finally, I went into the bathroom and took a long hot

shower. I brought the phone into the bathroom in case Tony called.

At a little after six, I was standing in front of my mirror, swiping on mascara. The phone rang, and this time I saw it was Tony.

"Laura Black, this is Tony DiCenzo. Is this a convenient time to talk?"

"Tony, it's fine. How's Max? Is he going to be okay?"

"I just had a conference with the doctors. It looks like Max is going to pull through. He'll be out of commission for a few weeks, but they say he's past the danger point. They say he'll fully recover. He's awake, and they have taken the breathing tube out already."

"Oh my God. Tony, that's such great news. I was so worried. Thank you so much for letting me know about Max."

"It's my pleasure to be able to bring you such good news. I hope you understand I have several other phone calls to make, but I wanted to call you first."

"Thank you, Tony. I was serious about what I said today. Let me know how I can help with your problem."

"Once again, I thank you. And no, Laura Black, I never doubted your sincerity. We'll be in touch."

As I hung up the phone, feelings of relief and happiness flooded throughout my body. Gradually, these feelings were replaced by a new set of feelings.

I now knew what I had to do. I vowed to myself that I would help Tony where I could, but I also vowed that I would do everything in my power not to get caught up in his life.

Max was also a problem I resolved. From now on, Max was only a casual friend and a co-worker. Nothing more, ever. No hugging. No kissing. And certainly, no sex. I have Reno, and he's a good man. That should be good enough for any woman.

You say that now, but what happens the next time you're alone with him?

I made it to Frankie Z's at about ten minutes after seven, almost on time. Frankie led me out to a corner table on the patio, where Reno was waiting for me. He'd already ordered two scotches, and they arrived when I sat down.

"So, you have three days off?" Reno asked. "I assume your latest assignment went well?"

"It was good, overall. Lenny's happy, and the client's okay. It wasn't the best possible outcome, but it was probably the best we could have gotten. It turns out the client's sister was the one we were most able to help. She currently lives in Chicago, but she's planning on moving down to Arizona to live."

"Sounds like it was a good assignment."

"How was your week?" I asked. "Everything go okay for you?"

"Yes, well, mostly okay. My lieutenant's happy, the captain's happy, and the bad guys are going to spend a long time in prison. So yeah, things worked out for me as well."

I held up my glass. "Here's to good weeks." We then clinked the glasses together, and we each took a long sip.

Dominic came over and took our orders. As usual, we each got our favorite. Reno stared into space for a minute, then started talking.

"From what I hear, the bomb squad's taken residue samples from the hotel ballroom. They aren't totally convinced it was only common fireworks or pyrotechnics. DiCenzo and his group aren't cooperating, of course, but there are some suspicions it could have been a bomb."

Reno then stared at me with his stony-faced cop stare for almost half a minute, and I swear he didn't blink once. I did my best to look both innocent and totally ignorant of the facts. Finally, he gave up and hung his head in defeat.

"Now, can you see why I worry about you?" he asked. "Every month, it's something new and horrible. Can you see why I want you to do something safe for a living?"

"But I wasn't even on an assignment. We were at a wedding. Besides, why do you worry so much about me? I'm a big girl, and I can take care of myself."

"I worry about you because I love you."

Oh, shit. Really?

"You do?"

"Of course I do."

What do I do now?

"Um, I love you too."

Oh, shit. What did I just do?

Reno didn't say anything. He only smiled and sipped his scotch.

Within a few minutes, Dominic brought out our dinners. We each ordered another scotch and dug into the food.

By the time we were done and sipping our after-dinner coffees, we were talking and laughing. I always have the best time with Reno. It gave me a good feeling for our future.

The bill came, and Reno paid it.

"Thanks for dinner," I said. "What's next?"

Reno gave me a smile. I knew that smile. It was the one that said everything was all right. Seeing that smile gave me a feeling of being warm and safe. It was the first time I'd felt that way since I'd danced with Max.

"Do you still have your overnight bag in your car?" he asked, the smile changing into a mischievous grin.

"Well, sure. But I already have a change of clothes over at your place."

Again, with the grin. "We aren't going to my place."

"Well then, where?"

We were lying on a bed in a suite at the Fairmont Scottsdale Princess Resort. Looking out the balcony door, all of Arizona was spread before us.

Lying next to me on the bed was my boyfriend, Jackson Reno, wearing nothing but a pair of red silk boxers. He was staring at me, breathing deeply with anticipation.

A wave of lust spread down my body in a warm shiver. Excitement rose as I lay back on the pillows and held my arms out to him.

Reno leaned his gorgeous face over mine. I put my arms around his neck and drew him close. I felt him press against me as our lips came together for a slow, deep kiss.

He placed his hand on the bare flesh of my stomach and hesitated, as if unsure of what to do next. To be helpful, I gave his hand a gentle nudge.

My heart pounded as his fingers slowly slid downward. I

stopped breathing and waited to experience the moment.

My cell phone started ringing. Reno was still smiling, but his hand had stopped moving.

The phone rang again. It was Sophie's ringtone.

No, no, no, not now!

Reno reached over to the nightstand and picked up my phone. He hit the power button and turned it off.

"Sorry," he said. "This time, Sophie can wait until morning. Now then, where were we?"

Yes!

As a special bonus, here's the first chapter of:

Scottsdale Scorcher

the fourth book in the
Laura Black Scottsdale Mystery Series.

Chapter One

August is a lousy time of year in Scottsdale. People are tired of being hot, tired of the monsoon rains, and tired of hearing about how great it is to live in a dry-heat.

This lousy August afternoon, I was watching a violent dust storm race towards me as I slowly baked to death on the top of a hill in the middle of the vast Sonoran Desert. I had climbed the hill to hide from a bunch of pissed-off guys who would almost certainly kill me if they found me.

I knew they were angry because I'd accidentally blown up their entire arsenal of military weapons, supplies, and ammunition. I looked to my left, back across the desert, and saw a column of thick black smoke billowing up from where I'd been, less than half an hour earlier.

The temperature on the hill was approaching a hundred and ten. My mouth was dry with thirst, my head pounded from inhaling toxic fumes, and my eyes burned from the glare of the desert sun. Due to dehydration, I'd stopped sweating and was becoming dizzy from the heat.

As I sat with my back against a rock, I looked to the right and watched as the wall of brown dust climbed high in the sky above me. The dust storm was a monster, even by Arizona standards.

The wall of flying sand and dirt was over a mile high and stretched from horizon to horizon. Winds of sixty miles an hour would act to sandblast anything caught in its path. I knew that within minutes, I would face the full force of the punishing storm.

As I waited for the first particles of sand to slam into my exposed skin, I thought about how I'd ended up here.

It had started innocently enough, the week before, on a Monday. I'd been sitting at my kitchen table, drinking an after-lunch coffee and flipping through a stack of unpaid bills, when there was a knock on my door.

I wasn't expecting anyone, so I grabbed my purse, which held my Baby Glock and went into the living room. Lately, I've noticed I feel more comfortable if my gun is nearby.

It was probably the result of being attacked too many times over the last few months. I stood off to the side and talked through the door.

"Hello?" I called out.

"Laura," came a soft woman's voice from the other side. "It's Suzi Lu. Do you have a minute to talk?"

I felt the tension leave my body as I opened the door and let Suzi in.

Suzi is a thin, athletic woman of Asian heritage. She has long black hair, expressive dark eyes, and a beautiful smile. She's a professor of computer engineering at Arizona State University, about five miles to the south in Tempe.

She's several years older than I am and lives on the second floor of my apartment building. In her spare time, she's a professional dominatrix called Mistress McNasty.

Suzi runs the business out of her apartment and has a steady stream of men who need to be punished and disciplined. I don't know her all that well, but she's helped me out with assignments in the past.

When I'd seen her previously, she usually wore provocative and revealing outfits. Today, she wore a simple blue V-neck knitted shirt and white denim shorts. She looked a little shaken and upset.

Suzi sat on the couch next to my cat, Marlowe. When Marlowe felt the cushions move, he woke up from his nap. Seeing a stranger in the apartment, he ran into the bedroom.

I went to the fridge, pulled out a half-full bottle of white wine from the night before, and held it up. Suzi looked at me with a smile of relief.

"Oh, yes. That would be great, thanks."

After pouring the remaining wine into two glasses, I came over and sat in a chair next to her. We each took a couple of sips and sat in silence for a moment.

"I'm not sure if you can help me," she said, "but I think there's a problem, and I don't know what to do."

"Tell me about it," I said.

"A client of mine is missing."

"Missing?"

"I don't know what else to call it. His name is John. He missed an appointment this morning and didn't even call. I know something's happened."

"John?" I asked, raising my eyebrows.

"No, it's his real name. I won't let any of my guys use an alias. It makes it more personal that way."

"Have you called any of his family or friends? If something's happened, somebody should know something."

"I called a friend of his. He's also a client, but he didn't know anything about it. You see, the thing is, John travels for business, and it's not unusual for him to take off somewhere on short notice. I'm not sure how long it will be before someone figures out he's missing and calls the police. It could be a week."

"Maybe he went on a trip and forgot he had an appointment?"

"No, impossible. He has an appointment every Monday morning from nine to noon. He's under strict discipline and knows the consequences of not letting me know if he needs to postpone. It's something else."

Suzi leaned closer to me and lowered her voice. "I never talk about business with my clients, but he mentioned a couple of times last week that he was worried that something was going to happen."

"Did he say what?"

"No, and I didn't press him on it. But I could tell something was weighing on his mind."

"I'm not sure what I can do to help. I work as an investigator at a law office. Missing persons usually go to the police. Why don't you call them and tell them you suspect something?"

Suzi shook her head. "I don't think it would be a good idea if Mistress McNasty called in his disappearance. Discretion is one of the things my clients value the most. If anyone found out I was talking to the police, it would be the end of my business."

"You could go to a pay phone and call in a tip."

"I've thought about that, too, but I don't think the police would take an anonymous call as something real. Besides, I don't even know where there is a pay phone in Scottsdale anymore. I was thinking if I went through a lawyer, they'd be forced to take it seriously. Plus, maybe I could keep my name out of it."

"You want to hire Lenny to tell the police your client's missing? I'm sure he'd do it, but he's pretty expensive. You'd be talking at least four or five thousand, probably more."

At that, Suzi's face lit up, and she started to laugh. It was a great laugh, and hearing it put me in a good mood.

"Laura, I'm sorry. I guess you don't know me very well yet. Do you have any idea how much I make? I have more money than I know how to spend."

"I remember the last time we worked together. You said the guy you were training was paying you a hundred dollars an hour. It seemed like a lot."

"Oh, that was just an introductory offer. The man you saw was in the process of auditioning to be one of the boys in my stable. The first couple of sessions are at a discount, so we can get to know each other and decide if it's something we both want to continue or not. Most of my long-term clients pay more, usually five hundred to a thousand dollars an hour."

You've got to be kidding me.

"Sometimes you'll need to tell me what it is you do to make them pay you that much," I said. "But no problem. As long as you have the money, I'm sure Lenny will be glad to take you on."

As if on cue, my phone rang with Sophie's ringtone, Rihanna's *S & M.* Hearing the music made Suzi cock her head to the side and smile.

"Hey, chica," I said when I answered. "What's up?"

"I think Lenny has something new for you and Gina. He wants you both here for a client appointment at four o'clock. He didn't say anything about you coming in early, so there's no need to rush. He has another appointment coming in soon, so he'll be busy for the next hour or so. But if you're not busy, come in early anyway. Gina's been out all day, and I could use the company."

"Okay, give me an hour, and I'll be in. Oh, I have a new client for him. When's his next free appointment."

"You pick up another stray? Lenny'll like that. It shows initiative."

I heard the sound of Sophie typing. "Let's see," she said. "He's free tomorrow morning at nine."

"Would nine o'clock tomorrow work?" I asked Suzi. She nodded.

"Perfect," I said to Sophie. "The client is Suzi Lu."

"Suzi Lu? The lady with the handcuffs and whips?"

"Yup."

"This should be interesting." I heard the sound of more typing. "Okay, she's in the book."

My name is Laura Black. I once had visions of becoming a world-famous movie actress, starring in all the summer action-adventure blockbusters.

I'd wear skimpy outfits while my handsome co-star and I fought on the side of good against evil drug lords and international terrorists.

My fallback career choice was to be the next Mother Theresa. I'd live a simple life of poverty, helping the poor and fighting for justice.

Now that reality's set in, I've found myself as an investigator in a small law office in Scottsdale, Arizona. The hours are terrible, the work alternates between being boring and being terrifying, and I'm not all that great at what I do.

But it pays the rent, and I've made some good friends along the way. Sometimes, I'm even able to make a positive difference in someone's life. That's enough to keep me going.

I locked my apartment, went down the stairs, and out to the back parking lot. I then hit the remote to unlock my car, a cappuccino-colored Accord.

Although I always try to take care of my car, my current line of work has caused a few cosmetic issues. The driver's side front fender is somewhat crushed, the mirror is loosely held on with duct tape, the door has some scraped paint, and there's a bullet hole in the rear quarter panel.

These modifications occurred while investigating some members of the Russian mafia back in January. They'd followed me down a highway and had forced my car off the road, causing the damage.

The passenger side had a large gash in the front fender. This happened in March and was caused by a hatchet thrown at my head by a guy from a Mexican drug cartel. At the time, he was upset with me because I'd just shot a stream of wasp spray in his face.

Fortunately, the hatchet missed my head. Unfortunately, it embedded itself in the fender.

My trunk lid doesn't close anymore because the latch is broken. This happened in June when my friend Chugger McIntyre used a crowbar to pop it open.

This had been fine with me since I'd been trapped in the trunk at the time and had already passed out from heatstroke.

Chugger felt bad about breaking the latch and gave me a bungee cord to hold down the lid.

Unfortunately, every time I go over a bump, the lid to my trunk loudly bounces up and down. I know I should probably get a new car, but all things considered, it still runs surprisingly well.

Besides, I'd hate to destroy a new car. With my job, it would be better to have this one slowly demolished, one piece at a time.

I drove to the office, parked in my assigned space, and went in through the rear security door. I dropped my bag off at my cubicle in the back offices, then went up front to talk to Sophie. Miss Sophia Rodriguez not only does the paralegal stuff and answers phones for Lenny, but she's also my best friend.

I opened the door to the reception area and saw the front door to the street was propped open. Sophie was nowhere to be seen.

I took two steps into the reception area and was hit with the stench of a wet dog mixed in with the reek of burning garbage. It only took me a second to place the smell.

I quickly walked out the open door to the street. Sophie was standing on the sidewalk with a look of misery on her face. Her mascara was smeared from her eyes tearing.

"Oh my God," I said. "Amber? What was Amber doing here?"

Amber was a train wreck of a girl Lenny had met at a nightclub a few months ago. She'd been looking for work, so Lenny invited her to interview for an open admin position.

During the interview, she seduced him and got the job. She then spent the next couple of weeks collecting a paycheck while doing no work. We eventually got rid of her, and I thought we'd seen the last of her, but I guess I was wrong.

"I wish I knew," Sophie said, wiping her eyes. "Lenny had an appointment in the book with Ambrosia Elliot and her counsel. I had no idea it was Amber until Miss Smells-Like-a-Toilet walked into the office with her lawyer. Is that the same perfume? It seems to stink worse this time."

"It's the same. A cross between a wet dog kennel and burning roadkill."

We heard Gina Rondinelli swearing in the reception area. A few seconds later, she also came out to the sidewalk.

Gina is the senior investigator and has been my mentor since I joined the firm almost three years ago. Before she started working for Lenny, Gina was a Scottsdale police detective. She's as tough as they come and doesn't take crap from anyone, well, except us.

"Amber?" Gina asked. "What was Amber doing back in the office?"

"Don't know," Sophie said. "Lenny put her in the book but didn't say anything about it. She went into the conference room with her lawyer, and they talked with Lenny for about half an hour. When they left, Amber looked smug, and Lenny looked pissed. He took off right after they did."

"I was afraid of that," Gina said, sounding a little frustrated. "I knew it was too easy to get rid of her the last time. I had the feeling she'd be back."

"You think she's coming back to work?" I asked.

"I'm thinking work is the least of our problems with Amber," Gina said. "But let's see what Lenny says when he comes back."

"It shouldn't be too long," Sophie said. "When he took off, he was mumbling about needing a pack of cigarettes."

"I thought he was trying to quit," I said.

"Looks like Amber has that effect on people," Sophie shrugged.

"I'm all for hearing what Lenny has to say," I said. "But I'm going to walk around back and open the rear door. We need to air out the place."

"God, yes, please do," Sophie said. "I'll take a hot office over that stench. When Amber walked in and her odor hit me, I threw up a little bit in my mouth, seriously. If I have to sit in that stink for much longer, I'll probably toss my cookies all over the reception area."

"Well, that'd be an improvement over Amber's perfume," Gina said. "But airing the office out would be a good idea."

Leaving Sophie at the open front door, Gina and I walked around to the back. She opened the door, and I propped it open with a cinderblock. We then walked back around to the front and waited almost five minutes before we ventured back into the office.

Lenny showed up about fifteen minutes later. He looked tired and defeated. The only other times I've seen him looking this bad was after he'd lost a big case in court. He shuffled past the three of us and stood in his office door.

"I'm glad you're all here," he said. "Give me a few minutes to get down a couple of shots of Beam and light up a cigarette. Then come in, and let's discuss how we're going to handle this Amber thing."

He walked into his office, and his door slowly swung shut.

"Wow," Sophie said. "Lenny looks like shit."

"I doubt Lenny will be able to handle this on his own," Gina said. "I'm sure it'll be up to us to dig him out of it."

"You mean like always?" Sophie asked with a giggle.

"Right," Gina said. "Let's treat this like any other assignment and start at the beginning."

"We need to dig into Amber's background," I said.

"I still have the paperwork she signed when she blew her way into the job," Sophie said.

"Let's start with the standard searches," Gina said. "Credit reports, public records, and employment histories. If that doesn't show anything, use the government software."

"I'll be glad to have the secret software take a crack at her," Sophie said. "I can probably have a preliminary report later this afternoon and the full report sometime tomorrow."

Our magic government software came as a result of a case the year before when we helped out the DEA. By entering a name and any other random things you have on someone, millions of files in a secret government database are sifted through, and you can find the background details on almost anyone.

We're pretty sure we still shouldn't have access to it, and we've been waiting for the Men in Black to show up and remove it. But since we still have access, we've been using it often.

Ten minutes later, the three of us walked into Lenny's office. He was sitting behind his desk with a half-full glass of Jim Beam on the rocks and a freshly lit cigarette between his fingers.

From the remnants in the ashtray, he was already on his third one. He seemed lost in thought and was startled when we walked in.

"How bad is it?" Gina asked as we gathered around Lenny's desk.

"Well, it appears Miss Amber Elliot wasn't very happy when we let her go," Lenny said. "She's now represented by counsel to pursue a case of physical sexual harassment and unlawful discharge against us. They've already contacted the EEOC, and it seems they are more than willing to take this to trial."

"But she was the one who seduced you into giving her the job," Sophie said. "How is that you harassing her?"

Gina slowly shook her head, a sad and knowing look on her face.

"Well," Lenny said, "harassment of the type alleged is typically difficult to prove since it's usually a 'he said, she said' situation. Unfortunately, Amber seems to have walked into the interview knowing full well what she was doing. According to her counsel, she 'accidentally' turned on the voice recorder function of her phone and recorded the entire thing."

"Uh oh," Sophie said. "That can't be good."

"During the interview, Amber repeatedly used the phrase 'What do I need to do to get the job?' According to her counsel, this is when I, um, encouraged her to perform a, um, physical act on me as an implied condition of employment."

"That doesn't sound so good either," Sophie said.

"And then," Lenny said, "according to Amber, I approached her after she started working and again demanded favors. She said when she refused, she was fired."

The three of us looked at Lenny.

"No, I didn't. Stop looking at me like that."

"So, she has a case?" I asked.

"Quite possibly," Lenny said, pausing to puff on his cigarette. "It's my own fault. No matter who starts it, there are some things you can't do when it comes to employment. I've opened us up for a tangled mess of harassment and employment actions."

"Did they offer you terms for a settlement?" Gina asked.

"Well, that's the strange part. They only offered one settlement option. We can go to trial, or I can let Amber come back here to work."

"Oh, please God, no," Sophie said. "Go to trial. You're *really* good in court. I'm *sure* you could win."

The three of us looked at her.

"What? I don't think I can handle having her back. I'm serious. I know Amber's perfume doesn't seem to bother the rest of you, but you don't know how close I was to tossing my breakfast all over the office when she walked in today."

"What's wrong with Amber's perfume?" Lenny asked. "I think it smells great. It sort of reminds me of being in a sorority house on a hot summer night."

"*Eeeeewww,*" Sophie and I said together.

"There must be more to it," Gina said, ignoring us. "Why would Amber go through all of this trouble just to get back an admin job? There's something we aren't seeing."

"I've been thinking the same thing," Lenny said. "But at the moment, I have no idea what it could be. She starts back here tomorrow. I need everyone to be polite and not antagonize her. Besides, now that Annie's gone back to school full-time to get her bachelor's, we do need another admin."

"We'll work on finding out what's really going on," Gina said. She had a soothing, almost motherly tone to her voice. "Sophie's going to do a background search. After she does that, Laura and I will track down whatever leads she digs up."

"Yeah, okay," Lenny said. "I like that. Let me know what you find out."

He looked over at Sophie. "What else do we have going on today and tomorrow?"

"You have that new truck company guy at four today and another new client tomorrow morning at nine."

"Shit, I don't know if I'm up for two new clients right now," Lenny said. "What's the one tomorrow? Another family law with a cheating spouse?"

"It's one I brought in," I said. "Her name is Suzi Lu, and one of her clients is missing. She wants you to go to the police and formally report him as missing so they'll make a serious attempt at finding the guy. She wants to keep her name out of it."

"Why? Is she a hooker?"

"Sort of. She works as a dominatrix and goes by the name Mistress McNasty."

"What?" Lenny's eyes opened wide. "Did you say Mistress McNasty? Are you serious? She's living in Scottsdale?"

"Yeah, there is," I said. "What about her?"

Lenny paused to take a couple of puffs on his cigarette and a long sip of his bourbon. His eyes got all dreamy and unfocused.

"I always thought Mistress McNasty was an urban legend, sort of like Bigfoot. I started hearing about her at cocktail parties around ten years ago. She's supposedly the best there is. From what I've heard, her clients are usually at the CEO level or above. What about this client of hers? What's up with him?"

"His name is John, and he didn't show up for an appointment this morning. She thinks he's recently been threatened by someone. She's concerned he could be in trouble and is willing to pay to get the police involved."

"Aren't all her clients named John?" Lenny asked.

"She said it was his real name."

"Is this the same Mistress McNasty who helped us out with the diamonds a while back?" Gina asked. "The one who lives in your apartment house?"

"What?" Lenny asked. "Mistress McNasty lives in the same building as you? Hold on. Are we talking about the same woman? You know, wealthy men, whips, shackles, blindfolds?"

"Why would a woman with that much wealth be living in your apartment house?" Gina asked. "No offense, Laura, I like your apartment, but it's not the kind of place where you'd expect someone like that to live."

"I don't know," I said. "I never thought about it. I guess we'll find out."

I looked at Lenny. "Sophie said you had something for Gina and me?"

"Oh, yeah. The new client, the truck company guy, is coming in at four today. Since you'll be booked for the next week or two, plus the Amber thing," he said, pointing at Gina, "this assignment will most likely be for you," he continued, now pointing at me. "But it would be good if you both could be here for the initial appointment."

"Sure," Gina said. "What kind of assignment is it?"

"It's an industrial harassment case that might need some legwork. The client's the office manager for a trucking company located in the Scottsdale Industrial Airpark. Have either of you heard of Arizona Transnational Express?"

We both looked at Lenny and shook our heads.

"Well, apparently, they're being harassed by one of the other trucking companies in town, Southwest Desert Transport. They've gone to the police, but the harassment is continuing. They think that bringing a suit against the other company may be the only way to stop the harassment. Other than that, I don't know a lot about the case. The client will be here at four o'clock."

Lenny looked down at his Rolex. "Shit, that's in about forty-five minutes."

"I'll be here," I said.

"Same with me," Gina added.

Lenny pushed the glass toward Sophie so she could take it to the dishwasher in the break room. "It would be good if you could also sit in and take notes," he said to her. "I always get a little lost in these initial meetings when the client starts throwing names at me."

He reached for the pack of cigarettes. "Okay, everybody, leave me alone for a while. Let me think about what to do about Amber."

The three of us went out to the reception area and shut Lenny's door behind us. We kept Sophie company while she went through the complicated database login procedure and started the search on Amber.

"How'd your date on Saturday go?" I asked as she typed. "Wasn't this the Arizona Cardinals guy? What was his name? Cobra or something?"

"It was okay. His name's Snake McCoy, and yeah, last

week, the Cardinals signed him to a one-year contract as an emergency backup quarterback. The date was sort of a group thing. There were three other couples, and we went to the Dakota nightclub to celebrate."

"I love that place," Gina said. "I haven't been there since we went with the Cougars a couple of months ago."

"Yeah, it was great," Sophie said. "One of the managers recognized me as a puma, and he let us sit at one of the big, reserved tables."

"He actually signed a contract with the Cardinals?" I asked. "It's been almost two years since he played at ASU. Is he still any good?"

"I don't know. He only got the league minimum salary, so I would say probably not. But considering he'll get almost half a million dollars for five months of tossing a football around during practice, he feels pretty good about it. Plus, if something weird happens and he actually gets to play in a game, he'll get a lot more."

"I'd feel good about it, too," Gina said. "What's he going to do with the money?"

"Don't know. He spent a couple thousand on champagne for everyone, and he got a Cardinals logo tattooed on his arm."

"Hopefully, he doesn't get traded," I said. "That could be awkward."

"Are you going to see him again?" Gina asked.

"Probably. He seems alright. But he's going to be busy with the training camp thing, so it'll be a couple of weeks before we can do anything. Of course, if the Cardinals do well this year, maybe I'll be invited to the Super Bowl. I've never been to one of those."

"What about Milo?" Gina asked. "Have you stopped

seeing him?"

Sophie gave a small snort of disgust. "I don't know what to do about him. We get along okay, and then he starts talking about getting serious and moving in together. I don't need that. Every time he asks, we get in a fight, I put him on douche leave, and I stop taking his phone calls."

"Well," I said, "until you start to get horny."

"Yeah," Sophie said, "that's usually when I break down and start seeing him again. The man does have his talents."

"Well," Gina said as she eyed both Sophie and me. "You know my advice."

"I know," I said. "Dating a criminal isn't very smart, and it will only lead to heartache."

"Yeah," Sophie said. "But dating any man leads to heartache, so really, what's the difference?"

Gina only shook her head and let out a small sigh of frustration.

The client arrived, and the three of us introduced ourselves. His name was Mike Malloy.

He was a thin and spindly kind of guy. He looked to be about thirty-seven or thirty-eight, had short dishwater-blond hair, and a nervous smile.

Lenny's door opened, and he walked out to greet the client. He'd composed himself and looked much better. I heard the sound of traffic coming from his office and knew he'd opened the window to help clear out the smoke.

We introduced him to Mike Malloy, then we all went into

Lenny's office. Sophie sat in the back by the open door in case her desk phone rang, or someone came into the office.

"Alright," Lenny said to the client after we'd all found a seat. "Tell me about your current situation and what you'd like to have happen."

"It's like I told you over the phone," Mike said. "My company has an office in North Scottsdale, at the airpark. We've been in the same location for almost fifteen years. We're one of the trucking companies taking advantage of something called the CANAMEX corridor that was set up two decades ago. We have direct routes from British Columbia and Alberta all the way down to Guadalajara and Mexico City. Going direct cuts our operating costs compared to companies who have to offload and reload every time they go over a border."

"When did the trouble start?" Lenny asked.

"Strange things started happening about three weeks ago. It began with graffiti and some slashed trailer tires. Last week, there were a couple of small fires. One was in an outdoor garbage bin, and the other was started in a pile of wooden pallets in the lot behind our warehouse. Neither of them spread to a structure but they certainly could have. I think they'll keep trying until they start a serious fire."

"Nothing before three weeks ago?" Gina asked.

"No, nothing."

"You think you know who's behind it?" Gina asked.

"I know some of the other transportation companies don't like the fact that we can undercut them on price. It could be any of them, but I suspect it's a company called Southwest Desert Transport."

"Based on what evidence?" Gina asked.

"I really don't have a smoking gun, but one of our drivers

got into a fight with one of their employees a week before the trouble started. Plus, I've seen some of their rigs drive past our offices at odd times of the day and night. We're nowhere near their offices, so it seems strange to see them."

"What else do you know about them?" Gina asked.

"They're a relatively new branch of a company in Mexico. I think they've had their Scottsdale location running for less than a year. They also run the same routes on the CANAMEX corridor."

"You've been to the police?" Gina asked.

"Yes, but they said they needed something more substantial to go on. They sent a detective out last week. He asked a lot of questions and took some pictures. Honestly, until someone gets killed or there's a major fire, I don't think they'll be all that interested. We've hired a night-time security guard and set up some cameras but still haven't found any evidence of who's behind it."

Lenny looked over at me. "Okay," I said. "I'll look into it." I looked over at Mike. "If you'll be there, I'll come over tomorrow morning and look around."

"Sure," Mike said. "Give me a call before you stop by, but I should be there all day."

"Assuming we can gather some solid evidence against them," Lenny said, "we can either confront them directly to have the harassment stop, or we can present our evidence to the police and push them for results. We'll also have the option of bringing a civil suit for any damages caused by the other company."

Although Lenny had only casually mentioned a civil suit, we knew that was his ultimate goal. Gathering evidence for the police would only result in some billable hours.

Sure, it would be a nice chunk of change, but not as much

as a multimillion-dollar judgment in a civil suit. From Lenny's point of view, the best possible outcome would be a large warehouse fire with solid evidence of who set it.

About the Author

Halfway through a successful career in technical writing, marketing, and sales and having four beautiful children, author B A Trimmer veered into fiction. Combining a love of the desert, derived from many years of living in Arizona, with an appreciation of the modern romantic detective story, the Scottsdale Series was born.

Comments and questions are always welcome.

E-mail the author at LauraBlackScottsdale@gmail.com

Follow at www.facebook.com/ScottsdaleSeries/